A
CLOCK
SHOP
MYSTERY

and

dagger

"Don't waste
another minute—
this is your new
favorite series."
—HANK PHILLIPPI
RYAN

JULIANNE HOLMES

Author of *Just Killing Time*

BERKLEY
PRIME
CRIME

$7.99 U.S.
$10.99 CAN

ISBN 978-0-425-27553-5

9 780425 275535

5 0 7 9 9

PRAISE FOR

Just Killing Time

"A fast-moving story, and a great start to an intriguing new series."

> —Sheila Connolly, *New York Times* bestselling author of
> the Orchard Mysteries, the Museum Mysteries,
> and the County Cork Mysteries

"Holmes creates the perfect contemporary cozy—with a smart and engaging heroine, a quirky and mysterious Berkshires town, and a cast of characters to rival any who live in Cabot Cove. Don't waste another minute—this is your new favorite series!"

> —Hank Phillippi Ryan, Agatha, Anthony, and Mary Higgins
> Clark award–winning author of the Jane Ryland series

"Delightful . . . The story, with a hunky barber, Ruth's childhood friends, and conflicts between the new town manager and the 'old' Orchard, winds up to a suspenseful and satisfying end."

> —Edith Maxwell, Agatha Award–nominated and
> national bestselling author of the Local Foods Mysteries

"Take one tightly wound plot, a charming clock shop in the Berkshires, a woman you want to be your best friend, and you have *Just Killing Time*."

> —Sherry Harris, Agatha Award–nominated author of
> the Sarah Winston Garage Sale Mysteries

"With its bucolic setting, engaging characters, and clever plotting, Julianne Holmes has crafted a mystery to stand the test of time."

> —Jessie Crockett, national bestselling author of
> the Sugar Grove Mysteries

"An intriguing premise, a fun mystery, and a town and heroine with heart."

> —Barbara Ross, author of the Maine Clambake Mysteries

Berkley Prime Crime titles by Julianne Holmes

JUST KILLING TIME

CLOCK AND DAGGER

clock
and
dagger

JULIANNE HOLMES

BERKLEY PRIME CRIME, NEW YORK

An imprint of Penguin Random House LLC
375 Hudson Street, New York, New York 10014

CLOCK AND DAGGER

A Berkley Prime Crime Book / published by arrangement with the author

ISBN: 9780425275535

PUBLISHING HISTORY
Berkley Prime Crime mass-market edition / August 2016

PRINTED IN THE UNITED STATES OF AMERICA

10 9 8 7 6 5 4 3 2 1

Cover illustration by Cathy Gendron; *Clock Face* © by harlowbutler/Shutterstock.
Cover design by Danielle Mazzella di Bosco.
Interior text design by Laura K. Corless.

Penguin
Random
House

To my sisters,
Kristen Hennrikus Spence and Caroline Hennrikus Lentz.
I am lucky to have you both as sisters,
and blessed to have you as friends.

acknowledgments

Writing may be a solitary pursuit, but getting published takes teamwork. What a team I have. Writing this series is a dream come true, and I owe thanks to so many folks. Some of them include:

Allison Janice, my editor at Berkley Prime Crime. Ruth Clagan is as much a part of her as she is of me, and I am so grateful for her insight, her work, and her thoughtfulness.

John Talbot, my agent. Thank you for your support.

The Wicked Cozy Authors: Barbara Ross, Jessie Crockett, Liz Mugavero, Edith Maxwell, and Sherry Harris. Their friendship and support are invaluable. I love being part of our blog and our community (wickedcozyauthors.com). Writing with Kimberly Gray, Jane Haertel, and Sheila Connolly is a lot of fun as well. Our readers are so terrific—I can't wait to hear what you all think of the book.

My Live to Write/Write to Live blogmates: Lisa J. Jackson, Diane MacKinnon, Lee Laughlin, Jamie Wallace, Susan Nye, and Wendy Thomas. Such a great crew—I love sharing ideas on nhwn.wordpress.com.

Sergeant Patrick Towle of the Bedford Police Department. Any mistakes are mine. His generosity about answering even the craziest questions made making up stories much easier.

The Roberts brothers at the Clockfolk of New England (clock folk.com). I look forward to clock tower lessons in the future.

Kimberly Gray bid on a Wicked Cozy Author basket at Malice Domestic three years ago, before I had a contract. I promised to name a character after her, and kept my word. Who knew Kim Gray would end up being such fun to write?

My first reader, Jason Allen-Forrest. Thank you, my friend. Your enthusiasm and thoughtfulness make a world of difference.

Sherry Harris, for her editor's eye. Even on deadline her own deadline, she takes the time to read and respond.

Scott Forrest-Allen, who came up with the title for this book. Thank you—and keep it up!

My friends and family who supported me all along this journey. I couldn't do it without all of you in my cheering squad. Thank you, Mum and Dad (Paul and Cindy Hennrikus), the Spence family (Kristen, Bryan, Tori, and Becca) and the Lentz family (Caroline, Glenn, Chase, Mallory, Harrison). Thank you to Amy, Emma, Evan, David, Rhonda, Deb, Ruth, Stephanie, Pat, Alex. To everyone who supported me, cheered me on, bought the first book, or said "That is so exciting!"— you'll never know what your encouragement means.

The mystery writing community is amazingly supportive. I am a proud member of Mystery Writers of America and the Guppies. Sisters in Crime, especially the New England chapter, has made all the difference in my life. I could name some folks, but would forget too many. Suffice it to say, you wouldn't be holding this book in your hands if I hadn't joined Sisters in Crime fifteen years ago.

chapter 1

I was running late. Again.

Tardiness is not an admirable trait in anyone. But for me, a clockmaker, it was just plain embarrassing. I knew how to create objects that managed time, but I couldn't do it for myself. I looked up at the row of banjo-style clocks that hung in a row. Five clocks, five different makers, made decades apart. And five very different prices. That was part of the new marketing strategy I'd decided on, making sure customers understood that owning a beautiful clock was within financial reach, while still emphasizing quality.

The fact that all five clocks were showing approximately the same time gave me a thrill. Anyone else would take it for granted, but Pat Reed and Caroline Adler, my collaborators in the shop, had a vague idea of what it took. They heard me complaining about it enough while I labored to get each of the clocks cleaned, in good working order, and able to keep time while overseeing renovations to both the shop itself and the cozy apartment upstairs.

I looked at the pile of three envelopes, two scraps of paper, and four Post-its scattered on the counter and thought for a moment how much sense it would make to compile all of this into one list. Then I shook my head. I'd need a personality transplant to make that work. Instead, I opened my messenger bag and swept the whole jumble into it. I hastily grabbed a pen and a pad of paper and added them to my stash. Likely there were several pens and at least one more pad of paper in the bag already, but who had time to look? I scanned the Cog & Sprocket, the shop that had taken over my life for the past two months. Where did I leave my scarf? The heck with it; I needed to get a move on. The clock was ticking. Or, in this case, the clocks.

Tonight was the first time I was going to open the doors to the citizens of Orchard since the renovation and I still had a million things to do before that could happen. Not many people could pull off this Herculean task in two months, but then, most people didn't have Pat Reed overseeing the project. I'd helped Pat out of a jam back in October, and he'd more than paid me back. The changes down in the shop were mostly cosmetic, though it had a much more open feel. Upstairs was where he'd really pulled off a minor miracle, turning a jumble of rooms into a home.

I didn't bother to button up my coat. It was cold out, certainly, but I was only going out to the car. Maybe it was the glow of the holidays doing a holdover, but today it was downright temperate, a balmy forty-five degrees. Hardy New Englander that I was, I never really considered it cold until mid-January, when the temperature went well below freezing and ice abounded on roads and sidewalks.

"Pat, I'm heading over to Marytown," I called up the back staircase.

"Drive safe, Ruth," he called back down.

"Will do." I closed the back door, locking it behind me.

I'd only recently started using the back door of the Cog & Sprocket again after my neighbor Beckett Green had complained about me taking up a customer parking space, which was supposed to be two hours only. I started parking out in back of the shop, not to make Beckett happy, but because Jeff Paisley, the chief of police in Orchard, had asked me to. Jeff, as I called him when he was off duty, had become a friend. He didn't want to start giving me tickets, and I didn't want to get him in trouble with the town manager, Kim Gray. She already had it in for both of us. I didn't want to add fuel to her fire.

I scurried down the stairs and hustled over to my car, hitting the button on my key fob to open the doors. Nothing happened. I tried again, but the doors didn't unlock. I used the key to open the door and slid into the driver's seat. The engine didn't turn over. I tried again, but nothing happened. Just a click.

"I did it again," I said, banging my hand on the dash and then resting my forehead on the steering wheel.

"Woof!"

I cracked open the door and looked up just as Blue, the Australian shepherd who lived next door, pushed his muzzle into the car, followed by as much of his body as he could fit. I couldn't help but smile, even as I thought of his gray and white fur shedding onto my black coat.

"Hey, Blue. How are you, sweetheart? I don't suppose you know how to jump a battery, do you?" I asked.

"He doesn't, but I do." I looked up at Blue's human and felt the color rise on my cheeks. Ben Clover, owner of the barbershop next door, was standing behind his dog, hastily picking up the trailing leash. The back alley was well traversed by all of the shop owners, so I wasn't surprised to see Ben there.

"Was Blue taking you for a walk again?" I asked as I climbed out of the useless car.

Ben had the good grace to look embarrassed, his reddish blond hair falling into his eyes. Blue owned him, not the other way around. My cat, Bezel, controlled my life, so I didn't have room to judge. Not that I would. There could be worse things than being owned by the sweetest dog in Orchard.

"He was," Ben said. "Since we have to walk back here, behind the shops, there isn't a lot of running space for Blue, so I let him off the leash to run by the river for a few minutes."

"Why do you have to walk back here?" I asked.

"Haven't you heard? Beckett Green found some ancient ordinance that doesn't allow dogs on city sidewalks, so we have to slink around in back alleys."

"Back alleys?" I said, looking around at the tree-lined road, well-paved street, wide enough for two cars, stunning river gurgling past. "Ben, you've been in Orchard too long. This is practically a country lane."

"You know what I mean," he said, raising his eyebrows. "I heard he was giving you a hard time about parking in front of your shop."

"He was. Two-hour customer parking only. I guess the excuse that I didn't want to park where my grandfather died didn't much matter to him." I looked over at the spot, where

Ben's car was parked. "I do really appreciate your switching spots with me, Ben."

"Listen, our shops are so close together, we practically shared a space already," he said. "So, what's up with your car?"

"I think the battery is dead," I said, resting my hand on the hood. "I used the headlights to light up the back stairs last night while I was moving a couple of more boxes back into the shop. I must have forgotten to turn them off."

"We need to get better lighting back here," he said.

"That one floodlight, over by the Sleeping Latte, really doesn't help us much here," I agreed. "Pat is going to put in a motion detector with lights. It's on the Pat Project List for the New Year. Of course we'll need to check the city ordinances first, so good old Beckett doesn't sic Jeff Paisley on us again."

"You'd think that Beckett would care more about what his neighbors thought, since he is about to open his bookstore," Ben said, watching as Blue trotted and snuffled about with the sort of enthusiasm reserved only for dogs exploring their outside world.

"You'd think. He probably doesn't understand how valuable word of mouth is in a small town like Orchard." The Berkshires are in Western Massachusetts—less than four hours from either New York City or Boston. Proximity helped for tourism in the summer and during leaf peeping season. But the rest of the year, the population shrunk to residents only, and Orchard was like dozens of other small towns in America where everyone knew one another, and one another's business.

"Or lack of word of mouth," Ben said. "Aunt Flo has decided we aren't even going to mention Been Here, Read

That aloud." It was a shame. I'd been so excited when I first heard that a bookstore was coming to Orchard. Then I got to know Beckett. "But back to the matter at hand. I don't have jumper cables. I bet Pat has some, so I can jump your car later, but I have to run over to Marytown right now."

"Oh, perfect."

"Perfect?"

"I need to go to Marytown, to the party supply store. Can I hitch a ride?" I made a little hitchhiker gesture with my thumb, and smiled. When Ben laughed, I immediately felt heat rise on my cheeks.

"Sure, let me put Blue back in the shop. Sorry, buddy, Ruth's going to sit in your seat today." Ben smiled his dazzling smile as he ruffled the dog's fur, and I felt myself blush again.

"So, where's Betty?" I asked, settling into the warmed seats of the SUV.

"Away for the winter, I'm afraid. Betty doesn't mind snow—it's the cold that gets to her," Ben said.

"Betty and I have that in common," I said. Betty was the name of Ben's car, an old, oft-repaired Volkswagen Bug that had apparently moved to Ben's aunt's garage for the winter. Like me, Ben lived in a small apartment over his shop, so occasionally borrowing his aunt Flo's car was a great option for him. I'd never tell Ben, but I preferred the heated seats, storage options, and quiet ride of the SUV to Betty's wheezing, bumpy ride and paper-thin floorboards. I pulled out my scraps of paper, and a pad, and started to consolidate my lists.

"What's that?" he asked as he pulled out onto the main road.

"I have four events in the shop this week. The open house tonight, Caroline's birthday party, New Year's Eve, and the official opening on January second."

"Don't forget the Town Hall celebration."

"If we have something to celebrate," I said, sighing. "I have another meeting with Kim tomorrow afternoon. She sent me a cryptic e-mail, referring to some ordinance issues if the town lease was going to be extended on the building."

"But the lease will still get extended on January first, right?" Ben said, shifting in his seat.

"That's the plan. Which means I have three days to deal with whatever new obstacles she wants to throw in my path."

In October, I had inherited the old Town Hall, a building that sat across the street from the Cog & Sprocket. The inheritance was a paper transaction—no huge sums of money were changing hands; we just changed the name on the title to mine—since the town had used the building for years, thanks to a favorable lease offered by the building owners, the Winter family. That deal was set to expire on December 31, four days from today. I'd offered to extend the same deal to the town of Orchard at the same rate: a dollar a year. But I'd added two caveats.

First, based on some input from Pat Reed and other folks, I asked that the town figure out a way to increase the budget for the building itself, so that it and its grounds could be properly maintained. Right now there was enough money to keep the doors open, but the old girl needed serious updates to make it more usable for the town in general. After some negotiation, the Board of Selectmen agreed, especially when it became clear that making some of the changes would make the Town Hall more viable and provide a revenue stream for the town. Harris University had expressed interest in becoming a partner in the operations, which helped make the deal more favorable to even its biggest skeptics.

The second caveat was personal. I wanted to rebuild the clock tower. During World War II, the clock tower's inner workings had been taken out and melted down to support the war effort. In the early '50s, as they were replacing the weights, cogs, and gears, a spark from a welder's torch caused a fire. At least that was the story everyone was told. My grandfather always hinted that it was something more nefarious—attempted arson. Thankfully, the fire was contained quickly, and the tower structure remained solid. The work to replace the clock itself was deferred over and over again, despite the fact that the Clagan family volunteered to maintain it once built. Small-town politics, petty grievances, and good old-fashioned New England orneriness didn't help discussions over the years. Still, my grandfather always dreamed of rebuilding the clock tower and had been working with Grover Winter to make it a reality. Then both men died within a year of each other. Now it was on me to see that the dream moved forward. Having decided to move to Orchard from Boston to take over my grandfather's business after my divorce was finalized, I was more than up for the task. I just hadn't expected the town manager to be such a barrier.

"What happens if you can't deal with them?" Ben asked.

"Then I own the building and all that entails, including having to pay the operating expenses."

"Would that be so bad?" Ben asked.

"I am trying to figure out how to keep the Cog & Sprocket

open, never mind the local white elephant. Insurance costs alone would wipe out all my savings. Running a building— not my area of expertise."

"Any chance that Harris University can help out? You mentioned that they were interested in renting some of the space."

"They are interested, and willing to pitch in a bit for repairs. But not until their new fiscal year starts."

"In January?"

"In July," I sighed. My ex-husband was on the faculty of a small college back in Boston, so I understood the glacial pace of decision-making for colleges. Still, it was disappointing when that avenue was blocked.

"Ruth, if anyone can figure it out, you can. I have total faith. Let me know what I can do to help," he said, giving me a quick sideways look as we paused at a stop sign.

"Thanks, Ben. That means so much to me. You're already doing a lot, being chairman of the board of the Clock Tower Fund. I'm not sure how G.T. talked you into that," I said, hitting him gently on the arm. "I still can't believe there's even a fund." G.T. was my nickname for my grandfather, short for Grandpa Thom.

"Thom's passion for the clock tower was contagious. I loved talking to him about it and learning what the work would entail. Besides, I like the community aspect of the project. After Grover died, it made sense for me to take over. I'm glad you're keeping it going."

"I'm glad we're both keeping it going. The Board of Selectmen is requiring a report at the next town meeting, this Friday. Are you ready for that?"

"Yes, we'll be ready," Ben said. "This is a house of cards

right now. We've got one grant if we can match the funding, so we need to raise the money to do that. Jimmy Murphy was trying to get us more time for that deadline. The tower fund doesn't have nearly enough in it, but we're working on it, as you know. If the town kicks in for part, it will put us over the amount we need."

"Lots of ifs."

"Again, I'm just going to say it. In Ruth Clagan I trust." Ben reached over and patted my knee, then he went back to driving.

I glanced over at Ben, studying his profile as his eyes remained steadily on the road. He was handsome. I'd noticed that the first time we met. But what made him even more attractive? He was a really nice guy. I kept waiting for him to do something that dissuaded me from that opinion, but so far, he'd proven himself to be a good neighbor and wonderful friend. Sometimes I hoped for more, but the ink on my divorce papers was barely dry, my business was taking over every waking moment, and I was still getting used to having a stepgrandmother in my life. Besides, Bezel could be very needy. *Friend* was good, for now.

I looked back at the pile of papers in my lap and continued working on the master list for the party store.

"Is it tacky if I use the same napkins for all of the events?" I asked Ben, chewing on my pen cap absently.

"Ruth, I'm not the guy to ask."

"Channel your aunt Flo. What would she say?"

Ben laughed. "Aunt Flo would tell you to get the same for all the parties, no doubt. She's a frugal Yankee, through and through. What colors did you all decide on for the Orchard Loyalty card?"

"Green and purple. And it's called the Program for Orchard Loyalty, POL for short. Get your acronyms straight." POL, the new business association for the businesses that made up downtown Orchard, had decided on a loyalty card so that we could support one another through the winter. Buy the featured local foodstuff at the Corner Market, get a free refill at the Sleeping Latte. Buy five coffees in one week at the Sleeping Latte, get a special gift at Ben's Barbershop. Show the card at the library and get a POL tote bag and an extra DVD rental. The hardware store was offering an amaryllis bulb kit with a purchase of twenty-five dollars. Go to all five shops, including the library, featured on the card, and get a free watch battery replacement at the Cog & Sprocket. The program was only good through April 1, and the hope was that it would encourage folks to pull on their boots, bundle up the kids, and come to town during the winter months.

"The barbershop is on the card, by the way. Your aunt Flo approved it."

"Don't I know it? Wait till you see what we came up with. It's genius," he said excitedly. "Hair product samples and a half-price haircut. With a little Flo magic in the mix—the packaging she came up with is a hoot."

"Your aunt Flo is a hoot," I said, smiling at the thought of the compact burst of energy that was Flo Parker. She'd moved back to Orchard to help Ben with his shop, and her effervescent energy pulled us all out of a dark time. She wore clothes that few others would dare to sport, even women half her age. Never mind that she wore them a couple of sizes too small. Still, somehow, zebra-print pants with floral-print shirts, or red pleather pants with a pink ruffled shirt worked. Flo often added hair extensions in coordinating colors that she teased into her trademark updo. Just thinking about her made me smile. "Those prizes sound great."

"The whole program is terrific. Everyone in downtown Orchard is on the card, except Beckett. I know you tried to talk him into it."

"Many times. I almost had Rina convinced, but Beckett wouldn't budge." Rina Sanske was a bit of an enigma. I surmised that she was Beckett's business partner, but neither of them had confirmed that. I did know that she went out of her way to smooth the feathers he ruffled, though lately even her best intentions couldn't keep up. "His loss. Anyway, the colors are purple and green. I guess those could be the colors for the decorations. That way we can use the extras for the events we are going to plan for this winter."

"You are really sweating the details of tonight, aren't you?"

"It's the first time anyone has seen the Cog & Sprocket since we closed on November first. I want to make sure we make a good impression."

"You've already made a great impression," Ben said, smiling over at me with that contagious grin of his. I smiled back and then looked out the window. So far the winter had been snowless, which was not ordinary for this time of year. The bleak landscape rolled by, still charming, but a bit foreboding. Green and purple would brighten things up considerably.

"Did you ever decide where to hold the rest of the classes this winter?" Ben asked. "I'm glad you're doing them, by the way. I'm really looking forward to the next one."

"I appreciated you coming to the test class," I said. My grandmother had held salons in the shop back in the '60s. As an homage, and because there was some interest in learning more about the clock collections in the shop, I'd offered to do a talk at the library. The audience overflowed the room, and I got talked into teaching a few more classes about clocks. "Something for folks to look forward to this winter," Aunt Flo had said.

"Hey, I'll admit, I was only there to offer support at first. But who knew that the history of the Willard family, and the banjo clock, would be so fascinating? Are you going to try and have the next one in the shop?"

"That was the first plan, but we already have a dozen people signed up for the Winding an Eight-Day Clock workshop. Moira offered to have it at the Sleeping Latte, but I hate for her to have to stay open late, even if it is only one night a month." Moira Reed owned the Sleeping Latte, the local coffee shop and café. She and I had been friends as kids, and we'd picked right up where we'd left off when I moved back to Orchard.

"It's genius. The lectures are fun, it gets people interested in clocks, and it's a great social event. It's a shame that you can't keep using the library."

"Mac Clark came to me about adding a food and wine component, which made a ton of sense both to attract people and to showcase the Corner Market's wares." Mac and Ada Clark owned the Corner Market, the local grocery store. Unlike the previous owner, Mac's cranky uncle, Mac and Ada thought of the Corner Market as more than just a place to get milk and eggs. They considered it a front for good food and took their job of supporting local businesses and agriculture very seriously. I was more than happy to work with Mac on his idea, even if it meant moving the classes out of the library.

"Maybe we could do one in the barbershop?" Ben asked.

"Maybe," I said, noncommittally. Ben's Barbershop was as close to failing as any business in Orchard, but Aunt Flo had some ideas to help him turn it around. I was fairly certain her ideas did not include clock classes. "Anyway, I'm going to figure it out, after the New Year." I turned down the heat on my seat and continued to look out the window at the trees and frost-tipped grass disappearing past us. Marytown was only ten miles east, but the roads had lots of curves and more than a few speed traps.

"Which is officially Sunday. Can you believe it?" Ben asked, as if he could barely believe it himself.

"Don't remind me. This week is packed. I'm glad it's only Tuesday, but what a Tuesday it's going to be. I thought we were more prepared—this list is crazy."

"Christmas derailed things a bit, for good reason. It was nice to spend a few days relaxing, don't you think?"

"It was," I said. "It's been a long time since I had so much to do over the holidays. My ex-husband and I used to go away to Mexico for Christmas. More traditional activities and just spending time with family and friends was great."

"You don't get much more traditional than the holidays in Orchard. Just be glad that Aunt Flo didn't drag you caroling. Next year you won't get off so easy. Now, back to your list. We'll get it done. This is a group effort, and it is quite a group. By the way, do you need anything at the hardware store? Aunt Flo gave me her own list."

"No, Flo checked in with me already. Anything I need is on her list, which, I'm sure, is completely organized. Mine, not so much, but I'll wing it."

"I have faith that it will be perfect, as always." Ben Clover was a wicked flirt. Maybe one of my New Year's resolutions should be to start flirting back.

"I wish I'd had a chance to run it by Caroline one more time," I said, clearing my throat and changing the subject.

"Where is she, anyway?"

"She's been flat out trying to learn how to use the online store that Nadia set up. She wants to be ready to show it off tonight."

"Nadia as a teacher. Can't say as I can picture that."

"Caroline gets along really well with her. She gets along well with the three of them, actually." I'd hired Nadia Wint in November, right after I'd decided to stay in Orchard. I'd posted the job at Harris University, hoping to find someone who had both marketing expertise and tech savvy, since part one of my business strategy for the Cog & Sprocket was to get us online. Nadia had both of the skills I wanted, and more that I didn't even know I needed. She'd talked me into hiring her boyfriend, Tuck Powers, to help with some of the photography and digital work. Another good move, especially since Tuck posted the job opening we had for a watchmaker on his Facebook page, and a high school friend, Mark Pine, had applied. Three new employees within a month. It had been a leap, but it had worked out well. For the most part.

I knew people like Nadia and Tuck from my days being a faculty wife. Very smart, hip, trendy, and too cool for school. I used to understand them a little better. Now Nadia and Tuck made me feel old. It didn't help that Tuck called me ma'am. Nadia called me Ms. Clagan. They both had a little edge in their voice, like they were bored at even having to speak with me. But their work was good, and I needed to keep a little distance as their employer. Still, it was exhausting. I felt older than my thirty years.

"I'm thrilled with the new website. Once it goes live, I know it is going to be terrific for business."

"You've made some great improvements," Ben said. "Thom would be proud."

My grandfather had inherited the shop from his father, who had inherited it from his father. My father got skipped. He had no interest in horology and no talent for clocks. The family legacy weighed on me as I rethought how to run the business or picked a new color for the walls. I knew my grandfather wouldn't have loved some of the changes, but I still wished he could be there to see them. "I hope so," I said.

"We're here," Ben said, pulling up to the curb in front of the party store. Marytown didn't have the building restrictions that Orchard had, and a few chain stores had moved in. Ironically, this party store was one of the most successful. Maybe it was because of the college population. Or maybe it was because it was the store that supplied color-coordinated party goods, including Mardi Gras beads in every color. "I'll call you when I am on my way back from my errands. Is that okay?"

"Perfect."

Now, what did I need to pull off four parties in five days?

chapter 2

I grabbed a shopping cart and stepped into the store. Green and purple helped limit my choices, but not by much. Plates, napkins, cups, cutlery, decorations, tablecloths—all available in a variety of hues. I was good at throwing parties. My skills were honed after five years as the wife of an ambitious faculty member. We hosted a lot of gatherings, and I'd become adept at planning. But four parties was pushing it, even for me.

I was excited about tonight, and rolling out the Program for Orchard Loyalty. Truth to tell, the POL card had been my idea. The town had come together to support me after my grandfather was killed. And I'd come to understand the role G.T. had played in town, and that I was expected to take on in his stead. His widow, Caroline Adler, had shown no interest in becoming the public face of the Cog & Sprocket, so I'd stepped in. The best part was, I'd come to really like my fellow business owners. All except Beckett Green.

I'd tried to like Beckett and to bring him into the fold. Even though I was the new owner of the Cog & Sprocket, the Clagan family had lived in Orchard for over a century. The Clark family had owned the Corner Market for the past fifty years. Mac and Ada were vast improvements over Mac's uncle Matt, and were part of the new energy people were bringing to the businesses downtown. Ben Clover was new to Orchard, but his aunt Flo was a beloved citizen. She'd recently moved back to help Ben and to reopen Parker's Emporium, an old-fashioned drugstore in the same building as the barbershop. Like the Cog & Sprocket, Parker's had been closed for renovations, but was opening for business January 2. Tonight it would be open for visitors, in lieu of the barbershop. But everyone knew that Ben's barbershop and Flo's drugstore were interchangeable for all intents and purposes, since Ben and Flo were family. Family histories were woven into the fabric of Orchard, and newcomers weren't always welcome. Which is why I'd gone out of my way to welcome Beckett Green, as much good as it did me.

Beckett had bought the old bank right across the street from the Cog & Sprocket, next door to the Town Hall. Apparently the purchase had been on a whim, done when Beckett's GPS sent him through town after a trip to Tanglewood last summer. He'd decided to make the old bank into a bookstore, calling it Been There, Read That. He told everyone that he was semiretired and this was his new hobby. It sounded great, until Beckett's plans started to steamroll the town right before Thanksgiving. Even though he forced Jeff Paisley to ticket the parking violators, he petitioned to have three spots on the street dedicated to his shop. He also filed papers to have a coffee shop in the bookstore, even though the Sleeping Latte was practically across the street. The parking spaces and the coffee shop were voted down by the Board of Selectmen at the last town meeting after a raucous discussion. Beckett hadn't taken the rejection well, and once more Rina tried to smooth things over.

Rina was a bit of a mystery to me, the biggest mystery being what she saw in Beckett. Beckett was average height, average build. His features were plain—he'd never be handsome, but he wasn't unpleasant to look at either. His best feature was his eyes, which were a deep green, unlike any eyes I'd ever seen. Nancy Reed was convinced that he wore colored contact lenses.

Rina was short, but she still filled a room when she walked into it. Her dark black hair had been dyed blue at the ends and cut into a perfect long bob that moved like silk when she walked. Her clothes were expensive and on the cutting edge of fashion. Most of the people I knew wore shades of blue and gray, or all-out black, in the winter, so Rina's bright red coat made her stand out, but she didn't need that prop. She naturally drew everyone's eyes to her. She was always waving at people during her daily run. She stopped by the Sleeping Latte every morning for her grande skim latte with an extra shot. From the look of her, the latte was her only indulgence.

I think that Beckett and Rina were a couple, as well as business partners, but I couldn't be sure. Beckett had moved into a bed-and-breakfast in Orchard and rented out the entire thing while renovations were under way at the store. Rina had moved into the B and B as well, but the owners weren't telling tales about the sleeping arrangements. Beckett's business was helping them pay for a new kitchen, and since an off-season windfall was both unexpected and welcome, they weren't about to cross him.

I looked into the cart, double-checking the number of napkins and plates. If worse came to worst, I could always come back to buy more supplies. I tossed in three more packages of purple napkins. I'd rather not have to come back. After tonight, the week just got busier for me.

I rolled my shoulders back and took a deep breath. I wasn't really nervous about napkins. Thinking about Beckett Green always made me tense. He was like dozens of people I'd met back in Boston, but I thought I'd left them behind, along with my old life. I pushed my shoulders down and focused on the shopping I needed to do. I tossed two more sleeves of cups into the cart.

Open house tonight, Caroline's birthday party after the open house, New Year's Eve, and the Town Hall celebration, and then the official grand opening of the Cog & Sprocket. I went to the birthday aisle and tossed in a package of "Happy Birthday" napkins and some candles for Caroline's cake.

I made my way over to the aisle stocked with serving platters. Nancy Reed had given me a very specific list of platters and bowls she needed. I found the slip of paper with her list and quickly found what she needed. I tossed in a few extras of each, just in case.

I was winding my way over to the checkout aisle, but got waylaid by the shiny New Year's decorations. Horns, crackers, clappers, disco balls.

"Who knew there were so many ways to celebrate the New Year?"

I looked over my shoulder to see who was speaking and started at the sight. The man towered over me, which was tough to do, considering I was five-ten. He had a wide-brimmed black fedora pulled down low on his forehead and wore dark glasses that covered the upper part of his face. I tried not to stare at the scars that sliced his pale right cheek, but it was hard not to. He was dressed all in black, a black shirt and tie peeking out from the top of his black trench coat, black jeans hitting the top of his black cowboy boots. The wavy gray hair that touched the back of his collar was the only variation on the dark theme, and it did nothing to make him less imposing. Despite myself, I shivered.

I turned back to the display. "I know," I said, trying to sound friendly. "I'm beginning to think my party will be lacking if I don't at least get some paper horns!"

"Sounds like you're planning a big party," he said.

"Sort of," I said. The business owner in me almost invited him to the open house. Almost. Something made me hold back.

"Say, is that you, here in the paper?" he asked, pulling a copy of the *Marytown Shopper* out of his pocket. I took it from him and unfolded the paper. The picture had been taken last week and included all of us working on the POL project. I scanned it quickly and noted that it mentioned the open house.

"It is," I said. "How did you recognize me?"

"That red hair of yours stands out," he said, smiling. I hoped he didn't see me shiver. His smile held no warmth, especially since I couldn't see his eyes. He held his hand out, and I handed him the paper.

"Hey, Ruth, how's it going?" Ben called from a few aisles away. "You won't believe the cover of the *Shopper.*"

"He showed it to me," I said, turning back to the man behind me. He was gone.

"Who?" Ben asked.

"I don't know," I said, looking around and lowering my voice. I couldn't see him anywhere. "This man started talking to me and showed me the paper."

"Did you know him?" Ben asked.

"I didn't. But it was weird. He almost seemed to know me." I shivered again. "He had the picture from the paper, maybe that was it. I know this sounds strange, but I got a bad feeling from him. He was a little creepy," I said.

"Point him out if you see him again. In the meantime, let's finish up here. I called Aunt Flo and told her about the paper. She said we'd better double up on the paper goods. She also wanted us to stop by the store and get another tray or two of hors d'oeuvres for Caroline's party, just in case we end up inviting more folks."

"Good idea. I'll get some more 'Happy Birthday' napkins too. Nadia said she'd get us some publicity, but who'd have guessed that we'd be on the cover of the *Marytown Shopper*?"

"Hey, that's big-time for these parts. C'mon, we also have to grab another dozen copies for Aunt Flo. I want to leave some here, so we'll need to try the liquor store down the street."

chapter 3

An hour later, Ben and I drove up to the back of the stores, ready to unload. The Cog & Sprocket was at the edge of downtown, on the corner across from the church and the town graveyard, just on the other side of the bridge. It butted up to the utility road that ran parallel to the river, which all of the businesses used for parking and loading along the back of the shops. Since my store was on a corner, I could walk around and peer at Beckett's store across the street. Or not. Today, I was just as happy to avoid seeing it.

"Let me help you get this in the store," Ben said.

"I can hear Blue barking from here," I said, looking toward his shop. "He probably wants to go out—go ahead and get him."

"You're sure?" Ben smiled and started to back up toward his door.

"Positive. But wait, take the trays of food with you. Make sure that Blue can't get at them."

"We're going to use the shop as a food staging station. I'll put them in there. Don't worry, it's a no-Blue zone. The river isn't, though, so I'm going to go up and give him a good run before he gets cooped up again."

The river had been both the lifeblood of Orchard and the cause of its near death. The currents had powered several mills, providing both power and water for crops and livestock. But then Orchard had almost been wiped off the map in the early part of the 1900s by a particularly horrifying flood. She'd been rebuilt over time, but most people had moved. Some well-placed dams helped control the river, but Orchard had never regained its prominence in the Berkshires.

I picked up as many of the shopping bags as I could and walked up the back stairs to the shop. I was halfway up when the back door swung open. Nancy Reed stood in the doorway, outlined by the warm glow of the workroom. She looked more like Moira's sister than her mother. Nancy's dark brown hair was flecked with gray, there were laugh lines on her face, and her figure was a little more filled out. But the brown eyes were the same, framed by dark lashes and strong brows. She didn't wear makeup; she didn't need it. Nancy treated me like her own daughter, which gave me no end of pleasure.

"There you are! Great timing—we just got the food loaded into the barbershop until the party. Pat is out buying more ice for drinks. I'd have thought by now we'd have some snow. Always so handy for keeping bottles cold during parties. Anyway, why don't you hand the bags up to me," she said, leaning over the top of the stairs.

"Are you sure?"

"They're paper, aren't they? The stairs are what kill me, not the lifting."

I handed her the bags, and she passed them to someone behind her. It didn't take us long to unpack the entire contents of the SUV.

"What's this?" Nancy asked, looking in the last bag and holding up the birthday napkins. "Great, glad you remembered them. I'll hide these till later. Remind me that I put them in the old grandfather case. We want to keep this a surprise."

Nancy Reed and I had decided not to tell Caroline about the birthday celebration we had planned for her later tonight. Caroline was a private person and wouldn't even let us post her picture on the website, never mind having a fuss made over her birthday. I'd given in to no picture on the website, but I was going to make a fuss about her birthday, albeit a small one.

I'd stayed with Caroline while the Cog & Sprocket was being renovated. Not really with her. Though there was plenty of room at the cottage, Caroline was desperately allergic to Bezel, the cat I'd inherited along with the shop. Bezel and I had become a unit, so I stayed in the barn. This wasn't a hardship. The barn only looked like a barn, to sidestep some building ordinance in Orchard. Inside, it had a fully functioning workshop, temperature-controlled storage, and a studio apartment for guests. The barn was built with one side facing the lake, and that side was full of windows. The views were stunning, and Bezel and I were very happy during our stay. At first I'd kept to myself, but soon Caroline and I had fallen into a routine of having dinner together, and we'd become friends.

I carried the last bag into the Cog & Sprocket and closed the door tightly behind me. I looked out toward the front of the shop and smiled at the sight. The renovations down here had been limited, but significant to the operations. Basically, we'd opened it all up and replaced walls with sliders that could be locked into place. The air-filtering system had been upgraded, since dust was the enemy of clock and watch repair. And we'd built a painting booth so that small clocks could be refinished without asphyxiating everyone else. Larger pieces would be worked on out at the barn. Given the huge inventory G.T. and Caroline had bought last summer, there was still a preponderance of clocks on display, and in storage. But now the customer visiting the Cog & Sprocket could come in and browse at their leisure. I was hoping to make the shop a destination where people could come and fall in love with clocks.

"Did you buy out the store?" Nancy asked as she unloaded the bags, putting the contents into different piles. Nancy Reed was a force, but a force for good. She and her husband Pat worked for, or with, most of the shops on the POL cards. I knew she was as nervous as the rest of us about the open house, and whether or not we could pull it off.

"I bought enough for all three events this week: tonight's open house, the New Year's Town Hall celebration, and the opening of the Cog & Sprocket. So, yes, I sort of did buy out the store. Is it wrong to hope we run out?"

Nancy laughed. "My fear is always to not have enough food, but at the same time, too many leftovers make me feel like a failure. Wish we knew how many folks to expect tonight."

"Did you hear about this?" I said, pulling a copy of the *Marytown Shopper* out of one of the bags.

"Wow, isn't that something. Your hair looks great in this picture. Does Nadia know?"

"I'm not sure," I said, self-consciously patting my hair, which was knotted on the top of my head. "She didn't say anything to me if she did."

"Does Nadia know what?" Nadia said, coming down from upstairs. During the renovations, we'd created a small work-space in the attic as an office space. Since the shop was more open, computer work that needed quiet now had a dedicated place. Besides, it got Nadia out of public view, since customer service wasn't her forte. Space was tight, but Pat Reed had created a hallway upstairs, with a lot of built-in storage for different clock pieces. It was accessible to everyone in the shop, but safe from nosy customers. The stairs to the attic were off the hallway, as was the door to my apartment.

"Nadia, did you know the *Marytown Shopper* published the story you pitched?" I handed the younger woman the paper. It was hard to read her eyes behind her horn-rimmed glasses, but I did detect a hint of a smile tugging at the corner of her mouth.

"Cool," she said quietly.

"Really cool," I agreed. "Great job. Let's hope it helps bring people out tonight. Did I read somewhere that the temperature is going to drop?"

"It is going to be in the thirties. Not bad at all by New England standards. We've been working the social media pretty hard. I think there will be a great crowd." Nadia sounded happier than I'd ever heard her. Letting her run the marketing for this promotion had obviously been a good move. Honestly, it had been my only move, since no one else could do it. I'd put a lot on her twenty-year-old shoulders, but she'd carried it all well.

"I think so too. Could you help us down here?"

"She's been a big help already," Nancy said. "She dropped off the cards and the displays, plus some postcards, to the library and the Sleeping Latte. Even helped some of us old folks understand how to use that little doohickey on the back of the card."

"QR code," Nadia said, laughing. "We want to make it really easy for everyone to use, no matter how comfortable they are with technology."

"You've done a good job."

"We've all done a good job," Ada Clark said. She took a breath and sat down on a stool.

"Ada, I didn't know you were here. Are you all right?" I asked. Ada's first baby was due in three weeks, but I for one didn't know how she was going to last that long. Everything about Ada was tiny, except for her belly, which seemed to grow every time I saw her. I could tell she was uncomfortable, though she'd never tell anyone. She and her husband, Mac, ran the Corner Market pretty much alone, and she was determined to keep working for as long as possible. Their business needed her.

"I'm fine. I came down here to help, but I guess I missed the unloading of the car." Ada rubbed her belly and closed her eyes. She had dark circles underneath them, which were highlighted by the paleness of her skin. "I think I need to get a nap in before tonight, though. Nancy, are we all set?"

"We are," Nancy said. "Each store is part of the scavenger

hunt Nadia and I organized for tonight. See these cards? Tonight only, if folks go to all six locations on the POL cards and get an employee in the store to sign off, they get a goody bag. When we give out a goody bag, Nadia wants us to post a picture of the winner to social media. She's walked us all through that, but you don't need help with that, do you?" I shook my head "no" and bit my inner cheek to keep from laughing. If Nadia could get Nancy to post pictures to Facebook she had more powers than I thought. "Anyway, we've made a hundred and fifty goody bags, and we're leaving a few in each store."

"A hundred and fifty?" I said. "Isn't that a lot?"

"We have no idea. We have everything to make more if we need to. If we don't need them all, we'll stick a Cog & Sprocket sticker on them and use them for your grand opening. Nadia, why don't you walk Ada back to her shop and help carry her postcards?"

"Aye aye, Captain Nancy. Then I'm going to find Tuck, go home, and get dressed. I'll be back by four to help set up." Nadia almost seemed excited. My apathetic, eye-rolling Nadia. Will wonders never cease?

chapter 4

"Ruth, what are you going to do now?" asked Nancy, arranging the last of the goody bags beneath one of the counters. "How about a cup of tea?"

I thought about the dozen things I had on my to-do list and was about to rattle off a few, but then I really looked at Nancy's face. She obviously wanted to talk about something, but unlike her normal straightforward behavior, she was hemming and hawing. I decided to let her off the hook and make it easier for her to talk.

"Sure, I could always go for a cup of tea. Let's go upstairs."

I grabbed my coat and bag and brought both with me. I unlocked the door to the apartment and held it open for Nancy.

"Oh my. Doesn't this look wonderful?" she said.

"You were here two weeks ago, helping me paint." I laughed.

"Hey, I was just painting, which I like to do, and second-guessing your color choices. Which I also like to do. I had no idea it would all end up looking like this."

I loved my new apartment. When I'd moved in, the space was cluttered with boxes, furniture, clocks in midrepair, walls that were in the process of being removed, and antiquated fixtures. Even though Caroline said I could stay in the barn as long as I wanted, the renovation had to be both fast and thrifty. I was anxious to move in above the store and to be able to walk down the steps to work. So the choices we made were to finish taking down the walls, change out the kitchen fixtures but keep the footprint, refinish the floors, and paint the walls. I'd decided on an open floor plan, with a movable screen that I could put in front of the bedroom area if I had guests. The only splurge I'd made was in the bathroom. I kept the old clawfoot tub, but had Pat Reed put in a separate shower. It was an indulgence, but heaven compared to the low, awkward shower that it replaced. If I was going to live here, there would have to be some special tall-girl accoutrements.

"I'm glad you kept the old woodwork," Nancy said. "I was afraid you were going to paint over it."

"I couldn't—it is too beautiful," I said as I set the kettle on the stove and chose my least chipped mugs down from the cabinets. "I remember my grandmother explaining that Harry, her father-in-law, kept tradesmen working during the Great Depression by offering them odd jobs in the shop if business slowed down. The cabinetmakers started to do upgrades around here, which is why there are so many great appointments."

"It all shows really wonderfully. As I said, I was doubting your color choices, but you obviously know what you're doing."

I blushed with pride. I had used shades of white on most of the walls. But I had accent walls helping define the space. Tomato red in the kitchen area, blue in the bedroom area, and yellow in the sitting area—just one wall of each. The colors, along with black and white, were used in fabric and accent pieces as well. The furniture was old, but the patterns were modern.

"It's a tiny space, but it's just me these days, so it's fine. Whoops, sorry, it's me and Bezel." As if on cue, the large gray beauty came out from the bedroom area, stretching as she walked forward and came over to say hello.

Nancy reached down, and Bezel walked over and head-butted Nancy's hand and rubbed her head in the palm. Nancy finished saying hello to Bezel in a voice she used on no one other than the shop cat. "Is she behaving herself on the furniture?" Nancy asked, looking up at me.

"She is. She's a very well-behaved cat, for the most part. When she isn't, it's usually for good reason. And my fault," I said.

Nancy laughed and stood up. "Your furniture is lovely. Was it all your grandmother's?" she asked. "I don't recognize some of the pieces."

"I got the couch and the kitchen table in my divorce."

"I'm surprised you wanted to keep them," she said, turning to look more closely at the table.

"Me too," I laughed, "but it's a nice couch, and a great table. I'm a girl on a budget."

"It all looks terrific, now that you've moved in. I still think it's a shame that you gave up some of the space in front."

"The shop is desperate for storage space, you know that. Plus, we decided to give me a little more privacy, since we added a bathroom and kitchenette on the first floor, and that required some structural building out. As I said, it's just me. Counting Bezel, us. This is plenty of room."

"It won't always just be you," Nancy said, raising her eyebrows.

"I don't know. I wasn't a terrific success at being married," I said, trying to laugh it off. I pushed away from the kitchen counter where I had been leaning to answer the squeal of the boiling teakettle. Truth be told, I'd probably still be married if my husband hadn't found a newer model. These days, the idea of being Eric Evan's wife made me sad, rather than wistful. Imagine what I would have missed? Moving back here, owning my own shop? Eric would have insisted I sell it. Life worked out the way it was supposed to, and for that I was grateful.

"I was lucky to meet Pat when I did. We've been very happy all these years. I guess I want you girls to be as happy as we are," Nancy said, sitting down at the table.

"We girls" were Nancy and Pat's daughter, Moira, and I. Moira was the only Reed daughter and the apple of her father's eye. She and her mother worked together every day, and were too much alike for it to be smooth sailing all the time. Still, Nancy's critiques came from a place of love, and Moira recognized that, most of the time. The when-are-you-going-to-get-married? mantra was getting pretty old, though.

"You know, Nancy, I can't speak for Moira," I said, dropping tea bags into the steaming mugs and placing one in front of each of us at the table, "but if I found someone who made me as happy as Pat makes you, I'd get married again. I can't wait for that to happen in order to be happy though, you know?"

"Yeah, I know. All right, I'll stop trying to fix you up

with Ben Clover. Oh, stop, don't act so surprised. He's the best-looking guy in town."

"Why aren't you fixing him up with Moira, then?" I asked, feeling another blush rise.

"Moira's got eyes for Jeff Paisley. You know that."

"I don't know that, Nancy. At least, she hadn't told me that." She didn't have to, of course. I'd noticed how she looked at him. Jeff Paisley was always all business, on the job twenty-four/seven.

Nancy played with her mug of tea and then looked up at me. This face, with the furrowed brow and anxious expression, wasn't what I expected from Nancy Reed. After everything that happened last fall, my relationship had moved to another level with Nancy. Now we were confidantes as well as friends. Though, I still, at times, wished she were my mother.

"Nancy, what's the matter? You look worried."

"Oh, Ruthie. I am worried. I'm worried about you. I'm worried about Moira. I'm worried about Ben Clover. I'm even worried about Flo Parker, for heaven's sake, and that woman has more business lives than a cat. You all, we all, have put so much of ourselves in these shops. What happens if this open house idea doesn't take off? Have you thought about that? I know that Moira is worried about cash flow this winter, especially if the roads get bad and the students stop coming by. You must have invested a fortune in the Cog. What happens if business doesn't kick in the way you want it to? I worry . . ."

"I know you do, and I love you for it. We talked about this after Christmas dinner. We'll all be all right for a while. So, what else is going on?" I said, sensing that there was still more she was holding on to.

Nancy sighed and ran her fingers through her hair. "It's Beckett Green. I heard about his latest idea to bring in customers."

"Since they shut down the coffee shop idea, I thought we were done."

"He's still going to serve coffee. For free, no less. A chain store in Marytown is going to bring over the coffee urns, so he won't have to make it on site. He blames you for that, by the way."

"I asked if the building was up to code for a restaurant. Simple question," I said.

"A simple question that stopped that conversation for now. Then, to spite us all, he went outside of Orchard to get a coffee vendor, rather than giving Moira the business. But he isn't stopping there. Apparently, Beckett has decided to expand his business a bit more. He's going to start selling clocks and watches."

I tried to laugh, but couldn't. The Cog & Sprocket was all about the art of horology and the craft of clock making. We'd even started to investigate fine-watch repair, since Mark Pine had apprenticed with a watchmaker and had interest in furthering his knowledge. But quality came at a price, and I was still trying to figure out how to keep us all employed. That was already hard enough without competition across the street.

"What kind of clocks and watches?" I asked.

"I don't know," Nancy said, staring into her mug. "All I know is that he has decided to put you out of business."

"Ruthie, you upstairs?" Pat Reed bellowed up the staircase, startling Bezel from her cozy perch on the back of the couch.

I tried to respond, but my mouth was too dry. I felt the color drain from my face. That rat—what did I ever do to cross Beckett Green? Yeesh. This I didn't need.

"We're both up here," Nancy called out.

I took a careful sip of tea.

"It looks like we're almost finished setting things up down here," Pat called up. I could hear stairs creaking under his weight. "Ruth, I'd like you to check out the placement of the screen downstairs. I want to make sure we show enough of the stock to be interesting, but that we make folks want to come back for the grand opening next week." Pat kept talking as he entered the room. He leaned over and gave Nancy a peck on her cheek. He turned toward me, and stopped.

"Ruthie, what's the matter? You're as pale as a ghost."

"I told Ruth that Beckett Green had decided to put her out of business. She didn't take it well."

"You told her what? For the love of Pete, Nancy, what are you trying to stir up?"

"I'm not stirring anything up. You know he has it in for her. He has it in for everyone. A terrible man, that Beckett Green."

"He does not have it in for Ruthie. Honestly, Nancy, sometimes I wonder about you."

"Pat," I said, "did you know that Beckett was going to sell clocks and watches?"

"I'd heard something about watches, from Mark. He went out of his way to tell me they were cheap plastic watches. I hadn't heard about the clocks, but I can't imagine they'll be high-end," Pat said. Pat was a peacekeeper, so I wasn't really surprised I hadn't heard this yet, but still.

"What's he doing?" I said. I hated how pitiful I sounded. Pat didn't seem to notice.

"Beckett is a self-important jackass who is trying to set his business up as a one-stop shop in Orchard," Pat said. "He'd be better off being a decent bookstore and leaving the other businesses to us. He'll learn soon enough, one way or the other. Don't worry about it, Ruth. Especially tonight." Pat gave me a wink, and I forced myself to smile back. A deep breath cleared my head. He was right, of course. Nothing I could do about this tonight.

"And you"—Pat turned toward his wife—"stop with the gossip. Moira talked to you about that. I know you're worried about the coffee business Beckett may take away from the Sleeping Latte. But we'll deal with that when the time comes."

"Pat Reed, some day you'll need to take off those rose-colored glasses and see what's happening around here," Nancy said, shaking her head.

"Trust me, I see what's happening. What's happening is that Beckett Green, and Kim Gray, are worrying my best girl too much. They aren't worth it, either of them."

"I wonder if Kim Gray will come by tonight?" I asked.

"Did you invite her?" Nancy asked. "'Cause I didn't."

"Of course I invited her," I said. "She's the town manager. She has to want this to work, doesn't she? Besides, if we didn't invite her, she'd tell everyone. Since we did, if she doesn't show up, it makes her look bad."

"Tonight is going to be terrific," Pat said. "You know I had my doubts, but this crazy POL promotion may work. Everyone I've seen today is planning on coming by. Now, let's see some smiles from both of you. What say?"

Nancy faked a smile, then sighed and glanced down at her watch. "Yikes, look at the time. I'm going to go check in with Moira, and then I'm heading home to get changed.

You coming, Pat?" Nancy got up and squeezed my shoulder. I gave her a smile and stood up as well.

"Let me do a walk-through with Ruth, and then I'll meet you down at the Sleeping Latte. Fifteen minutes, tops."

Pat and I walked Nancy to the front door. The windows on the front door were covered with old-fashioned blinds, the metal kind from the middle of the last century. When the shop was open, the blinds were raised, welcoming customers in and letting the rest of us look out at downtown Orchard. The Reeds stepped outside to the porch, which ran along the front of the shop, and exchanged a few words. I turned away, trying to give them some privacy. I looked around at the shop, from the point of view of a new customer. I smiled at the immediate impression of clocks, clocks, and more clocks. I needed to use the front entrance more often. I missed out on the "wow" when I used the back door.

I'd always loved walking into the shop. We hadn't had to do much work—it was already perfect, with beautiful oak-and-glass cases creating the customer counter. There was shelving that had acted as a wall to the back of the shop, with a gap in the center to allow someone to come from the back to the front when a customer came in. As part of the renovation, we took the back off the shelves, allowing for a peek into the workroom. We'd also taken down the wall to the right, opening up the tiny side space as a showroom. The shop was still tiny, cramped, and overflowing with clocks, but a new paint job, better lighting, and reupholstered chairs scattered about for customers to sit on made it more welcoming. It was perfect.

For tonight, Pat had created a screen that blocked both the shelves and the showroom area. We'd open them for the grand opening next week. We were going to use the front counter for food, drinks, and displays about the other shops. The side showroom featured some of our stock, all beautiful, but nothing too precious. I worried about some of our more expensive pieces being knocked off the wall or tipped over by exuberant visitors. Of course, that was if people showed up.

I looked over at one of the clocks. One minute to the hour. That's why Pat wanted me to come downstairs. This was a dress rehearsal for tonight.

I glanced over at Pat, who had come in and closed the door behind him. He looked as nervous as I felt. I held my breath as the minute hand clicked over. A cacophony of bells and chimes began to fill the space. I could tell that they weren't all in sync, and I made a mental note to move up the minute hand on the grandfather to the left of the door. Still, it was wonderful.

"That will knock their socks off, don't you think?" Pat asked.

"I do. Or scare them to death. Do you think we should hold off until the grand opening?"

"Nah. Let's give them a preview of the big show. For the opening we'll have a few more ready to go. Plus, folks will be able to see them all."

"I hope I remember to shut off a few of these chimes before I go upstairs tonight."

"I'm putting one of those sticky tabs on the doors of each one with a chime, so they'll be easy enough to shut off. Bezel doesn't love them, does she?"

"She really doesn't, poor thing. She shoots under the couch and hunkers down the instant the first chime rings out. But the new door upstairs is a pretty good sound barrier. So, Pat, what do you think? Will Kim Gray show up tonight? Is Beckett Green trying to put me out of business?"

"It's like a soap opera around here," Pat said, delicately sticking a little pink tab to a clock with his big, rough hand. "Of course Kim Gray will show up. I hope it's on the hour, so she can hear the chimes. It will help make the case for the clock tower, don't you think?"

"How so?"

"The chimes make you feel alive. You practically glow from the inside when they go off. They'll work on Kim Gray. Imagine if we can fill up Orchard with that sound?"

"Imagine that. I think you want this to happen as much as I do."

"Maybe more," Pat said. "Your grandfather talked about it for years. This last year, I'd begun to imagine how it would feel to work on it. Lost hope for a while, but you've brought it back. This will happen. We need to help Kim Gray see the light."

"Or hear the bells," I said.

"Who else is here?" I asked Pat. We were doing one more walk-through of the shop, trying to make sure everything was being shown off to its best potential.

"Nadia and Mark are going to put the watches in the front case, so folks can see them tonight," Pat said, explaining what the two of them were doing, huddled in the side room surrounded by boxes. It looked to me like they were holding hands.

"I thought she was heading home to get dressed," I said, half to myself.

"She went and picked up her clothes, and Tuck's. They're going to get dressed over at Ben's."

"Pat, you are a fount of knowledge, you know that?"

"No, I'm in the business of keeping the peace. Moira was looking for Tuck earlier, needed him for something or another. It threw off Nadia's schedule for the evening, so we all had to come up with a plan."

Pat and I were moving one of the mantel clocks to a safer space, away from where we were planning on putting the food. It was a beautiful old piece, hand painted to look like marble, with gold columns along the front. It was in terrible shape when it came to us as part of a collection. Not only was it not running, it had obviously not been tended to for years. I'd been working on it for a while, and I finally had it running up to my standards. Moving it was a risk, but it was a good test. I looked at it carefully and checked the time against other clocks in the area. I'd make sure it was still keeping time tonight, poor old thing. I couldn't sell it if it wasn't working well. Even if I was tempted to keep it, I'd need to get it running. That was the part of my work I really loved—bringing old pieces back to their former glory. I grabbed a rag and brushed out the smudges we'd added to the veneer.

I heard a tapping sound coming from the front of the shop. "Is there someone at the front door?" I asked as we put the clock down carefully and slid it toward the back of the countertop. I went over and peered through the blinds, feeling a grin split my face as I saw Ben standing on the front stoop.

"I found three bags of candy on the floor of the backseat. Since I didn't buy them, I thought they must be yours."

"Thanks, Ben. That's my just-in-case stash."

"'Just-in-case stash?'"

"My grandmother always had one. Some candy or nibbles she could put out just in case food was running low. The thought of completely running out of food was too horrible to imagine."

"There's fifteen pounds of chocolate here. That's quite a stash."

"Holiday candy, on sale but still seasonal. And you're right, I'm sure we'll do a fine job here in the shop if we don't open this up during the next week."

"Ben, you just missed the show!" Pat said.

"The show?" Ben said, coming into the shop and putting the candy on the countertop.

"I don't want to ruin the surprise, but let me say this. Be here on the hour at some point tonight. You won't be sorry."

Ben smiled. "Mark and I have a surprise tonight too."

"You and Mark? Really?" I asked.

"Yeah. Mark and I cooked it up last week while we were painting the red wall in the showroom for the twentieth time."

"Don't exaggerate. It only took five coats," I said.

"'Only five coats,' she says. Pat, it seemed like twenty coats, didn't it?"

"Ruth had a specific color in mind. That takes some work. You've got to admit, that accent wall looks terrific. Makes the clocks really pop."

"Thank you, Pat," I said. "Anyway, while you were painting you hatched a plan?"

"A secret plan. To take place right after the open house, right before Caroline's party."

"You're not going to tell me anything, are you, Ben?" I said, squinting at him accusingly.

"It's a secret, Ruth. You're not good with secrets, are

you?" Ben and Pat both laughed, and I pretended to. But he was right—I wasn't good with secrets. I could say that the switch had happened when I discovered my ex-husband was having an affair, but that would be a big lie. I'd never liked secrets and had always done everything I could to uncover them. No matter what the cost.

"By the way, Moira brought the cake over," Ben said. "I put it in the shampoo area of my shop—right where we usually put towels, so if Caroline goes by to get something, it isn't in plain sight."

"Great, I'll go over and get it before the birthday party," I said.

"Does Caroline have any idea about the party yet? Between Nancy and Flo, it is hard to keep a secret like that," Ben said.

"So far she has no idea," I said. "She probably wouldn't come if she did. She thinks we're gathering to unveil the new website. Which we are, sort of."

"I'm really looking forward to that," Ben said. "I'm amazed at how much material you've all been working on for the new site. Makes my static page with directions and hours seem pitiful, and I haven't even seen the finished product."

"Still not sure why you needed me to do those videos," Pat said. "Can't see how seeing my old face is going to help us sell clocks."

"Nadia thought they would help with some of our marketing efforts. I'll admit, I was skeptical, but they are really terrific. Tuck did a great job with the editing. I wish Mark and Caroline would have agreed to do a couple of them."

"Some folks are camera shy," Pat said.

"So, what are these videos?" Ben asked.

"Short videos on some of the clocks, or how to wind a grandfather, or naming the different parts of a clock. We're going to rotate them out on the site, and I'm hoping it will be something to drive traffic."

"So no videos of Pat tap-dancing around the shop?" Ben said, nudging the older man with his elbow.

"You heard Ruth. We're trying to drive people to the shop, not away from it." He turned toward me and smiled. "You sound like a marketing expert," he said. "Nadia's rubbing off on you."

"I'm becoming one. Being a small business owner is a huge learning curve for me. Sometimes I wish I could just fix clocks, but I really have to sell some of them too."

"Lots of them, actually, to pay for all of this," Pat said, gesturing around the shop. It was hard to see with all of the curtains masking the back of the shop. I could easily have skipped the cosmetics down here, left the back closed off, the floors scuffed, and the woodwork worn down. But if not now, when? I needed to make the upstairs habitable, and doing all the work at once made sense. Sure, my bank account was pretty anemic. But it was all going to pay off. It had to.

"Pat, if I didn't have you, all of you, to help me, I never could have pulled this off. Look at what you did in a few weeks. It's amazing. I can't wait to show it off to the world."

Pat and Ben left together, and I locked the door behind them. I grabbed the three bags of candy off the counter. I needed to hide them in plain sight and not in my apartment, or fifteen pounds of candy would be fourteen in no time. Chocolate was my downfall.

I walked through the curtains to the back of the shop. This area was, perhaps, the least changed. My grandfather's presence was still omnipresent, and I wouldn't do a thing to change that. Not for anything. I stepped to the right, planning on putting the candy in one of the cubbies where we kept the work that was ready for customer pickup. I had a lot of choices for where to stash the stash. That had to change.

As I turned the corner, I caught another glimpse of Mark Pine and Nadia Wint, still bent over a piece of paper, arms touching. They didn't hear me come in, and I was tempted to back away rather than interrupt this intimate moment. Mark Pine personified shy, at least with me. Obviously, Nadia had a different effect on him. I couldn't help but wonder what her boyfriend, Tuck, would think.

A part of me would be fine with Nadia and Mark being a couple. Tuck and I didn't really hit it off. His hipster disdain for me was palatable. It wasn't only for me, though. He was too cool to show enthusiasm for much, including, in my opinion, Nadia. His work was good, and he was fairly reliable. Still, he made me feel like I was missing a joke. I didn't like the feeling.

As an employer looking at a week of business openings, this love triangle, if that's what it was, would be way too much of a distraction. Adding drama to an already tense week—not good for my stress level. I had a lot riding on those three people. I hated that I was worried about Tuck being able to take photos tonight, about the website work Nadia still needed to finish before we went live, about Mark's focus on the jobs he'd taken on. Hopefully, the romantic drama wouldn't interfere.

One of the bags of chocolate slipped from my arms and

smacked onto the hardwood. Nadia and Mark jumped apart. Mark had the good grace to blush as he pushed the papers they were looking at back in the folder. Nadia looked annoyed, but she always looked a little annoyed. I wanted to wipe off Nadia's dark eyeliner, pull her hair back from her face, and tell her to smile. But I held off.

"Whoops," I said, plastering a smile on my face as I scooped up the bag. Nadia shot me a look that could fry ice, but I ignored it. "Hey, just so you both know, this chocolate is in case we run out of food tonight."

"You're kidding me, right? We have, like, ten dozen clock cookies."

"I know." Boy, did I know. Caroline and I had spent the last week rolling them out, frosting them, and then using a stencil to dust them with a shimmery clock face. Last night we'd had a bagging party—putting each cookie in a cellophane bag, tying it with ribbon, and attaching a Cog & Sprocket card to the bag. My fingers still ached from curling ribbon.

"Do you really think we'll have that many people come by tonight?" Mark asked.

"I have no idea. I'd love to think so. Otherwise, we'll be eating cookies for days."

"We're all over social media," Nadia said. "I posted a picture of the cookies. Having food will definitely help get folks to come by. Otherwise, and don't take this the wrong way, getting people to party at a clock shop might be a hard sell. This is a great opportunity to get some fun video and pictures and let people know the party starts here. No need to freak out."

"Okay, I won't panic. Until I'm eating clock cookies for the next month."

Nadia laughed and looked shocked at the sound. "We

need to get a group shot tonight. Maybe at Caroline's party afterward?"

"Sounds like a plan. Now, I think I'm going to go up and get dressed. Unless you need me down here?"

"As a matter of fact, I wondered if you had a couple of minutes to talk," Mark asked.

Nadia reached over and squeezed his arm. "I'm going to head out and find Tuck," she said. She didn't look at me when she walked out through the back of the shop.

Just when everything was falling into place. Please don't let this be bad news.

chapter 5

"Please don't let this be bad news," I said to Mark after the door closed behind Nadia.

"It isn't. At least, I hope it isn't. Beckett Green offered me a job."

"What? Doing what?"

"Fixing clocks."

"Fixing clocks?" Nancy had been right; he was trying to put me out of business.

"He told me that he had an opportunity to buy some antique clocks and watches. He wanted to hire me to get them ready to go on sale. Part-time. He said I didn't have to tell you."

"What a weasel," I said.

"Yeah, definitely uncool," Mark said. He sounded so sincere, I had to smile. He wasn't that much younger than I was, about five years. Part of his soul seemed so much older. But then there were these times, when he seemed like a kid.

"What did you tell him?" I said.

"I told him I was working for you and that meant I wasn't working somewhere else."

"Thank you, Mark. That means a lot. You're a valued member of the team, that's for sure. Did you look at the clocks? I wonder . . ."

"I saw some pictures, but only saw one in person. The clocks looked like some of your pieces. You know, the banjos." Banjo clocks were invented by Simon Willard, right here in Massachusetts, around 1800. The wall clocks had a round face, an elongated neck, and then a rectangular box on the bottom. There were only four thousand or so true Simon Willards produced, but there have been hundreds of replicas made over the years by members of the Willard family, and other companies. There wasn't a chiming mechanism built into original Willards, but they were still beautiful clocks. We had dozens of examples of banjo clocks, but I had yet to work on a Simon Willard. I went to the museum in Grafton a couple of times a year, trying to charm the director.

"But you couldn't tell the era?"

"No, sorry. Yesterday, he showed me pictures of a couple of watches. Again, couldn't tell the details, but they looked authentic. One looked like it could be a Patek Philippe. You know them: Patek was Polish, Philippe was French. They founded a company in 1851, one of the premier Swiss watchmakers. The Stern family has owned the company since 1932 and—"

"Slow down, Encyclopedia Brown! I remember them." I

almost hated to cut him off—his love of horology was so earnest and pure—but this chocolate was heavy.

"Well, last year a Patek Philippe sold for twenty-four million dollars."

"Twenty-four million dollars?"

"It was a Supercomplication pocket watch. Nine hundred and twenty components. Man, I'd love to take a look at that baby."

I had to smile, since I recognized the look on Mark's face. I wore it myself when I thought that one of the grandfather clocks in the shop was a rare find a few weeks back when I was unpacking. It wasn't, but it was still a thrill to work on.

"The watch Beckett showed you was a Patek Philippe?"

"Looked like one, at least. Like I said, he said he'd gotten his hands on a huge shipment of clocks and watches at a good price. He needed someone to help him look over the collection. A good quality watch, like the one he showed me, could be worth thousands, maybe more."

"Why does Beckett Green have watches worth thousands of dollars?"

"He said he had a friend who stumbled across them at an auction and gave them to Beckett to put in his shop, sort of like decorations."

"Did Beckett say why he wanted to decorate with clocks?"

"No. Honest, Ruth, I have no idea. He was showing me one of the clocks, so I showed him how to wind it up, talked him through it, explaining a little bit how it worked. He was fascinated. But I guess you understand that."

"I do. All too well. I wonder why he didn't bring one by the shop? I'd have been happy to give him an estimate."

"I suggested that, but he acted kind of squirrelly. Today, he upped the pressure. He told me he needed to hire me to get the clocks ready for sale, but like I told you, I turned him down."

"Even though you were itching to look at those watches. It's okay. I know you love them. Listen, as I said, I really appreciate your loyalty. You know I have more than enough work to keep you busy, but I can't stop you from taking on other jobs," I said half smiling. I didn't want him feeling pressure from me too.

"Thanks, Ruth, but I've decided I want to work for you right now. If that's all right?"

"Of course it is." I studied Mark, who was specifically not looking at me. I added *Get to know the staff better* to my internal list of New Year's resolutions. Mark was holding something back, but I didn't have time to pry it from him now. "Tell you what. My grandfather had several pocket watches he always meant to get to, but he never did. How about if I bring them in for you to work on? They'd be a good challenge for you, I think. Especially since they haven't worked in years."

"Did your grandfather work on watches as well?"

"He did, or he meant to. Whenever he bought an estate, he'd hold on to the watches, promising himself, and me, that we'd work on them."

"Why?" he said, looking up.

"He thought I should know a bit about watches, in case business slowed down. Old habits passed on by his father. During the Depression, the Cog & Sprocket couldn't make it as just a clock shop, so they brought in other craftsmen to work on watches. My grandfather was young, and he learned how to do repairs from some of the people in the shop. He preferred clocks. To each his own, I guess."

"To each his own. I'd love to take a look at those watches.

Don't worry too much about Beckett Green. He's worked himself up to a tizzy. Rina tries to talk him down, but it is going to get worse the closer they get to opening. At this rate, he's never going to open if he keeps getting distracted by other people and crazy ideas. He isn't anyone to worry about."

I hoped Mark was right. In fact, I was banking on it.

chapter 6

I loved my new bathroom. It was the biggest indulgence of
the entire renovation. The old clawfoot tub was perfect for
baths. When I moved in, there was a contraption that turned
it into a shower as well, but it was always a nightmare trying
to keep the circle of shower curtains from attacking me. At
five foot ten inches, the five-foot-tall showerhead was also
way too short for me to get my curly red hair really washed,
never mind rinsed. Adding a shower stall, one that I could
stand up in, and move around in if so inclined, was a luxury.
A luxury made affordable by the fact that the shower bed
didn't match the color of the tiles, and the glass door had a
scratch. The scratch-and-dent reject section of every store
was more than adequate for me, and perfect for my budget.

Much as I wanted to linger, my shower was quick. I did
wash my very curly hair. I knew it was never going to dry

in time for the open house, but since I planned to wear it up, the only hope of taming it was starting all over with the conditioner-and-product balancing act that kept my curls controlled for very limited periods of time. Wintertime was the worst. Hat head combined with static equaled a very scary hairstyle.

I finished up my ablutions, including layers of lotion and a lot more makeup than I normally wear. The natural look took a lot of effort. Layers of powders, blending, outlining, and smudging. Lipstick came last, once my dress was safely over my head. I wrapped myself in my robe and went to get dressed.

I walked back to my bedroom area and closed the curtain that gave me a semblance of privacy. Even though I'd locked the door to my apartment, I was well aware of the other people who worked in the shop, and had keys. *Better safe than sorry* was my motto about privacy. The living area had needed the most work when I decided to move in, mostly because it had been a hodgepodge of half-torn-down walls that had morphed a small apartment into a storage area that had been filling up ever since my grandfather had moved into the house Caroline still lived in. We'd taken down all of the walls and then used shelving and cabinets to divide up the space. I hung a curtain between the two cabinets that created the doorway into the bedroom area so that I could close it for privacy, but Bezel, my roommate, could move about freely.

Bezel was the shop cat my grandfather had adopted last spring. She was a mixed breed, but looked and acted a lot like a Russian Blue. Her headbutts were a force. The only way to stop them from breaking my nose was to kiss her head as she moved in. She'd look at me with disgust, turn, and walk away. But she'd always look back, as if to wink, before she settled down on the nearest soft, flat surface. I could hear her purring from across the room.

Even though I'd made the design choices upstairs, Bezel had been part of the plan. She needed windowsills, safe places for her food, privacy for her litter box, and plenty of space to roam. After a break-in last fall, I also needed to make sure I could lock us both in the apartment. That said, I recognized that living above your shop meant people would come in and out more often than usual, hence the curtain.

I looked down at the black knit dress I'd laid out earlier, and sighed. Gray hair. I was always wearing gray cat hair. I took out the lint roller and did what I could to remove traces of Bezel. Caroline was terribly allergic to her, so de-Bezeling had become part of my routine. I put on my undergarments and pulled up my tights. Last step: I needed to get the dress on without ruining my hair or makeup. I unzipped the back and stepped into it, pulling it up carefully. Navigating it over my hips took a moment, but the give of the fabric worked with me. The dress was a simple shift with a sweetheart neckline. Flattering, but not too dressy. Bezel jumped up on the bed and blinked her eyes at me. I blinked back and she smiled.

"What do you think?"

"Meow," she said.

"Thanks," I said. I looked at myself in the mirror I'd hung up on the back of the wardrobe. Aside from at my grandfather's funeral, I don't think anyone in Orchard had seen me this dressed up. No wonder. I'd given it up the day my divorce papers had dried, leaving my faculty-wife costumes in my rearview mirror, along with my ex-husband.

I futzed with my hair, pulling damp auburn spirals out of my bun to frame my face, and took a deep, shaky breath. I was nervous. But not only about the open house. As much as I hated to admit it, even to myself, I was nervous about seeing Ben while I was dressed up, and what his reaction would be. I wanted it to be positive. Not too positive. I wasn't ready to start dating. But I was ready to start thinking about it, and Ben was an interesting prospect.

I struggled to reach the back zipper. I should have paid more attention in yoga class—I couldn't reach it.

"Bezel, can you help?"

She sighed, and I joined her. This was the hard part about being single. No zipper help. A rare need, and one for which there surely had to be a modern work-around. There is a fortune to be made on personal zipper-pulling inventions. I reached around by my waist and tried to get the zipper inched up. A couple of inches. Still couldn't reach it over my shoulder, so I twisted again. A couple more inches. I could almost grab the zipper, and somehow thought jumping up and down would help. Bezel meowed and moved to the other side of the bed. I finally got the dress zipped, but now my hair needed fixing. But when didn't it?

I was mid curl wrangling when I heard the shop phone ring in the kitchen. I was glad I'd had an extension installed up here, and even gladder that I could turn off the ringer if I wanted to. I was tempted to let it go to voice mail, but decided against it at the last minute. Maybe Nancy needed something, or Caroline was running late?

"Hello. Cog & Sprocket. How can I help?" I said.

"Caroline?" a voice whispered.

"No, this is Ruth. May I help you?"

"Ruth? Are you Thom Clagan's granddaughter?"

"Yes."

"My name is Zane Phillips. I am, I was, a friend of your grandfather's. Perhaps he's mentioned me? Or Caroline has?" The voice was still whispering. Maybe he didn't want to be overheard? Or he had a cold?

"I think so," I said. The name was familiar, but since I'd become immersed in the business of the Cog & Sprocket, I couldn't be sure.

"I'd love to come by the shop. I haven't been there for years, and I read about the open house in the paper. I didn't realize that you were Ruth until I read the article more closely. I saw you—"

"We are going to reopen next week. On January second," I said. I didn't want to rush him, but trips down memory lane took time, and I was running late. No big surprise, but still, I couldn't be late to my own party.

"Please, tell me. Is Caroline about?"

"No," I said. I didn't elaborate. Something about his voice sounded familiar, but my gut said to hold back until I could talk to Caroline directly. She was so private, it was contagious.

"Is she going to be at the open house?"

"She isn't feeling well, so I'm not sure she's going to make it." I'd run the name by Caroline first. Not that it was my job to protect her, but still.

"I'm sorry to hear that. I was hoping to stop by tonight. When you talk to her, please tell her I called and am in the area. I'd love to see her."

"May I have a phone number where you can be reached?"

I reached for a scrap of paper and wrote down the numbers he rattled off.

"If I don't hear from her, I'll call back," he said. "Perhaps you could give me her home number?"

"You know, I don't know it off the top of my head," I lied. "I have it programmed in my phone, which is downstairs, charging. Sorry about that."

"I'll try back later in the week. Please do pass on the message. I'm sure she'll want to see me." With that, Zane Phillips hung up. I wrote down his name and put the paper in the pocket of my dress. All of my dresses had pockets—a prerequisite for purchase. I heard one clock chime, and then others join in. Five o'clock.

Yeesh. Once again, I was running behind time. A heckuva habit for a clockmaker. If anyone asked, I'd blame it on the zipper. The party started in a half hour. I looked longingly at my beat-up Dr. Martens nestled in the corner before I zipped up my slick, high-heeled-for-me black boots, and slashed on some red lipstick. I was tempted to try and fix my hair again, but gave up. It would have to do. I closed the door behind me as the clocks finished their five o'clock show.

I closed, and locked, my apartment door, which was an unusual move for me, especially since I'd moved back to Orchard. But the shop was going to be full of strangers tonight, and some might decide to explore. I worried less about a burglar than I did a curious visitor letting Bezel out.

The steps down to the shop were wide and not terribly steep. The entire building was designed with hatches, trapdoors, and movable walls. I needed to explore the history more, and kicked myself for not asking my grandparents more questions while they were alive. I'd spent a lot of time with them, especially during high school, but I'd always taken the marvel that was, and is, the Cog & Sprocket a little for granted. No longer. During the renovations, Pat Reed and I had agreed that not a single hatch was to be nailed shut and any wall safes were to be kept in use. Though we'd configured the attic space to be storage and office space, we both were surprised by the number of hiding places we hadn't known about. We hadn't finished exploring loose floorboards and boarded-up eaves upstairs, and exploring and archiving the contents of the basement had been delayed. The onus had been on getting me moved back in, and the shop open, and we'd met those goals, or were pretty close. Who knew what treasures we still had left to discover?

I stepped off the final step to the stunning wide pine planks of the shop floor and felt the now-familiar pang of joyful pain. Joy at being at the Cog & Sprocket, and the pain of not being able to share the joy with G.T. His death, his murder, was still a fresh wound. That his murderer was behind bars was of some comfort, and I was pleased that I had played a small role in making that happen. But the ache was still there for me, and I know it was still fresh for Caroline. We'd left the wooden pegs by the back door, and one of G.T.'s plaid wool work shirts still hung there. The sight gave me comfort, and last week I'd caught Caroline burrowing her face in the fabric, undoubtedly looking for the scent of Old Spice, pipe smoke, and machine oil that were the memory markers of the man who'd worn the shirt.

I walked through the workroom and then took a left into the showroom. This space had been a forgotten pocket a few months ago, but now it showcased some of the more beautiful clocks, while giving customers a place to sit while waiting. We'd even added a restroom and small kitchenette toward the back for both customers and staff. Family story had it that my great-grandfather had served "special tea" in this room during Prohibition. I looked over at the picture of Harry Clagan from the '20s, smiling at the mischievous grin on his face as he stood in front of the Cog & Sprocket. From what my grandmother had told me, he was not as gifted a clockmaker as his father or his son, but he was a gifted town leader and a wonderful man. His was one of the many ghosts I wanted to welcome back to the Cog & Sprocket.

I looked around at the old family pictures interspersed among the impressive clock collection. Deciding what to put in the showroom had been a difficult decision. Because of the two estate purchases G.T. and Caroline had made last winter, we had a lot of inventory, including some really stunning pieces that were worth a great deal of money. But, as Nadia kept reminding Caroline and me, the Cog & Sprocket wasn't a museum, it was a shop. Customers needed to see a range of clocks, some of which they could afford, others which they needed to aspire to. Caroline had pushed me to include a couple of my own creations—part clock, part art pieces. I'd created one I called the Cog & Sprocket, a large piece that evoked the spirit of the shop. I'd started working on it before I came back to Orchard and finished it right after I'd moved back. To the outside observer, it looked like something a clockmaker would create instead of scrapbooking. But looking more closely, there was more to it. The clock was an eight-day mechanism that worked perfectly. Each cog had a name, or memory, or date etched on it. Some were well known to the town, others were personally meaningful family dates. I'd hand painted all of the pieces on the clock, most of which moved throughout the day. I was proud of the Cog & Sprocket clock, and knew it would help people envision what was possible to create in the new clock tower. Pat had installed it on the back wall, near the kitchenette and restrooms, hoping it would do its job and draw people farther into the showroom.

The showroom was cramped, overcrowded, and wonderful. Nadia's website included more of the inventory than we had on display, with promises that more would make it to the shop, but all was available for sale. There was a lot riding on this new online presence. The shop had needed to step into this new century. The website was a leap.

I heard the front doorbell chime, and saw Nadia and Tuck come in. The door chime was new, and a vast improvement over the buzzer that had been installed to let people know that customers had come into the shop, but it was temporary. With the new open configuration, we could see the customers come in, though we still needed something to remind us to look up. Pat Reed promised to design a more spectacular door chime and to install it by the opening. He wouldn't tell me more, but promised I would love it. Trusting Pat had served me well so far, so there was no real reason to stop now. It's just that I was very particular about the door chimes.

"Don't you both look terrific," I said. I wasn't lying; they were both dressed to the nines. I hoped Orchard was ready for the Gothic steampunk fashion statement they were making. Nadia's black velvet dress, bustier, fishnet stockings, and high-heeled ankle boots were offset by a red ruffled coat. I was really pleased to see that she was wearing the pair of earrings I'd made her, fashioned out of clock parts and dangling to her shoulders.

Tuck was wearing a crimson smoking jacket, white

pleated shirt, and string tie over blue jeans and black cowboy boots. His mustache was waxed to create impressive curves, and the soul patch on his chin was well groomed. It was a lot of look for the twenty-five-year-old to carry off, but he was trying. As always, he barely smiled at me, but did nod, acknowledging my compliment.

"Thanks, you look great too," Nadia said with a hint of that elusive sincerity that I had seen earlier. "How's it going? Are you surveying your empire again?"

"I was, am," I said, feeling a blush rise. "I do love this showroom."

"I picked up the new brochures," she said. "I know we were going to wait till the opening, but I thought maybe we'd want to put some out tonight." She handed me the trifold brochure she'd been working on for the past three weeks. I'd thought that it was an old-fashioned idea, creating a printed piece, and was surprised that Nadia had suggested it. But looking at what she'd created, I understood the value. A picture of the shop on the front, a map to our location on the back, and inside a scavenger hunt for customers, inviting them to come and find the grandfather clock with the moon face, the banjo clock with the carriage scene painted on the door, and other pieces that we would always display and never sell. The brochure balanced old-fashioned, with muted sepia tones, with modern touches, including our social media icons running along the bottom. Our website was prominent, as was our Twitter handle of @ClaganClocks. She'd included a QR code for people who wanted to take a virtual tour of the shop.

"Nadia, I love them!" I said, and meant it. I wasn't usually as energetic in my praise, but I always pushed my enthusiasm around Nadia, hoping it would become a virus she'd catch. So far, I'd had little success, though I did see a faint smile. "Yes, let's put them out tonight. All of these events are feeding into one another, so let's not waste an opportunity."

"Agreed," she said, smoothing her dress. "Did the rest of the clock cookies arrive yet?"

"Caroline's on her way, I'd imagine. The rest of them are with her."

"I'm going to go up to the office and drop my stuff. I'll be right down," she said. We all turned toward the tinkling sound of the door chime, and stopped when Beckett Green walked in.

Beckett Green had been the first person to welcome me to Orchard in October, and I'd taken him to be a mild-mannered, milquetoast man. I'd liked him at first. The last time I'd been so mistaken by a man was when I met my ex-husband.

"Beckett," I said. It came out like a hiss, and Nadia snorted a laugh.

He stopped and looked around the shop. "It doesn't look that different, does it?" he said. "After the weeks of work, I'd expected more."

"Most of the work is upstairs, in my apartment. Only friends have seen those changes," I said.

"Living in your shop. How quaint," he said through a thin-lipped smile. "Seems to be a trend here in Orchard."

"Not all of us can afford to live in a B and B like you and Rina do," Nadia said. "Tell me, do you prefer the pancakes or waffles for breakfast? Or both?"

I couldn't help glancing down at his belly, which was pushing over his belt buckle. I glanced over at Nadia and raised my eyebrows. I knew engaging with Beckett would prolong his visit. Besides, a part of me still hoped it could all work out.

Beckett sucked in his stomach and glared at us. "Ben lives over his shop too, doesn't he? Of course, if business doesn't pick up, he can move into the shop itself and rent out his place for some extra income." Beckett laughed at his own terrible joke. Nadia and I didn't crack a smile. I looked around for Tuck and noticed he was prowling around the back of the shop.

"What can I do for you, Beckett? We're about to start the downtown open house. There's still time to be a part of the new POL card," I said. I'd added a *Visit the website for more special offers* tagline to the bottom on the off chance he'd change his mind.

"As I said, I don't see the business strategy of supporting one another with discounts," he said, leaning in close to squint at a clock on the wall by the door. "We all know my shop would take the biggest hit, and supporting the rest of you with my cash isn't in my best interest."

I sighed, but didn't take the bait. My family had deep Orchard roots, and I understood the community. And that it was a community. We all looked out for one another, and kindness counted. Beckett didn't understand the power of paying it forward, but he'd learn. His bottomless bank account would keep him in business out of spite, but his local customer base was eroding every time he opened his mouth in public. Tourists would only get him so far, and they'd get him nowhere in the winter.

"Again, what can I do for you?"

"I'm looking for Mark Pine," he said. "He left me a ridiculous voice mail, and I need to talk to him."

"He's not here, though he will be soon," I said. "He and Ben were working on a project. Did you try the barbershop?"

"I'm not going to traipse all over town looking for him. Tell him to come over and talk to me in person. I'll make it worth his while."

"He's not going to work with you," Nadia said, crossing her arms over her bodice. "I was there when he called you, and he was pretty clear."

I heard a small crash and looked back at Tuck, who was restacking the paper cups. I was surprised that the back of Nadia's head wasn't smoking from the glare he was giving her.

"Every man has his price," Beckett said smugly. He looked at me. "I assume you had something to do with this?"

"Me? No, though he did tell me about your new sideline of clocks. An interesting business strategy," I said. My heart pounded in my chest, and I resisted the urge to raise my voice.

"A good businessperson takes advantage of opportunity when it comes, even if it's unexpected. Anyway, tell him to come and see me, for his own sake. Now I must be off. The caterer is due any minute."

"The caterer?" I asked.

"I'm going to be offering some repast on my front porch. Surely, you won't begrudge me that?" he said, smiling down at me as if he were indulging a small child.

"Beckett, I don't begrudge you anything," I said as graciously as I could. "Have a great evening."

Nadia and I stood shoulder to shoulder and watched him leave. Nadia was six inches shorter than me but my boots didn't have too high a heel, and her platform boots had a four-inch heel. We were almost the same height, tonight at least.

"What. A. Jerk," Nadia said when the door was almost closed. She didn't lower her voice one decibel.

"Seriously," I agreed.

Nadia took her cell phone out of her coat pocket and dialed. "Hello, Nancy? It's Nadia. Did you know that Beckett was going to serve food on his front porch tonight? I know, right? Anything we can do about that? Hmmm, right, that's a great idea. You'll take care of it? Thanks."

"What was that?"

"I called Nancy," she said. "We've been expecting Beckett to try and pull something, so I wanted to let her know what he was up to."

"Why does the idea of the two of you hatching a plan make me so nervous?"

"Hey, Nancy's great. She's going to call the police station and make sure he has a vendor's permit for giving away food. You know all the hoops that Kim Gray made us all jump through just to have the block shut down tonight? Seems only fair."

Part of me didn't like small-time, petty town politics. The other part was thrilled that Nadia and Nancy were on my side. Both of my selves were winning right now, but I felt it necessary to be a grown-up. "I doubt Chief Paisley will like the idea of shutting down Beckett Green over a vendor violation." Our chief of police, Jeff Paisley, was by the book, but he also understood that his job was to keep the peace in Orchard. His past training as a SWAT commander wasn't needed much in these parts. At least not yet. Jeff and I had become good friends over the past few weeks since I'd moved back to Orchard.

"That's the beauty of the plan. The chief is in Boston, at

some family event in Dorchester. Officer Ro Troisi is in charge, and there's no love lost between Beckett and Ro. Especially since he didn't hire her brothers to put in his new heating system." Small towns. Family businesses. No-brainers on who to hire, or at least call for a bid, especially when you were new. "Nancy will take care of it."

"That's what I'm afraid of." My palm itched for my own cell phone, to call Pat and let him know what his wife was up to. I resisted the urge. Pat couldn't stop Nancy once she had her mind set. Besides, the open house started in five minutes. Showtime.

chapter 7

The open house was supposed to go until eight o'clock, but it was almost nine, and the party was still in full swing. I took out my phone and send out a group text, checking in once more with Ada from the Corner Market, Moira from the Sleeping Latte, Harriet from the library, Max from the hardware store, Flo from her Emporium, and Nancy, who had been roaming the streets with Pat and Ben, moving food from place to place and replenishing supplies.

Send everyone outside in five minutes. Surprise almost ready to go, Ben's text said.

Where's Mark? he texted me privately. Where indeed? Caroline and I had been holding down the fort at the Cog & Sprocket, with Nadia jumping in and then disappearing when she got texted instructions from Nancy. Caroline was innately shy and had spent most of the evening toward the back, fussing with cookies, refilling the punch bowl, and talking to neighbors. My years as a faculty wife had again served me well, and I worked the crowd, meeting and greeting, distributing the POL cards and brochures, and answering a lot of questions about clocks. More than one person promised to be back for the opening.

Not sure. You need him? I texted back.

All good. Pat is here. See you in three minutes.

"Are you typing someone?" Caroline arrived by my elbow. Caroline looked as put together as always. Hair in a perfect twist, more gray than brown now that she'd decided to let her natural color show. She was wearing a gray wool sheath dress with a black cardigan. She wore her regular pearl earrings and choker, and smart but sensible black wedge shoes. She was also wearing the brooch I'd made her for Christmas—a combination of cogs and wheels that I'd painted in washed-out shades of red and pink. From a distance it looked a bit like a flower. It was the only pop of color she wore, and I was really pleased she'd made the effort to wear it tonight.

"Texting. Yes, Ben wants everyone to go outside in five minutes for a surprise."

At that moment, Nancy Reed walked through the front door. "Hey, folks, come outside. We've got the capper of the evening about to take off! And don't forget, the Cog & Sprocket opens next week, so come back then!" She went back outside, the Pied Piper of Orchard. I grabbed the basket of clock cookies and made sure everyone had one on their way out. Most folks added them to the tote bags they'd picked up at the library, which were filled with goodies from each of the shops they'd visited tonight. Everyone oohed and aahed and wished us luck with the shop.

"It looks terrific," Phyllis Bourdon said, flashing her impish grin. "Honestly, I think more folks were in this shop in the last two hours than walked through the doors over the past ten years. Good for you, Ruth. Thom would be pleased to see this."

I laughed. "Now, Phyllis, we both know that he would have hated tonight. But my grandmother would have loved it."

"She would indeed. Boy, I still miss her something fierce." She reached over and squeezed my arm. I blinked back tears and smiled.

"Me too," I said. "But Caroline's terrific."

"Yes, she is," Phyllis agreed. "So are you, Ruth Clagan. So are you."

"I'm sorry Howie didn't make it tonight," I said.

"The grandkids wore him out over Christmas. He'll be here for the opening."

"Bring him a cookie, and tell him I said hi. See you next week."

Phyllis was the last one out the door, and I glanced over at Caroline, who looked as tired as I felt.

"Well, that was a resounding success," she said.

"You think?"

"I know. Congratulations, Ruth," she said, wrapping one arm around my shoulders and squeezing.

"Congratulations to us all, Caroline. I suppose we should go outside and see what this surprise is all about, don't you?"

"I suppose so," she said, buttoning her cardigan up. "Are you going to get your coat?"

"I'll wear G.T.'s jacket," I said, walking back and taking the wool shirt off the hook. "Are you all set?"

"I have my wrap," she said, grabbing the large shawl from behind the counter and wrapping it around her shoulders." We won't be out for that long, I shouldn't imagine."

"No, not that long. Remember, we're having a light dinner afterward."

"I don't know, Ruth, I'm fairly done in. I think I may head home."

"You can't!" I said. Caroline started at my urgency, and I lowered my voice. "Caroline, folks will want to see you."

"Ruth, this isn't about my birthday, is it?" she asked, her hands on her hips. "I told you not to fuss."

"Let's go outside, see the surprise, and then we'll come back in and enjoy the rest of the surprises." I held open the door, and Caroline went out, rolling her eyes. I double-checked that I had my keys, and let the door lock behind me.

There had to be at least a hundred people huddled in the middle of the street. I looked over and thought I saw a very tall figure dressed all in black hovering toward the edge. Was that the guy from the party store? Looked like the *Marytown Shopper* really worked. I'd need to tell Nadia. I looked for her, but then I heard my name.

"Ruthie, over here," Nancy bellowed toward me. Caroline pushed me over, but held back at the edge of the crowd. Though it was dark, the warm glow of the streetlights helped me recognize some familiar faces. I walked toward Nancy, and looked over the crowd toward the dark Been There, Read That store across the street.

With a wicked grin, Nancy glanced over her shoulder and then back at me.

"You didn't shut him down, did you?" I asked.

"Me? No. That wouldn't be very neighborly. No, old Beckett didn't think things through. Remember when he talked Kim Gray into moving the streetlight?"

"Yes, he wanted one of the gaslights installed closer to his shop."

"Right, well, that ran into a snag with the gas line. So, no streetlight. And he hasn't installed his own outside lights yet. So it was darker than the inside of a pocket over there. Old Beckett's going to be eating canapés for the next week."

"Serves him right. So what's going on out here?" I asked.

"Nancy, Ruth, come over here. Please," Ben called out. "Where's Caroline?"

"She's right there," I said, looking over to where I'd left her. She wasn't there.

"Never mind, you both will do," Ben's aunt Flo said. Flo did not need a microphone or megaphone to make her voice heard, which she did now. "Hello, folks. Could I have your attention, please? On behalf of the business owners here in downtown Orchard, we'd like to thank you all for being part of the POL launch tonight. The Program for Orchard Loyalty was the brainstorm of Ruth Clagan, and we're all thrilled to be part of it. To commemorate the launch, we're going to have a launch of our own. We're sorry that Kim Gray couldn't join us tonight." A few folks in the crowd giggled. To her credit, Flo kept a straight face, though the sparkle in her eye told the whole story.

"Where is she, anyway?" a young man shouted. I recognized him as one of the reporters for the *Orchard Gazette*, our local weekly newspaper. I'd heard rumors that they were going online in the New Year and were looking for more content.

"I've been told that she was called into a dinner meeting in Marytown. Something about a chain store lease?" There were a couple of groans from the crowd. Kim would be extra sorry she missed tonight's event when she saw the next issue of the *Orchard Gazette*. Flo was careful to add enough fuel to the fire to scorch the town manager. "We're delighted that the members of the Board of Selectmen are here, and we're grateful for their support of our businesses. Folks, if you could all come up here and join us business owners, we're going to light these paper lanterns and launch them."

Pat handed Ben a paper lantern with a flame flickering, Ben handed one to Nancy, and then took another one from Pat and handed it to me. Within a minute, there were twenty lit lanterns glowing in the little square, illuminating the faces of all of the people I had come to love in these few months since I'd settled in Orchard.

"One, two, three. Happy launch!" Flo said. We all let go of our lanterns and watched as they floated gently into the December night sky. The crowd was silent, and then someone started to clap. Everyone else joined in, and then a few cheers erupted. I looked around and couldn't help but smile.

Ben had walked up next to me and squeezed my hand and then, to my dismay, let it go.

"This is wonderful," I said, smiling up at him. "Your idea?"

"No, Mark's idea. Just wish he was here to help me pull it off. Did he get stuck obsessing about a clock in the back of the Cog all night?"

"No, I haven't seen him since this afternoon," I said, wrapping my grandfather's old shirt around me tightly.

"Thankfully, Pat was around and able to help me put these

lanterns together. Of course, once we got going I finished three of them, and Pat did the rest. I'm glad you liked it."

I leaned up and gave Ben a kiss on his wonderfully square jaw. "The whole night was wonderful."

We looked at each other for a moment too long, and then I broke the mood.

"Caroline's not going to last long. She always gets sleepy," I said. "How about if we serve a reverse dinner and start off with the cake?"

"Sounds like a plan," Ben said, rubbing his hands together. "It's over in my shop. I'll go get it."

"No, I'll go. You go gather the troops, especially Nancy and Pat and your aunt Flo. Won't be a party without them!"

I made my way through the crowd toward the Cog & Sprocket. I loved downtown Orchard, all of its stand-alone buildings that came from different eras, made of different materials and painted different colors, but gathered together to create a town. Ben's store was built around the same time as the Cog & Sprocket, but it hadn't fared quite as well. Too many well-intentioned but badly designed additions and changes made it look like a mid-1800s gem with a few cancerous growths. Ben had been working hard to bring the building back, but now that Flo was back in town, anything could happen.

Ben's Barbershop and the Cog & Sprocket shared a small parking lot in front of the stores. There was a small path down the center that led to the back alley. I walked down it to the side entrance of Ben's Barbershop on the right toward the back of the shop. I noticed the door was slightly ajar.

Not surprising, since the food had been stored in his shop for the event, but still. I hoped a small animal hadn't decided to stop by and partake of birthday cake. Blue had been left at Flo's house for the night, otherwise I wouldn't have had to worry about that. Blue kept the place protected.

I pushed open the door and reached toward my left, and then to my right, for a wall switch. There wasn't one. Of course there wasn't. Up until a year or so ago, the barbershop had been two separate shops, one for men and one for women. The stores may have been merged, but the building systems were still separate. I stepped into the shop, but I didn't know it well enough to know where else to look. I took out my cell phone and hit the flashlight app. I did a sweep of the area back near the hair-washing sinks and saw a pile of towels on the floor. No obvious lights. I walked to my right and swept the rest of the store. The closest lights were by the front door, so I made my way over. I bumped into something and almost knocked it over. I dodged a couple of those old standing hair dryers and some carts of rollers. I turned on the front lights and blinked twice to get used to them. Yeesh. Ben needed to work on the lighting in here. These overheads were way too bright, and not very flattering for the shop or, I imagined, to its customers.

I walked back toward the sinks, hoping that the cake was where Ben had left it. The shop had been the way station for the open house, and it showed. Bottles of ginger ale, bags of ice, paper products, trays of food. We'd stacked them all neatly earlier in the day, but now the debris was strewn all over the shop. We'd need to get a cleanup party together for this.

The pink cake box was supposed to be over by the sinks. There was a pile of towels on the floor, and I shook my head.

What had happened in here? I walked back, but slowed down as I got closer to the pile. There was a shoe peeking out from under a pile of towels that had been toppled over. I peered around, looking for what, or who, the shoe belonged to.

"Hey, buddy, nap time is over," I said. Great. Someone was passed out between the sinks. I didn't think it was that kind of party, but there was always someone. I got closer, and slowed down. The pink box that had contained Caroline's cake was in a heap facedown on the floor next to the left-hand sink. Terrific, just what I needed. I took a step closer and nudged the foot with my boot. No response. I stepped closer and moved around to the side of the sink near the cake so I could see what pillar of Orchard society I was dealing with.

"Mark," I whimpered. Mark Pine was lying on his side, partially covered with towels. If he was asleep, his eyes would be closed, but they weren't. Instead, they were staring at me, but not seeing me. I stood up quickly and jumped back, almost sliding on the cake that was covering the floor.

"What's taking so long?" Ben said, stepping into the shop behind me. "Did someone steal the cake?"

"Ben, go back," I said. "Call the police and then find Jeff. We need him here. Now. Something's happened to Mark. He's dead."

chapter 8

I stayed with Mark for as long as I could. Not right with him, but outside the barbershop, making sure no one else went in. Ro Troisi had asked me to stay put when she came by, and I had agreed. She was trying to secure the scene before the state police came in and took over. Ben came out of the back door of the Cog & Sprocket and brought me my coat and the pad of paper I'd asked him to get for me after he'd called Jeff.

"Why don't you come in here?" he asked.

"Ro went back to the station to get her gear, and she asked me to stand guard for a few minutes."

"Are you all right? Can I do anything?"

From his strained tone, I could hear how much he needed to be useful, but there was nothing. "No, and no. But thank you. Poor Mark."

"'Poor Mark' is right. I wonder what happened to him. He's pretty young to have a heart attack."

"Maybe he had a seizure or something," I said, "and hit his head. I couldn't tell. That pile of towels was on him so I couldn't see if he had any injuries." I hated the way my voice shook.

"Jeff had to call in the state police, but he's on his way back."

"I know. Ro told me." I reached into my pocket and took out a pen, clicking it open. I drew some circles on the top sheet of paper to make sure it worked.

"What's the paper for?" Ben asked.

"I watch way too many TV crime dramas," I said. "I'm going to write down everything I did when I went in the shop, while it's still fresh in my memory. Just in case."

"Just in case?"

"Just in case it wasn't an accident."

Ro returned at the same time as the state police arrived. I watched the turf-war tussle, but it didn't last long. In the Berkshires, the state police were on call overnight or on weekends. Or they were supposed to be. In the two years Jeff Paisley had been the chief of police, he'd always answered every call.

It was cold in the back alley between our shops, so I rubbed my arms to generate some heat. The state police officer took my statement and asked me a few questions. He barely introduced himself, and I didn't ask him to repeat his name. I could have invited him into the Cog & Sprocket, but I didn't. I sensed he'd move in, and that just wouldn't do. I'd talk to him now, but I'd wait for Jeff to share any ideas I came up with.

The officer ignored Ro, but she didn't leave. She'd pass on information to Jeff as well. Good woman. He asked about how I'd discovered the body, and some other information about the evening, before coming back to Mark himself.

"How did you know the victim?" he asked.

"He works for me, over at the Cog & Sprocket. It's the clock shop next door."

"Did you know him well?"

"No," I said, choking up a bit. "I didn't. He only started working for me about a month ago."

"Do you know who his next of kin is?"

"I'm sorry, I don't. Tuck Powers, he works for me as well, he knew Mark from high school. He'd have more information."

"What did the victim do for you?"

"Do for me?" I asked, confused by the question.

"What did you hire him to do?"

"To fix clocks. He was a clockmaker. He'd been an apprentice up in Vermont for the past few years and was looking for his next training opportunity."

"Does he also fix watches?"

"No. Not for me, I mean. We'd been talking about that this afternoon—"

"We?"

"Mark and I."

"Really? Interesting."

"Why 'interesting'?" I asked.

"Did Mr. Pine have a drug problem?"

"Drugs? No, of course not. Not that I knew of anyway," I said unsurely. Now that I thought about him I didn't know Mark all that well.

"You'd be surprised, Ms. Clagan. There's an epidemic out here."

"Not at the Cog & Sprocket. Why do you ask? Do you think he died of an overdose?"

"No, he was probably strangled," Ro said.

"That is not for public consumption," the officer snapped. "Officer Troisi, perhaps you could help . . ." The officer touched the earpiece he was wearing and then looked back at me. "Got it." He turned toward me and looked back down at his notes. "Ms. Clagan, Chief Paisley has arrived, and we need to regroup. I have your phone number. There will be more questions, so we'll need to be in touch. Don't turn your phone off."

"I won't. Trust me, I want to help however I can."

I had a text from Ben, asking me to meet everyone at the Sleeping Latte when I was done. I went over to the Cog & Sprocket quickly to double-check the back door. It was locked tight, and I knew the front was. Instead of going down the street, which was packed with crowds and media trucks, I decided to go down the access road. There were police everywhere, setting up lights and walking around. It was only a couple of blocks, but I walked them quickly.

Poor Mark. I wiped away a tear and tried to remember him alive, rather than staring through me from the floor of the barbershop. I couldn't. I knew I would eventually. At least I hoped so.

The back door of the Sleeping Latte was closed, and the shade was drawn over the window. I saw light leaking through, and knocked. Nancy Reed peeked from behind the shade and then unlocked the door.

"Is Jeff here yet?" she asked, gathering me in a tight hug. "Saw a bunch of staties swarming the place."

"He just arrived, but I haven't seen him yet. Ro Troisi was working with the state police. How's Caroline?" I said, carefully disengaging from the hug and looking around the room.

"She's in rough shape. We're all in shock. What could have happened to Mark? You don't think it was drugs, do you?"

"Drugs? No, not Mark. He was a straight arrow." I loved Nancy, but she was the hub of all gossip in Orchard. Time to cut that off now. "We'll know what happened soon enough."

"You're right, of course. Come on in. We're all sitting in the kitchen. Don't want folks to think the Latte is open. All those looky-loos. They should be ashamed of themselves, waiting outside, hoping to see something untoward. Just terrible."

"Why did you all come here?" I asked.

"Once Ben told us what had happened, we locked up your shop and came down. You know me, Ruthie, I cook when I'm stressed. Besides, none of us had dinner tonight. Won't do any good if we all keel over, will it?"

"I guess not," I said. I walked back into the kitchen. Caroline was bent over a cup of tea, both hands wrapped around the mug. She looked up when I came in, and held a hand out. I went over and reached down to give her a hug first, then I took her hand. Her normally calm demeanor was gone, and her eyes were puffy.

"Are you all right, Caroline?" I asked.

She nodded. "What about you? It must have been awful."

I nodded too, and sat down on the chair Pat brought over. I looked around at my friends, the other shop owners here in Orchard. Ada Clark was absentmindedly rubbing her pregnant belly, and her husband, Mac, sat next to her, an arm protectively around her shoulders. Pat Reed sat himself on a stool by the stove, where Nancy was busy frying, scooping, and stirring. Moira was taking the wrapping off some baked goods and putting them out on plates. Ben was sitting next to his aunt Flo, who dabbed her face and tore at the tissue in her hands.

"Where's Nadia?" I asked.

"I'm not sure where she and Tuck are," Moira said. "I've been texting and calling, but she isn't replying."

I pulled out my phone and texted Nadia. *Call me ASAP* was all I said. I stared at my phone, but no return text came through.

"Anything?" Pat asked.

"No, and that's unusual for Nadia. I don't think I've ever gone more than two minutes without a return text from her. Let's assume she's all right. No news is good news, right?" I said, hoping I sounded more confident than I felt.

"So, Ruth, tell us what happened," Nancy said, plunking a mug of tea down in front of me.

"Nancy," Pat said.

"What? We all want to know, so let's hear it. She'll leave out the bad parts."

I looked around the room. I'd sort of promised not to tell the details, but I had to tell them all something. Everyone here knew Mark and wanted to know what had happened to him. I told them about finding the body, but I left out the details about the cake. And that he was strangled. Not my details to share. I looked over my notes to see if I had missed anything I could tell them all.

"What's that?" Ada asked.

"I wrote down everything I saw," I said. "Just in case."

"What's the matter, Ruth? Are you saying this wasn't an accident?" Caroline asked, smoothing her hand over her neatly styled hair, pushing a few errant strands back into place.

"I don't know. It's a feeling I had—something wasn't right. I'm sure I'm wrong, but since Jeff isn't here, I thought I'd better take notes."

"We were all talking about that earlier, trying to think about when we last saw Mark and who was where," Caroline said.

"I saw him around four or so, at the shop," I offered. I turned the page on my pad of paper and wrote it down. "He told me that Beckett had offered him a job."

"The clocks. Of course," Nancy said, dropping a spatula on the frying pan.

"Did everyone know about the clocks before I did?" I said, looking up from the notes I had spread out in front of me.

"No, only since Mum found out," Moira said.

"Hush, you," Nancy said. "Pat and I saw him around five. He came by for a cup of coffee and some food. A pesto and mozzarella sandwich, with what passes for tomatoes this time of year."

"Mum, I doubt anyone cares what kind of sandwich he got," Moira said.

"And he also got a sliced meatball panini with a side of sauce. His favorite."

"So the pesto was for someone else," I said.

"I'd guess, but I don't know."

"He came by the market afterward to get a Moxie soda," Ada said. "He had the bag and was sipping the coffee. I joked that he needed another hand." She started to cry softly, and Mac rubbed her back.

"Yeah, I talked him into some chips," he said. "I gave him a bigger bag so he could carry it all."

"I saw him a few minutes after that," Flo said. "I stopped him to ask him to bring me some brochures from the Cog & Sprocket over so I could put them out. He promised he would, but didn't come back. That was right before the open house started. It started out a little slow—I was nervous, let me tell you—but then about fifteen minutes in, it really picked up. I can't say if I noticed him again after that."

Everyone agreed that once the open house started the crowds took the focus, but no one remembered seeing Mark after that.

"What a terrible way to end a great night," Nancy said, adding part of an omelet and some hash browns to a plate and handing it to Pat, who put it in front of me.

"I'm not hungry," I said, pushing the plate away.

"But you have to eat," Pat said, putting it back in front of me with one hand and sliding a plate in front of Caroline with the other. "We all have to eat. I, for one, am going to wait up for Jeff to come by, so I might as well eat now. It's going to be a long night."

I lifted my fork and picked at a bit of potato. I took a small bite, and then a bigger one. I was hungrier than I realized, and I polished off the plate before long. Pat silently picked it up and got me some more potatoes. We all ate in silence, at least most of us did. I looked over at Caroline, who was moving her food around.

"Eat something," I whispered to her. "It will make you feel better."

Caroline looked over, and smiled uncomfortably. I heard

a knock on the back door, and Pat went to answer it. He came back, followed closely by Jeff Paisley.

Jeff Paisley had moved to Orchard to become the chief of police, a sideways career move. I rarely saw Jeff out of uniform, never mind dressed up in a nice suit like he was wearing today. The gray wool was cut perfectly, and his white shirt was still pressed. His tie was loosened, and on closer inspection, I saw a small stain in the middle. We were about the same height, but he was in much better shape. His brown hair was cropped short, and had flecks of gray at the temples. I knew that his brown eyes would crinkle at the edges when he laughed, but I also knew we wouldn't see that tonight.

Moira stared at him, but not in a happy-to-see-him way. When he turned toward me, I could see why. There was a red lipstick mark on the side of his brown face. I also noticed glitter and confetti on his shoulders.

"You got here fast," I said.

"I was already on my way back when Officer Troisi called. I understand you found the body . . . Mark." I nodded. "You all right?"

"Better now that you're on the case," I said.

"Not really on the case," Jeff said, sighing. "The state has taken over, since I wasn't here."

"But you'll be in charge, right?" Nancy said. "We want our own chief to be on the case."

"I'll be helping out. Especially since it is being treated as a murder case."

chapter 9

"Murder?" Caroline said.

"It's an unattended death," Jeff said. He walked toward Caroline, and she put her hand out. He took it and squatted down, speaking directly to her but in a voice loud enough for us all to hear. "They are going by the book."

Everyone started asking questions at the same time. I kept silent, knowing that it was, in fact, murder, but still having a lot of trouble wrapping my brain around that fact.

Jeff stood again and looked around the room, and then rested his gaze on me. I nodded, letting him know that I'd keep the news to myself. Ro must have filled him in on everything. "Since we need to treat this like a crime scene, your shop is going to be closed for a few days, Ben."

"What about Aunt Flo's shop?" Ben asked, looking up

from the food that he had been steadily consuming since I'd walked into the room.

"We're going to work on getting you get back in there as soon as possible. Flo, you have my word on that. We want to make sure we do right by Mark."

"Of course," Flo said. "You do what you need to do, Jeff."

"I'm going to need to ask some questions about where you all were . . ."

"Ruth's already on that," Flo said.

"Oh, she is, is she?" he said, raising his eyebrows.

"Yes, well, I thought it would be helpful for us all to try and remember when we last saw Mark, in case you needed a timeline for that. Here, I've been taking notes while we've all been talking. I can transcribe them if that's easier."

Jeff took the pad of paper from me and then he slowly took his reading glasses out of his inside front pocket. I thought about the time I'd spent with Jeff over the past few weeks. I can't say it helped me know him any better, but it did create paths for us to build a friendship. I knew little about his family, except that they lived in Dorchester and that his grandparents on his mother's side had emigrated from Jamaica many years ago. He hadn't mentioned to me that he was going to visit them today. I wondered if Moira knew. There were sparks with her and Jeff, but neither of them acknowledged them, nor did they act on them.

"This is helpful. Thank you, all. Listen, Officer Troisi has to come in and take brief statements, then she'll let you go home."

"Chief, I'd like to drive Caroline home," I said. "She was at the Cog & Sprocket the whole time, with me. Does she need to stay?"

Jeff took a deep breath and ran his hand over his closely cut hair. He let the breath out on a deep sigh. The state police had jurisdiction; he'd already told us that. I wondered if they were going to let Jeff in, or if he was going to have to play second fiddle. I also wondered how I could help.

"All right, listen. Ro will get the statements done, and I suspect you will all be going home. We'll need you more tomorrow. Ruth, why don't we head back to your shop. I have some specific questions I want to ask you. Then you can come back and get Caroline. How's that sound?"

That didn't sound like a suggestion, so I got up and grabbed my coat.

"Thanks for the food, Moira. I really needed that," I said.

"I hope to see you for breakfast" was all she said. "Both of you."

"Jeff, why would Mark be murdered?" I asked as I closed the back door of the café behind me. I called Jeff "Chief" in public, but had started calling him "Jeff" in private, or in front of Caroline. After a man saves your life, and you help him catch a murderer, you start using first names.

"Ruth, why did you think it was murder?"

"I was there when the state police officer—I don't remember his name—when he told Ro and me Mark was strangled. Or maybe Ro told me?" I had to try to cover for Ro; Jeff was her boss after all.

"Not that. Ro told me you knew. Good for you for keeping it quiet, by the way. I meant when you found him, why did you think it was murder?"

"I didn't," I said.

"You secured the crime scene. Wrote down what you did when you went to turn on the lights, and wouldn't let anyone else in. One of the state police techs commented on it."

"I could tell he was gone right away." I cleared my throat and closed my eyes tightly to block out the image. The night was still, but it had gotten considerably colder in the past few hours. Or maybe I was feeling it more. There was a buzz of activity coming from Washington Street. Even our little parallel access road was busier than normal, with vans parked and lights being erected to help the officers gather evidence. "I remember seeing him, and I guess I thought it was odd for him to be dead, so I acted. Does that make sense?" We'd reached the back door of the Cog & Sprocket, and I let myself in. Jeff followed and locked the door behind him.

"You've got good instincts. What I am about to tell you isn't public, but I'm going to need your help with this. As you know, it looks like Mark was strangled. We'll know more after the exam. I'd like you to take a look at something. Right now all I've got is my cell phone photo. The lab will be forwarding me better images soon." Jeff flipped through the images and then handed the phone to me. "What can you tell me about this?"

I looked down at the photo and used my fingers to zoom in. The pocket watch was oversized and thick. Possibly old, very old, before parts got as miniaturized as they were now. The filigree pattern on the watch case was faded in parts, as if it had been handled a certain way over the years.

"This is a pocket watch, not my area of expertise, but I know a little about them. This looks like a railroad watch, could possibly date back to the 1800s."

"Railroad watch?"

"Clocks and watches have always striven for accuracy, but there was leeway for a long time. Who really knew if your clock was five minutes off?"

"I guess that makes sense. I always wondered who decided what time was what?"

"Oh, Jeff, don't even get me started. I can fix clocks, but I study time. I love the history of how humans have been trying to manage it for years. We'll talk about that another day. Anyway, railroad watches. A few minutes of inaccuracy worked until there were trains, and schedules. Keeping accurate time became critical for conductors to keep trains from crashing. So, there got to be a standardized, and accurate, watch. It became a stamp that a lot of watchmakers used, but not everyone adhered to."

"This looks pretty ornate for a conductor," Jeff said, pointing to the wrapped vines that wound around the cover.

"The clock guts could be housed in different cases, and cases could be changed out. Maybe this owner liked a little more decoration? Or a wife or girlfriend picked it out for him? Looking at the inside would answer a lot of questions. Research could be done on the history of the watch to determine age, ownership, history. I could tell you more about it if I saw it, but, again, watches aren't my area of expertise."

"You do know people who could help?"

"Of course. But you know, Mark was one of those people." I pursed my lips to stop them from trembling. Mark could fix a clock, but he loved watches. I knew the minute I saw him clean one of them that he had a gift. "Where did you find the watch?"

"It was nearby, under the sinks. It may have nothing to do with his death. Mark might have had it and dropped it.

Or it may have been placed there. Ruth, what are you think-ing?" It was like he could see the gears turning in my head.

"I'm thinking," I said, concentrating, "that if someone wanted to ambush Mark, they could use a watch to distract him. He's a lot like me. He was. Yeesh, this is hard. You know me, once I get seduced by a clock, I'm a goner. He was good at all of this, you know. He had great talent." I wiped a tear that ran down my cheek.

"Do you know how we can contact his family?" Jeff asked, taking his phone back from me.

"I don't, I'm sorry. Caroline will know—she does payroll for the shop."

"You never talked about family with him?"

"Not specifically, no. He must have known about what happened to G.T., and didn't want to bring it up. Or maybe he didn't have family. He did spend the holidays in Orchard. Even had dinner with us, at the Reeds'. I don't pry about personal matters, but maybe I should start. Right now, I've got nothing. I should have cared enough to ask him more questions."

"Ruth, don't blame yourself for any of this, all right? We all know you care. Some folks are private about their fami-lies. Besides, for all we know, it was his watch. Or someone else dropped it earlier. Okay if I keep asking you questions as we find out more?"

"Of course. I want to help." I reached over to Caroline's work area and grabbed a tissue so I could blow my nose.

"For the record," Jeff said, "I was visiting family tonight. I know I don't talk about them much, but we're very close. I have two older sisters, both married. One of them has grown kids, two girls. The other one has twins, a boy and a girl. They're eight. They all live around Boston. They think the Berkshires are in another country, but my mother made noises about coming to visit soon."

"Which one of them wears red lipstick?"

"What are you talking about?"

I grabbed another tissue and wiped the side of Jeff's face. He looked down at the lipstick smear and grimaced.

"That looks like my sister Angela's shade. I know this will surprise you, but I'm not a very demonstrative person." Jeff smiled, and I smiled back at him. "My family likes to make fun of me. Hugs and kisses when I arrive, and when I leave."

"The horror," I said. "A family who loves you."

"Yeah, I know. I'm a lucky guy. I've got a good family."

"They're pretty lucky too. If, when, your mother comes to visit, we'll have her over for dinner, Caroline and I. How does that sound?"

"Sounds good. Tell you what—I'm going to let you go and get Caroline and take her home."

"Wait. Why is it so bright in here?" I said, suddenly aware of the light streaming in through the windows. We both looked around. We'd turned on some lights, but they weren't really needed. Activity over at the barbershop was spilling into the Cog & Sprocket. The noise was a loud hum, with occasional shouts. "I might as well stay out at the cottage tonight, what do you think? I doubt I'll get much sleep staying here."

"It is pretty chaotic next door," Jeff said.

"Tell you what—why don't you use the shop as your base of operations? I'll get you the extra key to my apartment. There's food up there. Just don't let Bezel out."

"—Bezel out." He said the last two words with me.

"Thank you," he said. "It would be helpful to stay put and get to work. The state police are determined to take jurisdiction, but Orchard is my town. I need to be on site, and staying next door is easier. I can probably make do down here; won't need the upstairs."

"Take the key, Jeff. Make yourself at home. Take a nap. You just drove back from Boston!"

"Thanks, Ruth. Don't worry, I'll watch out for her majesty if I do need to go upstairs."

"Let me go up and pack an overnight bag," I said.

I started to walk toward the back stairs, but stopped when I heard steps coming downstairs.

"Did you hear that?" I turned toward him, but he obviously had. He moved past me, gently pushing me to the side. Someone was coming down the stairs, and Jeff Paisley was the welcoming committee.

chapter 10

"Freeze!" Jeff Paisley said. Where did the gun come from? I hadn't noticed a holster, but then again, I wasn't looking for one.

"What the?" Nadia came downstairs and stood on the bottom step. "What's going on?"

Nadia looked terrible: mascara streaks down her face, her hair smashed on one side, bloodshot eyes, carrying her boots, the cuff of her coat torn.

"Where have you been?" Jeff asked.

"We came back here during the lantern ceremony."

"We?"

"Tuck and me."

"Where is Tuck?"

"He's right behind me. Can we come downstairs? Or are you going to shoot us?" she said, sarcastic even at gunpoint.

Jeff lowered his gun, but didn't put it away. He stepped back and cleared some space.

"Yeesh. That was a little extreme, don't you think?" Nadia said. Tuck followed her, his head lowered. His clothing looked as disheveled as Nadia's did.

"Why did you come back here? What was the time?" Jeff asked again.

"I don't know. Nine or so? Why we came back is private," Tuck said. He looked up at Jeff, and I noticed the blood down the front of his shirt. It looked like his nose was broken, and he had a black eye.

"Listen, the two of you, answer his questions. Have you been upstairs this entire time?" I asked. Tuck always made me feel like a schoolmarm with no sense of humor.

"I kept bouncing around, making sure everyone had what they needed. I was over at the Corner Market, helping Mac, but Tuck came by, and we started talking. My bag was here, so we came back to get it. We came in the back door and went upstairs. Everyone was busy, so we didn't say hi. When we got up there, we started talking more."

"Talking?" Jeff asked, looking at them both.

"Okay, arguing," Nadia said.

"Nadia, you don't have to tell them anything," Tuck said, gingerly touching the bridge of his nose. "It's none of their business."

"Of course I do. They've probably heard all about it. The whole town probably has, the way you made such an idiot out of yourself."

"I made an idiot out of myself?"

"That's right. Getting into a fight with Mark. Idiot."

"You and Mark Pine fought tonight?" Jeff asked.

"I was over by the Sleeping Latte, and I saw him kiss Nadia. She left out the part of the story where she left the Corner Market with Mark. I'll admit it, when I saw them, I lost it," Tuck said. His color rose as he spoke, accentuating his bruises.

"It wasn't a *kiss* kiss. It was a friend kiss. He brought me dinner! You're such a jerk," Nadia said.

"I don't kiss my friends like that," Tuck said. Nadia stopped talking. "So I took a swing at him—who'd blame me? Why, what's he saying? Is he pressing charges? Is this why we are getting the third degree right now?"

"He's not saying anything," Jeff said. "He's dead. He died earlier this evening."

"He's what?" Nadia said, her eyes wide. I rushed to her side as she began to crumple. I put an arm around her and lowered her onto a chair.

"Tell me more about this fight," Jeff said, keeping his distance. Tuck didn't move to Nadia. Instead he turned and addressed Jeff directly.

"Hey, listen, I said I took a swing. I never connected. The guy was some sort of martial arts master. Before I knew what happened I was flat on my back and my nose was bleeding."

"Where did this happen? Outside the Corner Market?"

"No. He and Nadia were heading back here. I caught up to them past the Sleeping Latte, closer to Ben's shop. A little before nine o'clock. Anyway, he knocked me flat. He wanted to talk to me about it, but I couldn't deal with him then. I needed space so he went his way, and Nadia and I came back here. To talk."

"Is that when Nadia's coat got ripped?" I asked. Nadia was useless, weeping in my arms. We were sitting together in the chair and a half I'd located near the back of the store. It was a tight fit, but she wasn't letting go. Neither was I.

"She tried to stop me from fighting with Mark. Her coat got ripped. It was an accident." Tuck turned and sat at one of the stools at a workstation. Jeff remained standing, his eyes never leaving Tuck.

"Is that true?" I whispered to Nadia.

"Yes," she said, nodding her head.

"Where did you go next?" Jeff asked.

"Up to the attic office."

"That was over three hours ago."

"We fought for a while, then Nadia went and got me a cloth for my nose. I must have fallen asleep."

"How about you, Nadia? Did you fall asleep too?"

Nadia nodded her head, but she still couldn't speak. She was sobbing, and I kept my arm across her shoulder.

Jeff finally secured his gun into the holster beneath his jacket. He pulled out his cell phone and hit a button.

"Ro, I'm over here at the Cog & Sprocket. I need you to come by and take a couple of statements. Yes, now." While he was on the phone Nadia got up and went into the bathroom. She never looked over at Tuck. Once the door closed, I heard her start to wail.

"You can't keep us here," Tuck said.

"I can make this more official if you'd like," Jeff said, his patience waning. "I assumed you would want to help me find out who killed your friend. He was your friend, wasn't he, Mr. Powers? Didn't you get him this job?"

"We went to high school together. Sure, of course I want to help. It's only that Nadia is so upset, I should get her home." Tuck started to rise, but Jeff gestured for him to stay put.

"Tell you what. After we get your statements, I'll have someone drive you both home."

"Do you want me to stay?" I asked, getting up. "I can make some coffee."

Jeff shook his head. "Go and get Caroline home. We can touch base again tomorrow."

I could tell I was being dismissed. I went upstairs and changed out of my dress. Yoga pants and a hoodie were much more comfortable. I fed Bezel and explained the situation to her as I packed. She was more interested in her food than my explanation, so I picked her up and kissed the top of her head, holding her reassuringly warm bulk for a few moments longer than I knew she liked. Even as she wriggled away from me I was comforted by that brief moment of contact. I grabbed my spare key and went back downstairs with my overnight bag, brushing fur off the front of my hoodie.

Nadia was back sitting in the chair, crying more quietly. Ro had pulled up a chair next to her, her cell phone on the arm of the chair and a half, a pad of paper on her lap. She was taking notes and nodding. I walked toward the front of the shop and noticed Tuck had moved to one of the chairs in the showroom. He wasn't looking at the clocks. Instead, his elbows were on his knees and his head was in his hands.

Jeff Paisley was standing by the front counter of the store.

"I'm going out the back," I said.

"Good idea. There's still a crowd out front," Jeff said.

"Here's the spare keys. This one is to my apartment, and this one is to the office, in case you need anything there."

"So, Nadia and Tuck couldn't have gone into your apartment?"

"No, neither of them have a key."

"Did you go up to the office?"

"No, I thought you'd want to do that." Actually, I hadn't thought of that. Shoot. I was more tired than I thought.

"So, I have your permission to look around?" Jeff Paisley sounded more official than he had all night.

"You do. Are you sure you don't want me to stay?"

"No, go take Caroline home. And take care of her; she was fond of Mark."

She was indeed. We all were, or so I thought.

chapter 11

I went outside and pushed the unlock button on my car. Sigh. My car battery was still dead. Caroline's car was right next to mine, but I didn't have a key. I walked back down to the Sleeping Latte and knocked on the door again. Pat Reed answered.

"I was getting ready to send out the search party," he said.

"Sorry about that. The chief wanted to ask me a couple of questions, and then we heard a noise upstairs. Nadia and Tuck had been up in the office ever since the open house was over."

"What were they doing up there?" he asked.

"Fighting and sleeping, or so they say."

"Just fighting and sleeping?" Pat said, raising his eyebrows.

"Oh please, don't put that in my head," I said, hitting him on the arm. "Anyway, Jeff is questioning them both. He's using the Cog & Sprocket as base camp and it looks like this investigation is far from over for the night. I'm going to bring Caroline home. It's probably best to let this go through the grapevine without help from us—what do you think?"

"I agree. Plus, this would wind Nancy up, and I don't have the energy."

"Is everyone still here?"

"No, Ro took all of our statements, and Ben took Flo home. Ada and Mac left too. Ada's exhausted."

"Of course she is. Not sure how she is going to make it for three more weeks."

"Moira took some coffee and sandwiches up to the police officers, and then she was heading out. Nancy and I are going to close up and go home."

"That's good," I said, absentmindedly. "Sorry, I zoned for a second."

"That's okay. This wasn't an accident, was it?"

"They aren't sure, but it doesn't look like it," I said. A half-truth. The full truth was going to get around town before dawn anyway.

"Not again," Pat said, rubbing his arm. "Are you okay, Ruthie?"

"I'm shaken up. You?"

"Sleep will help us all. Where's your car?"

"Up at the shop. Battery's dead. We'll take Caroline's car."

Pat held his hand out. "I'll take care of your car."

I shook my head. "I can call someone," I said.

"No, let me do this for you, Ruth. Go get some rest."

Pat walked us both to Caroline's car and made sure it started before he took my car keys and went back to the Sleeping Latte to pick up Nancy.

I drove slowly out to the cottage. There weren't a lot of streetlights, and I couldn't tell if the shiny spots up ahead were ice or water, or my eyes playing tricks. We hadn't spoken yet, but the silence was comfortable, though heavy with sadness. "Caroline, you holding up?" I asked.

"He was a lovely young man. They think someone did this to him?" she said, her eyes wide. She was normally so composed, but I could tell she was really feeling this.

"That's what people are saying."

"The thought that someone may have wanted to hurt him? I can't fathom it."

"Neither can I. How about if we talk about something else? How did you think the open house went?"

"Lord, that seems like days ago, doesn't it? It went well, really well. We talked about it a little, after you'd left with Jeff. Everyone was pleased." Her voice broke, and she looked out the window again.

"Oh, hey, I forgot to mention this. Someone called today. Zake Phillips?"

"Zane Phillips?"

"Zane, right. Come to think of it, I might have seen him earlier too. Tall, thin, white guy?"

"With a scar on his right cheek?"

"Yes, that's the one."

"Zane is a clockmaker. Knew your grandfather," she said, half smiling despite the dry tears lining her cheeks.

"I don't think I've ever met him."

"You wouldn't. He's been under the radar for years. He closed his shop a few years ago, thinking he'd retire, but it didn't suit him. So he started working for other clockmakers and doing his own work on the side. That's how he got the scar."

"He got that scar from clocks? Calluses, maybe. A rotator cuff injury from winding clock towers—I can see that. A bad back from squatting and twisting and lifting when you are fixing a grandfather clock? Been there, done that. A scar across the face, from a clock? This you have to explain."

Caroline laughed. "Zane was always trying to push the boundaries of clocks. He decided to make a clock out of knives."

"Knives? That's crazy!"

"I think it was a commission of some sort. For a restaurant. Anyway, the balance was off on the pendulum, given the knife he was using, actually a machete—"

"A machete? Yikes."

"Yikes indeed. He was working on the balance and got too close to the clock and was cut. He was so stubborn he wouldn't go and get it sewn up, so he got a terrible scar. It made him look scary, but he's actually the sweetest man I know. He's been a good friend to me over the years."

This story didn't jibe with the feeling I'd gotten from Zane earlier. But then, I wasn't always the best judge of men. Example one being my ex-husband. Example two being Beckett Green. Given my history, Zane Phillips probably was a saint, and I'd misjudged him.

"He's in town and wants to have dinner."

"Now, that gives me something to look forward to. Do you have his phone number?"

"I do. In my dress pocket. Which is in my apartment. Sorry, I'll get it to you tomorrow."

"No worries. Much as I'd love to see him, I want to focus on Mark for a bit."

"I hear you, and I agree. We'll do what we can to make this right."

I reached over and grabbed Caroline's hand, giving it a squeeze. I navigated the turns, avoided the ice, and finally pulled into the driveway. The moonlight sparkled on the lake in the distance. The porch light was on, welcoming us back to the lovely old Cape. It was so peaceful out here, a sharp change from the chaos in Orchard. We were home.

I gave up trying to sleep around six thirty. I thought I'd be the first one up, but Caroline had still beaten me. She was sitting at the table fully dressed, her hair swept back in her customary twist. The unopened paper lay in front of her, a coffee mug clutched in one hand and a crumpled tissue in the other. She was staring into space, and I coughed softly from the doorway before I came into the kitchen.

"Oh, good morning, Ruth," she said, dabbing her eyes and clearing her throat.

"Good morning, Caroline," I said. "You all right?"

"I didn't sleep very well last night."

"I know what you mean," I agreed. Every time I'd closed my eyes I saw poor Mark Pine lying in Ben's shop, but I didn't tell Caroline that. I suspected it was Mark that kept her up as well. She'd taken a real shine to him.

I put the notebook I carried down on the table, then I walked over and poured a cup of coffee. I sat down at the table across from Caroline and opened the large sketch note-book I used for everything—sketches of clocks, lists for every event, shopping lists, recipes, notes from meetings. I went through one every few months and then indexed what was in it for future reference, adding a table of contents. I'd inherited the notebook habit from my grandfather. I'd developed the table of contents habit after I'd spent some time trying to catalog his old books, to no avail. I was at the tail end of this book, but I hoped to stretch its use out to the New Year and the reopening of the shop in just a few days' time. I felt guilty even thinking about that. I looked over the notes I'd written last night right before I went to bed, the ones I'd re-created from memory. I'd had to give the originals to Jeff, and it hadn't seemed appropriate to ask to make a copy. Finding Mark Pine's killer was another task I'd added to my to-do list.

I turned the page and looked over the watch I'd sketched the night before in the guestroom after Caroline had gone to bed. It was rough, and from memory. I'd sketched the twisted vines on the side, trying to remember the exact pattern. I wondered if Jeff Paisley would let me look at it again. The watch might hold some answers.

"What's that?" Caroline asked.

"This?" I said. "Just a watch I saw somewhere. Why, do you recognize it?"

"No," she said softly. I was fairly certain she was lying, but I didn't push. Caroline was a lovely woman, but her guard was up all the time. I wasn't about to toss stones though, since my house was glass. I was fresh from a divorce, forging a new life in a town that was both familiar and foreign. I knew Caroline had a son I still hadn't met, but the rest of her life before marrying G.T. was a mystery to me. I'd asked a few questions, but she didn't offer answers, and I didn't push. We were both opening up, slowly, but neither of us was given to effusive sharing of feelings. We had time.

She was still staring at the watch, so I gently turned the page back to the list of things I needed to do this week.

"Caroline, do you think you could give me a ride to the shop? I hope Pat jumped my car. I need to go back to Marytown and the party store yet again. We went through almost all the paper goods I bought."

"So, everything will still go on as if nothing happened?" she said, stiffly folding her hands in her lap.

I took a deep sigh and looked at Caroline. "I thought about this a lot last night. On the one hand, it feels wrong to plan to reopen the shop on schedule, what with what happened to poor Mark. On the other hand, he worked as hard as anyone did to get the shop ready to open. The best tribute I can make to him is to show off his work."

"I'm sorry, Ruth," she said. "You're right, of course."

"I don't know if I'm right, but I don't know what else to do." I took a sip of my coffee, surprised by how bitter it tasted. "Caroline, do you know anything about Mark's family?" I asked.

"Nothing, I'm afraid. He changed the subject anytime it came up."

"Had he filled out the employee information sheet?" I asked. We were new to being employers, and had taken a one-day small business owner 101 course a couple of weeks ago.

"No, not yet. Remember, we were going to ask Kristen to look it over first."

"Right, I remember." Kristen Gauger had been my grandfather's lawyer, and she'd been walking Caroline and me through the legal minefields of running the Cog & Sprocket.

I took another sip of coffee, more for the caffeine than the experience. I tried not to wince.

"It's terrible, isn't it?" she said. "It's reheated from yesterday."

"Reheated?" I said. I took another sip. "Sad, because reheated still tastes better than mine. Though this is pretty bad." Caroline smiled, and I smiled back.

"We need to keep moving forward," she said. "Besides, maybe you can help figure out what happened to Mark. Oh, don't give me that wide-eyed, innocent look. I see the gears going—you have a glint in your eye. You know that if it weren't for you, Pat Reed would be going on trial for your grandfather's death. I saw you last night, making lists, trying to make sense of everything."

"I doubt Jeff Paisley needs my help," I said.

"Everyone needs help," she said. "I'll tell you what. I'll go over to Marytown and pick up the paper goods. I have a couple of other errands I want to run, and then I'll meet you at the shop."

"Sounds like a plan. Thank you, Caroline."

"Let me go up and pull myself together. Pat's out in the workshop. Why don't you go out and say hello."

I almost told Caroline she looked pulled together to me, but I looked more closely and noted the crooked lipstick and the strands of hair that were falling out of her twist—a look far more my style than hers. Maybe she did need to spruce up.

chapter 12

I grabbed my coat and went out the kitchen door, onto the deck. The deck was a new addition, and it wrapped all around the side of the house. I stopped for a moment, and took in the view, and smiled. When I was growing up, I spent summers with my grandparents. It was the happiest place in my childhood, this lake, this house. This view. I learned about clocks, and fixing them. I also escaped the benign neglect of my academic parents, who had no interest in the family business.

The workshop was even newer than the deck, and a wonderful addition to the house. It looked like a barn, and the building permit had been for a storage unit. It was, technically, a storage unit. A storage unit that you could live in, happily.

I walked out to the workshop and found Pat Reed in a very familiar pose, gently and carefully examining the case

of an old clock. My grandfather and Caroline had bought
out two estates last summer, and there were dozens of clocks
in each collection. We'd gotten a few clocks ready for a quick
turnaround in order to get cash flowing into the business.
We were still assessing the other clocks. There were a few
beautiful replicas that needed some tender loving care and
replacement parts, and Pat was focusing on those.

"You're here early," I said.

"Rhonda Whatshername. You know, the one from that
design firm in Boston?"

"Rhonda Nichols."

"Right, that's the one. She's coming by tonight to pick
this one up for her clients," Pat said. "I wanted to come by
and give this beauty one more buff and get her ready for
transport." He ran his hand along the oak case of the grandfather clock. Not priceless, but Pat was right, she was a
beauty. "Perfect for the dearest dining room on Beacon Hill,"
Rhonda had said. Rhonda spent a lot of time looking at our
clocks and trying to imagine new homes for them with her
long list of wealthy clients. She was a bit pretentious, but her
checks cleared and she gave us a lot of business.

"Need any help?" I asked.

"No, I've got this. I haven't had time to get your car
jumped, but I'll get to it as soon as I get back."

"No worries," I said, masking my disappointment with
a grin that I hoped read as cheerful. "Caroline is going to
give me a ride into town. Have you been there yet this
morning?"

"No, not yet. Nancy and Moira headed in first thing to
open the Sleeping Latte. Nancy called me, and Ben's shop
is still closed; police are still there. She said the Latte was

packed, but I'd imagine she's found out what there is to find out by now."

I laughed, but then sobered up.

"Listen, Pat, do you think we should go on with the opening, like nothing's happened?"

"No, not like nothing's happened. But we should stay on track. We've spent a lot of time, and money, letting folks know we were going to have an opening party. Won't do anyone any good to keep the shop closed any longer than necessary."

"That's what I was thinking. But I feel so heartless."

"Tell you what. We can change the plans as needed. Maybe do something to honor Mark. Has someone been in touch with his family?"

"I don't think he has family, at least not so they're in touch. He'd have gone to visit them instead of spending Christmas with all of us, don't you think? Tuck would know—they went to high school together. I should have asked him last night. Anyway, we may need to help make arrangements. Why are you looking at me like that, Pat?"

"Ruth, you've got a lot of your grandmother in you, you know that? The young man worked for you for just a few weeks, and now you're determined to do right by him."

"He was a good guy," I said as I struggled to hold back the tears pooled beneath my eyelids. "Besides, someone has to take care of him."

"Let Jeff Paisley take care of finding out who did what, all right? You hear me?"

"Yes, sir, I will let Jeff do his job. I promise." Didn't mean I wouldn't do what I could to help, though.

My phone buzzed in my pocket, and I took it out. A text. From Kim Gray.

"Kim wants me to call her."

"Call her? At seven in the morning?" Pat asked.

"That's what the text says. I still can't believe she didn't come by last night. For all we know she's sitting on a beach somewhere, calling it all in."

"I haven't seen her for a while, but she avoids Nancy like the plague, so that doesn't surprise me."

"Nancy did threaten her job at the last town meeting. Publicly. On the record."

"She did indeed. And she'll do it again at the next town meeting. If nothing else it gets folks attending them. Kim probably has another hoop she wants you to jump through before the thirty-first."

"Without a doubt," I said. When Grover Winter left my grandfather the old Town Hall in his will, he must have assumed a few things. First, he didn't count on being murdered, so he expected more time to iron out details. Second, he would have expected that Kim Gray would act in line with his wishes, since he handpicked her for her job. He either underestimated or misunderstood Kim Gray's motives and intentions.

I didn't. Kim Gray had a vision for Orchard that included adding tourist dollars by getting rid of the historic downtown area and starting fresh with a bunch of chain stores. We had been able to scuttle parts of her plans, but she still had some technicalities on her side. Even though we were only days away from the deadline, I wasn't sure what was going to happen when the old Town Hall reverted to me on the last day of the year.

"You want me to make the call for you?" Pat asked. I smiled and shook my head.

"No. Thanks, Pat."

"Don't trust me to keep my temper?"

"It isn't that. As it is, getting the clocks ready to go will be a lot of work to do in a short amount of time, and we both know that meeting with Kim throws you off your game for hours."

"She does wind me up, that's for sure. I'm getting as bad as Nancy."

"I wish Kristen was back already. I'd like to have a lawyer on this call, but she's on the road today."

"Hopefully you won't need one."

"With Kim Gray, you always need a lawyer."

"What do you mean I need to come up with a plan? What do you call the hundred-page document I delivered to your office, as requested, three weeks ago?" I said loudly. I wasn't quite shouting, but I was coming close, closer than was helpful. I took a deep breath and lowered my tone. "Explain the ordinance you are talking about."

"The proposed changes you submitted to the Town Hall go against the historical nature of the building and need to be voted on by the Board of Selectmen as well as the Town Historical Council."

"What Town Historical Council?"

"We formed it at the last meeting. You should have been there."

"If I knew when the meetings were, I would have been there. Since you didn't announce it in public seventy-two hours in advance, as is stipulated in the town charter, I doubt that this meeting, or this Town Historical Council, will hold up in court." Kim coughed a few times, and I knew I had her. Of course, I had no idea if what I'd said was true or not, but it sure sounded good.

"It was an emergency meeting, held on December twenty-fifth."

"Over dinner, no doubt," I said. "Where was my invitation?"

"Over dessert, actually. I believe that Heather Goody invited you for dessert, did she not?"

She did, indeed. But I'd decided to spend the day with the Reeds, and Heather Goody did not extend the invitation to them. Small-town politics. I was off my game.

"The Town Historical Council is a group of concerned citizens determined to keep the integrity of downtown Orchard intact. As you know, the old Town Hall is one of the oldest buildings in Orchard that is still standing."

"I do know that," I said. I didn't need a history lesson from Kim Gray. Orchard had been devastated in a flood and then flattened by a fire a few years later. The old Town Hall had remained standing, due to the fact that the building itself was made of stone. In New England, getting rid of stones in farmer's fields was a difficult and necessary task. The stones were used in walls, foundations, and, in some cases, buildings. In the case of the old Town Hall, the outside of the building was covered by clapboards, but the structure was solid stone.

"Your plan does not maintain the historical integrity of the building. As you know, the clock tower was added much later and is not historically accurate. Since rebuilding the tower is integral to your proposal to the town, the plan itself cannot be approved without modifications. Town funding has been pulled from the project until this issue is settled."

"Funding is pulled? And what modifications?" I said. Orchard wasn't putting a lot of money into the project to begin with. Most of it was tied to upgraded electric and heating in the building. But still, we were trying to make an end-of-the-year goal.

"The Town Historical Council will come up with recommendations by the end of the day."

"That gives us a day to get ready for the meeting on Friday. That isn't enough time."

"I suggest that you speak with the head of the council. Beckett Green."

"Beckett Green? Is he even a resident of Orchard?"

"He is, and an important business owner in addition to a student of history."

In addition to a thorn in my side. What had I ever done to Beckett Green?

chapter 13

Caroline dropped me off at the back of the Cog & Sprocket, just in case any looky-loos were still lurking, and then continued on to Marytown. I'd told her about my conversation with Kim Gray, but I tried to keep concern out of my voice. I had a feeling Kim and I were becoming locked into a game of chess, and I was losing. I needed a better strategy. Who could help me with that? The first name that came to mind was Ben Clover, but he had his own troubles right now, including a murder in his shop.

I let myself in and checked the clocks on the wall. Friday was winding day, so everything was running, though not at the same pace. Normally, that was the first conversation I had every morning with Mark Pine.

"How are the patients doing this morning?" I'd ask him, and he'd report back.

"Ugly cherub lost a minute," he'd say. "The pastoral scene's chime still sounds sick." Mark had taken to nicknaming the clocks. We were working on several banjo clocks right now, so specificity about the painting on their door or the decorative style helped us keep track. Mark did the naming, and some of them made me laugh. They were the first signs of his quirky sense of humor, and I'd taken it that he was feeling more comfortable and opening up. My heart ached, and I shook my head.

I needed more coffee, and some breakfast. I considered going straight down to the Sleeping Latte, but decided to employ my own cooking skills this morning. I wasn't up to conversation. I needed to sort some things on my own.

I poked my head through the door to the front of the shop and saw Jeff Paisley sitting in the chair and a half in the showroom. I took a couple of steps forward and noted his outstretched legs and his head resting on the back of the chair. His reading glasses were on, and he was still holding his cell phone in his right hand.

I tiptoed backward, and went upstairs to my apartment, letting myself in. I half hoped that Bezel would run out to see me, but she barely lifted her head when I went back to the bed to check on her. Bezel was not a morning cat.

I decided to skip the shower for now, and did what I could with my hair. There wasn't much I could do, since my hairstyle had gone from curly to frizzy at some point last night. I pulled some product through the tangles, trying to tame it back to curly, and then I washed my face. A sweep of blush, a little eye shadow, some mascara, lip gloss, and I began to look human.

I pulled on some lined leggings. I reached for a brightly flowered tunic, but then reached farther into the wardrobe and pulled out a black dress with white flowers. More subdued, and appropriate for the day. Earrings made out of clock parts and my clogs completed the look.

The coffee was brewing and the omelet was cooking, so I went back downstairs. Jeff Paisley was still sleeping heavily in the chair. I hated to wake him up, but it had to be done.

"Jeff," I said quietly, touching his shoulder.

He sat up so quickly I jumped back and put my hand on my heart.

"Sorry," we both said at once.

"Do you always wake up at attention?" I asked.

"They didn't finish up next door till around five," he said, taking in his surroundings. "I came back here to check messages. I must have fallen asleep. What time is it?" He looked down at his cell phone, but it didn't respond when he turned it on. He stared at the blank screen.

I tapped the top of his phone, and made a sweeping gesture with my hand. At least a dozen clocks announced the time from the walls and surfaces immediately in front of him. "It is just about eight. The clocks will start chiming any minute. Did they wake you up last night?"

"I got used to them around four o'clock." Jeff put his phone down and rubbed his fingers over the corners of his eyes.

"Tell you what—I made some eggs and coffee. Come up, plug in your phone, and have some food," I said.

"I should get into the office," he said, running his hand back over his hair.

"We both know this is probably the only food you'll have for hours, and you can't do anything if your phone doesn't work. Don't be stubborn."

"You sounded like my mother just then," he said. "Her nickname for me is Mule."

"Sounded like your mother?" I said, putting both hands on my hips. "You're a smooth talker, you know that?"

Jeff laughed and picked up his tie and jacket from the chair beside him. "It's early. Besides, my mother is a great lady. Okay, you win. Coffee and eggs, made by Ruth."

"Don't sound so surprised. Or is that cautious?"

"I've never tasted your cooking. And you yourself have said that your coffee-making skills were lacking."

"I've got my game back. Bought a better coffeemaker and I'm playing it safe with the French roast. But you can be the judge."

I poured Jeff another cup of coffee, his third. His eyes were still red, and he had dark smudges underneath, but he looked better. I was still nursing my second cup, but I felt better too. The food had also helped. Simple fare: eggs, cheese, and some roasted vegetables I had left over from lunch the day before. Simple, but plentiful and filling.

Jeff checked his phone, which was still plugged into the wall. He swiped past some messages, but didn't jump up and rush out the door.

"How is it going?" I asked.

"The state police are involved, so the investigation is in their office."

"Even though it happened in Orchard?"

"I wasn't here, and Kim Gray called them in."

"Can she do that?" I asked.

"She can do whatever she wants to do," he said.

"Tell me about it. She's trying to throw another wrench in my plans. Says that the Town Historical Council won't approve them."

"Who, or what, is the Town Historical Council?"

"Seems like it is Beckett Green."

"That guy knows how to make friends, doesn't he?"

"Has he crossed you too, Jeff?"

"Crossed. Not sure I'd use that word in public, but between you and me, yes. He has put several complaints in with Kim Gray about the way I handle citations in Orchard. Seems I'm not strict enough for his liking."

"Funny, there are a few folks who think you're plenty strict enough. Especially lately."

"I know. Parking tickets—that's what I've come to. Kim sees them as a way to increase town funds. I see them as a way to get citizens to avoid using businesses down here. I can't make anyone happy on this front."

"It does seem like parking tickets aren't the best use of your skill sets. Mark Pine's death is, don't you think?"

"Doesn't matter what I think. The state is in charge, I'm supposed to follow their lead."

"The state being the state police."

"One and the same."

"Pat Reed calls them staties. So do I, come to think of it."

"Not very respectful," Jeff said, though he had a small smile.

"I won't call them that to their face. Anyway, we both know that you are the best man for this job," I said. "I want to find out what happened to Mark, and why. So what do we do next?"

"*We* don't do anything. I keep on investigating and keep the chain of command informed of what I find."

"As part of your investigation, how about if I take a look at that watch, see what I can find out? Unless you're going to use Beckett Green as your watch expert?"

"Beckett Green? Never mind. I don't want to know, unless he's breaking the law. I could use your help on figuring out the watch. You sure it wasn't Mark's?"

"So the watch is a clue?"

"Depends on who you ask. There are lots of threads to the investigation. I'm following up on the watch. Do you think it was Mark's?"

"I'm not sure. It was a watch he wouldn't mind owning, that's for sure. I know you know this, but if it was his watch, his fingerprints would be on the release clasp, on the winding mechanism, and on the case. I'd need to look at it more closely to see if it needed to be wound daily, or weekly. If it's an eight-day watch, it will run out on Saturday. Friday is winding day."

"Why Friday?"

"Mark had some very, very precise habits. Friday was winding day in his world. He was obsessive about it. Also, if the watch was his, you probably won't find his fingerprints on the crystal or on the bezel. He was obsessive about keeping them clean."

"I thought bezels and crystals were the same thing."

Bezel was motionless, peering out the window, but at the mention of her name, her ears flicked around and the tip of her tail twitched.

"No, bezels are the ring that hold the crystal in place," I said, impressed with his clock knowledge. "You can determine a lot by the bezel, and the designs on it. I'd love to see this one."

Bezel's ears flicked forward again, back to more interesting things.

"So would I. I'll see what I can do to get you photos. How does that sound?"

"Could you send me the pictures of the watch you took?"

Jeff opened up his phone and flicked through the pictures.

"I'll send them to you later," he said.

"Why not now? They aren't official photos, are they?"

"Ruth, they are of the crime scene. I'd rather you didn't have to see Mark like that. How about you give me time to crop a couple of photos, and then I'll send them to you."

"Thanks for being worried about me. But you forget, I'm the person who found him. I kept seeing him every time I closed my eyes last night. I can't believe I missed the watch."

"It was a mess over there, and you were in shock. Anyway, at some point you may need to testify about what you found. You'll probably get questioned about it. Won't help anyone if you have photos that can be studied. Give me an hour or so. I'll get you photos of the watch."

"All right, I guess I understand."

"Thanks for that. I'm sorry that you didn't sleep well, Ruth. We'll find out what happened to Mark, but you're not going to unsee him for a while. Let me know if you want to talk about it. You suffered a trauma last night; you need to take care of yourself. Or let other folks take care of you. Agreed?"

"Thanks, Jeff. Agreed. I guess it's starting to hit me. It's so sad." I took a minute to regroup, and Jeff waited. It was one of the things I liked best about him. He didn't try to fix emotions, or brush them aside. I took a deep breath and went on. "I promise, if I need to talk, you're my first call. And please, let me help you however I can. That's probably the best medicine possible."

Jeff went in to wash his face, and I cleaned up the kitchen area. I wondered if I would ever take my new galley kitchen, and its lovely appointments, for granted. Probably not. Pat sought out, and found, a number of bargains that made my new kitchen affordable. Like in the bathroom, small scratches on the refrigerator, a dent on the dishwasher, a chip on the counter, a faucet hose that didn't retract automatically, and two different types of cabinets. All new to me, and much nicer than my budget would have allowed so I didn't mind that they weren't perfect.

I followed Jeff down the stairs and went to open the front door, which was double keyed. He walked over to the chair that he'd used as a workstation and began to gather his things. His backpack lay on the floor.

I opened the door and found Ben standing there, holding a huge bouquet of flowers and reaching forward to knock on the door.

"Ben," I said. Brilliant conversationalist, that's me.

"Morning, Ruth," he said, smiling that easy smile of his. "I hope it isn't too early."

"I'm going to head into the office. I have an extra uniform there," Jeff said, walking up behind me. "I'll get you the pictures as soon as I can. Oh, hey, Ben. I didn't know you were here."

"I didn't know you were here, Jeff."

"I ended up staying here last night," Jeff said, pulling on his jacket. "Thanks again for breakfast, Ruth. I'll get you those photos before noon. Wait—let me give you your key back."

"Why don't you keep it? You may need to come back when I'm not here. You're always welcome," I said.

"Thanks. Remember, call me," Jeff said, pointing at me.

"I will, I promise."

"Ben, are you around today?" Jeff asked.

"Not at my shop, but you already know that," Ben said, his hands clenched around the bouquet of flowers. "I'll be out at Aunt Flo's. You've shut her down as well."

"I haven't shut anyone down, Ben. You know that," Jeff said. "I'll see what I can do to get her store back up and running, but it is in the same building as your shop. They have a right to keep it closed down while the investigation is still active. I'll call you later and give you an update."

Ben didn't say anything, and Jeff left. I imagined that Jeff was used to people not being happy with him, but Ben was radiating animosity. You'd think he blamed Jeff for Mark being killed in his store.

"Come in," I said. "It's cold out there."

"Yeah, it's fine. I've got to get back," he said, shuffling his feet a bit on the welcome mat.

"Oh well, those are lovely flowers," I said. The mixed bouquet was in shades of white, a welcome change from the red and green that had covered every surface over the holidays.

"They're not for you," Ben said quickly. "They're for Caroline. For her birthday. We never did get a chance to celebrate it."

I was taken aback. I didn't expect them to be for me, though a girl could hope. Why would they be? We were friends, just friends. But still, he didn't have to bite my head off.

"Last night was hardly a night for celebration," I said, immediately regretting my tone, and softening it. "At least at the end. The first part of the night was great. I'm sorry I didn't get a chance to tell you how wonderful the lanterns were."

"As you said, the night ended up pretty badly, at least for most of us. I won't keep you any longer."

"Ben, don't rush off. Maybe we should talk?"

"I've been talking all night, to the whole town, it seems like," he said, rubbing his scruffy chin with his hand and looking more tired than I'd ever seen him. "I'll see you around, Ruth."

With that, he turned and walked down the front steps. I went to close the door and saw Beckett Green watching the scene from across the street. I'd talk to Ben later. Right now, I had business with Beckett.

chapter 14

Beckett had to have seen me coming, but that didn't stop him from turning, and half running into his store. I quickened my pace. Not only was I as tall as he was, I was in much better shape. I caught up with him as he was about to close his front door. I pushed my way in, and turned, ready to give him a piece of my mind.

The words all caught in my throat as I looked around the store, taking it all in. Cartons of books were everywhere. A few had been shelved, but the ones that were unpacked were laid out on tables, in piles. A coffee station in the corner, surrounded by overstuffed leather chairs. A round customer service station anchored the center of the space, with a few computer stations on it, and shelves below filled with magazines, candy, fruit-and-nut mixes, and other assorted sundries. The wall to the left of the store was painted deep red and had a dozen clocks hanging on it. The ticking was audible in the silence of the room.

"I wouldn't have believed it, but it's true. You are trying to be all the shops of downtown Orchard in one place, aren't you?"

"What do you mean?" he asked, his color rising.

"Your magazine rack looks like the one over at the Corner Market."

"Good for impulse purchases. Bookstores are risky businesses," he said, tapping his foot impatiently. "I need to make the customer happy."

"Coffee?"

"Why should folks have to walk down the street?"

"Never mind that if you'd agreed to be part of the POL card, you could have said with a purchase of so much money, folks could get a free cup of coffee at the Sleeping Latte? Or a free candy bar at the Corner Market?"

"You sound like Rina. She's been all over me this morning about that blasted card, and the open house. Have you two been talking? I still don't see the value of discounting."

"What don't you get? That's the point of the program, to get the businesses to support each other, not to take away sales."

"I have no idea what you are talking about," he said, straightening a pile of paperbacks on a nearby table.

"And what about these? And this?" I asked.

"What?" he said, not looking up.

"The clocks," I said. He flinched when I said the word *clocks*, and he should have. I sidestepped him, again not difficult, and walked over to the wall of clocks. Lovely banjo clocks, examples that rivaled my own collection. A few Viennas. A Seth Thomas.

There was a sign affixed low on the wall, underneath the row of clocks.

"'Have a clock that needs to be fixed? We can help! The Clock Doctor will be in on Wednesday afternoons.' Who, exactly, is this clock doctor?" I scoffed.

"None of your business."

"None of my business? You are offering a specialty service across the street from my shop, and it is none of my business? You've got to be kidding me." I couldn't decide if I wanted to laugh or scream.

"If I am able to offer comparable service for a fraction of the cost, that is simply good business strategy. You have to admit, you overcharge for your services. Just like I hear your grandfather did."

"My grandfather and I both undercharge for our services. Do you have any idea what it takes to be a horologist? The years of training? The apprenticeships? The costs associated with opening a shop, keeping the right parts in stock, finding vendors to make parts, the hours that a repair can take? Even a simple cleaning is anything but. I know that you offered Mark Pine a position, and he turned you down. So who did you hire? Who's your clock doctor?"

"How do you know about Mark?" he said, meeting my eyes for the first time since this ridiculous conversation began.

"He told me, of course. The last time I saw him, alive. I saw you looking for him later. Did you find him, Beckett? How angry were you that he turned you down? Angry enough to hurt him?"

"How dare you? Get out of my shop. Now."

"I wonder if the police know about your fight with Mark. I need to give Jeff Paisley a call and let him know. I think I told him last night, but maybe I didn't."

"Never mind. I'll call him myself, unless you leave right now." Beckett walked over to the customer service desk and picked up the phone. He stood and stared at me. I shrugged and turned back to the clocks.

I opened the door on the third one in, a lovely antique. The card said it was a "Biedermeier Vienna Regulator Wall Clock dated 1865." A beautiful clock, rosewood. Brass pendulum, working. Grande sonnerie movement, if I wasn't mistaken. In less than five minutes the quarter hour was due to chime. The clock should be better protected from customers, but I wasn't going to tell Beckett that. I took out my cell phone and turned on the flashlight app, sweeping it inside the clock. Beckett grabbed at my arm, pulling me away.

"That clock is worth thousands of dollars," Beckett said. "Get away from it."

I turned to look at him, and knew that he believed what he said.

"Don't get your panties in a twist," I said, shaking him off. "I'll leave. I've seen enough. But listen to me, Mr. Historical Council, you should probably know what you're talking about before you start making judgments on historical accuracy."

I wish I'd been able to look at all the clocks more closely, but it didn't matter. I'd already seen enough.

Beckett Green was selling fakes.

chapter 15

I left Beckett's store and walked down to the right, to the Corner Market. I needed more cat food, but also wanted to check in with Ada and Mac Clark.

Mac had inherited the Corner Market from his uncle, but he and Ada had made the store their own. With an emphasis on locally sourced and organically grown food, it was hip enough for foodies to flock there. But they also carried staples like eggs, milk, cheese, and bread. Not enough junk food, but I had noticed they'd started carrying a few more bags of chips. They were responding to customer demands. This customer, at least.

I'd learned early on, never just carry a basket through the aisles. Get a cart. Even when all you want is cat food, you'll find a half-dozen other things you didn't know you needed. Today's case in point, half-priced sourdough bread and a grapefruit that was the size of a softball. I had barely gotten in the front door.

I found Ada Clark in the condiment aisle, trying to stock shelves. What was normally second nature had become a chore for her, as she tried to navigate around her enormous belly. From the back, she looked much the same, but when she turned around it looked like she had swallowed a basketball. Or two.

"Ada, can I help you with that?" I asked. I bent over and handed her the bottles and jars she had in her cart.

"Was there a run on mustard?" I said, taking note of the labels as I handed them to her.

"Last night got a little crazy. We offered people three percent off their bill as part of our promotion, and boy, they took us up on the offer."

"Three percent could really add up, couldn't it?"

"Mac is running the numbers now. It could, especially on items that are expensive for us to carry, like some of the specialty cheeses. But there are other items that have a decent profit built in, and folks were buying them as well. I think we had a really good night. Up until the end, of course."

"I know what you mean," I said. "It feels like there are two different nights. One before we let the lanterns go, and one afterward, when I found Mark. We're all so focused on the afterward it is hard to remember the open house."

"I wonder if we'll ever stop thinking about the night and feeling sad?" she said, holding a jar of fancy, spicy mustard in each hand.

"If you want something to help move you to another mood, go over to Beckett's store and look at his checkout counter. See yours, the display of candy, magazines, mints, water, all that? His looks like that."

"What do you mean? I thought he was selling books?"

"Books, and sundries. And clocks."

"Clocks."

"Clocks. Then there's the free coffee."

"Free coffee?"

"I'm telling you, Ada, you'd think he was the only store in town. I'd be surprised if he didn't start selling eggs and milk."

Ada laughed and sat down on the stool that was nearby in the aisle, likely for that express purpose.

"Sorry, I know it isn't funny. What is he trying to do? Someone should explain how a small town works," she said.

"He thinks he has it figured out. He's got Kim Gray in his pocket."

"How do you know?"

I told Ada about my conversation with Kim, and she thoughtfully rubbed her belly. Ada and I were almost the same age, but she seemed years younger. When we'd first met, I envied her happy marriage and her impending motherhood, both things I'd always wanted. Now we were friends, and I was excited about the arrival of Baby Clark, knowing that I would play a role in his or her life.

"We need to tell Mac about the meeting with Kim. You know we'll help however we can. What happens if the deal with the town doesn't go through?"

"Then I own the Town Hall. I can figure it out, but I don't want to. I know that I sound like a wimp, but taking care of the Cog & Sprocket is enough for me to deal with right now. The old Town Hall is Pandora's box. Who knows what's inside?" I said, opening the last box full of mustard bottles in Ada's cart.

"We're all here to help—you know that. I can't believe Beckett is selling clocks."

"Right? I don't think he knows what he is doing. He had mislabeled the one I was able to get a good look at. I didn't even get a chance to look at them all."

"Mislabeled, like wrong name or year? Or mislabeled, like pulling the wool over customers' eyes?" she asked, shifting uncomfortably on her little perch next to the packaged pastas.

"Pulling wool."

"Yeesh. How can you call him out on that?"

"I'm not sure. I should probably let Jeff know, since he is looking into . . . Hey, what are you smiling at?"

"You and Jeff Paisley," she said, smiling and shaking her head.

"What about Jeff and me?"

"I heard he stayed at your place last night. And he had breakfast this morning."

"Wow, what time is it? Not even nine o'clock, and the gossip mill is in full gear? Please, Ada, Jeff and I are friends. I spent the night at Caroline's." Was that what was wrong with Ben? It couldn't be. Surely he'd know better.

"I know. Look at me, I'm turning into something I despise. No, please, don't explain anything. Your business is your own. I promise, I won't be part of the gossip mill. It doesn't suit me."

"But you should know . . ."

"I should know nothing. Again, I'm sorry. Thanks for your help with the mustards. I have to go to the ladies' room—big surprise there. Can you help me up? Thanks. Let me see if Mac can come out front and chat with you."

"That would be great. How about if I put these boxes back in the cart for you?"

"I'd appreciate it. Harder for me to stock shelves these days."

"Happy to help. Anytime. Really, just ask."

"You're a good neighbor, Ruth. Make sure you tell Mac about Kim's plans. I'm done being the nexus of information."

With that Ada waddled toward the back of the store. I picked up the empty mustard boxes and put them in the cart, pushing it to the side.

"Y ou looking for a job?" Mac said.

I turned away from the condiment section, where I had been finishing up Ada's work and straightening the labels.

"I would become obsessed by this," I said. "I was moving one jar to the right shelf, and next thing I know, I'm finding out how satisfying lining up labels can be, and moving everything forward."

"It's called facing. Anytime you want to work out your obsessive tendencies, come on down. Once Ada has the baby, I'll need all the help I can get for a while."

"Are you hiring new staff?" I asked. I knew that was a tricky question. Hiring staff for small businesses, especially on a short-term basis, was difficult during the winter.

"We've got enough folks filling the shifts. I'll need to keep up with the ordering and the inventory though. Nancy Reed is going to help out."

"Nancy Reed? Does she have time?"

Mac laughed. "I know, she's everywhere these days. She already helps us keep stocked on baked goods and sends over sandwiches for us to sell after the Sleeping Latte closes in the afternoon."

"Moira's thinking about starting to serve dinner," I said.

"Not till the summer, when there's more traffic in town. Anyway, Nancy kind of works for us already. We're making it more official."

"We're all in this together," I said, shrugging.

"All except Beckett Green. Did you hear about the readings he is going to be holding at the store?" I nodded my head. That was part of his business plan.

"Guess who's going to be catering them?"

"The Sleeping Latte?" Mac shook his head. "You guys?"

"No. He's going to a chain over in Marytown. Not even a small business, which would be bad enough. A chain."

"How do you know that?" I asked.

"Tuck told me. We did a proposal for him—all discounted prices and fair rates— and when I didn't hear back I went by. Tuck was working in the store, unpacking boxes, and let me know. Of course, Beckett didn't have the guts to tell me himself."

"Tuck works for Beckett now?"

"Didn't you know that?" Mac asked.

"I don't think I did," I said. "We hired him for some odd jobs through Nadia, but not enough to live on, really. I guess I never asked. I wouldn't have cared, really. Until today." I told Mac about the clocks, only telling him as much as I'd said to Ada, about Beckett's deceptive labeling. I wasn't sure why, except that I felt that Jeff Paisley should be the first person to hear the news that they were full-blown fakes. Then I realized that he hadn't heard about my phone call with Kim either, so I repeated that story as well. I was beginning to think I should just print up a newsletter every time anything happened so I could just hand it to each friend at the beginning of every conversation to catch them up.

"Whatever you need, Ruth, let me know," he said, his face serious as he thought over everything I just related to him. "I'm behind your plans for the old clock tower one hundred percent. It's the best plan for Orchard. It keeps the building open and available for town use. The clock tower project is exciting and could get folks to visit, which is good for all of us. Kim Gray and Beckett Green are awfully short-sighted, if you ask me."

Or they were both playing a different end game, one that I didn't understand. I had to wonder—did their game have anything to do with Mark Pine's death?

chapter 16

I called Jeff as soon as I left the Corner Market, and told
him about the clocks. I sat down on one of the benches
outside the market, surveying Orchard while I talked.

"You did say you only wanted me to talk about Beckett
if he was breaking the law," I said when he didn't respond.

"I did. Not sure that misrepresenting clocks is breaking
the law. Are you sure what you saw?"

"I'm sure about the one I looked at, but I didn't have a
chance to look at the others."

"How could you tell?"

"The regulator wasn't—"

"Never mind, Ruth. I wouldn't understand if we were
standing right in front of it. Was it a good fake?"

"Pretty good, yes. I'd love to look at the other clocks in
the shop. Can you help me with that?"

"I can't help you, but I can see what I can find on my own."

"You don't have the expertise to know what you are look-ing at."

"I do know someone who does have that expertise, and I'll ask her for it."

"But—"

"But nothing, Ruth. There is a murder investigation going on right now in this town. Don't go poking around—you never know where the bees are hiding."

"Interesting phrase."

"Promise me."

"I promise," I said, fingers crossed.

"Now promise me you'll call me with anything you find out."

"Whoa, Jeff, that was cold. Don't you trust me?" I squeaked.

"Just promise," he sighed. He really had me figured out.

"Promise." This time I didn't cross my fingers. Keeping Jeff in the loop could save lives. "Are the state cops still in charge?"

"You know it," he said. "Speaking of which, I've got to invite myself to a briefing."

"Hang in there," I said. "Oh, and one more thing."

"What is it?"

"Ada Clark heard that we were dating."

"We're what?"

"I think I stopped that rumor in its tracks. But just so you know."

I could almost hear Jeff's head shaking as I hung up the phone.

After I hung up with Jeff I crossed the street, in the crosswalk, having looked both ways beforehand. I didn't want Beckett to give me a citizen's citation for jaywalking. I turned back to look at Been There, Read That, and saw him standing on his front porch, talking on his cell phone. I smiled and waved. It was hard to read his expression from that far away, but he quickly went back inside.

I pivoted to go into the Sleeping Latte and almost ran over Rina. She could trademark her look: black bottoms, today running tights; red tops, right now a fleece jacket; a headband that provided both warmth and fashion; tinted glasses that got darker in the sun, but that she wore every time I saw her; deep plum lipstick. She exuded money and class, yet she still somehow fit right into Orchard daily life.

Today her hair was pulled back into a ponytail, but it was still glossy and completely in control. Rina was always in control. She was an excellent foil for Beckett. Bringing her into the business had been his best move so far. I smiled when I saw her. I noticed that she had a POL bag from the library and was looking at the card she carried.

"Hi, Rina," I said.

"Hey, Ruth! Good morning. Are you getting refueled as well? I'm addicted to Moira's lattes."

"Nobody makes better coffee than the Sleeping Latte," I said.

"I'm trying to figure out their secret," Rina said.

"So you can steal it for your store?" I said, instantly regretting it.

"What are you talking about?" she said, looking up with her eyes narrowed.

"Sorry, that was harsh. I didn't get much sleep last night. I'm sure you heard about what happened to Mark Pine."

"I did," she said, relaxing a bit. "Terrible story. The police came by to check in with Beckett and me about anything we might have seen last night."

"They asked me the same thing. Did you remember anything helpful?"

"After Beckett and I realized we couldn't very well serve our food in the dark, we went back to the B and B to put it in the fridge and then headed over to Marytown to grab dinner."

"You missed a great party. Up until the end."

"Ruth, what did you mean by stealing the coffee recipe?"

"I went over to Been There, Read That this morning. I noticed the coffee corner. And the clocks. Beckett's making a mini downtown Orchard right in his own store."

Rina scowled a bit and looked back down at the POL card in her hand. She raised it up and shook it in front of me. "You all have the right idea here, with this card. Beckett is used to being a corporate raider—that's how he made his money. He'll see the light. I promise you, by the time we open, Been There, Read That will be a bookstore. Only a bookstore. All right, with games and puzzles too. But that's all. No coffee."

"And the clocks?"

"I'm working on that too. Trust me. Those clocks were a mistake. A big mistake."

I was tired, stressed, sad, and frustrated. Mostly because of Mark's death, but Kim and Beckett certainly deserved a fair share of my ire. And they were getting all of it today. I didn't want to start a war with Beckett, but I would. Selling clocks. Across the street from the Cog & Sprocket. Please.

I wasn't actually hungry, but knew I'd get a sympathetic ear at the Sleeping Latte. I really didn't want to be alone yet and I could also grab a sandwich for later. I hadn't bought anything that needed refrigeration at the Corner Market, and had restrained myself so I only had one bag of groceries. Good thing, since the Latte was packed. Two of the student workers Moira had brought on were busy behind the counter, and the line was six people deep. Moira was busing a table, and I walked over to say hello.

"You can't sit here right now," she said, not looking up.

"What?"

"There are customers who've been waiting awhile. You can't just come in and sit."

"Moira," I said, a little taken aback by her abrupt tone. "I wasn't going to sit. I came over to say hello and see how you are."

"Right. Sorry," she said, stacking up plates with one hand and gathering crumpled napkins with the other. "It's been a heck of a day. We haven't had a break in business. Reporters, cops, curious folks. They all want to eat and drink at once."

"Do you need help?" I asked. I'd helped in the restaurant a couple of times. I wouldn't trust me to make a latte, but I could use a register.

"No, we're all right. Listen, I need to get these dishes in the dishwasher, so I can help out front."

"I can do that," I said. "Seriously. I'm good at it. How about if I put my groceries in the office, and then I'll take the dishes back, put them through the wash, and say hi to your mother."

"Whatever," she said, shaking her head like I was a

mosquito buzzing in her face. "Thanks, I guess. But you don't have to."

"I know I don't have to," I said. So much for that sympathetic ear.

Moira shrugged and left the tub of dirty dishes on the chair. I watched her walk away, but didn't wait too long. I dashed to the office and stowed my groceries and my giant purse out of the way. Then I went out front again and grabbed the gray tray of dirty dishes and walked through the door to the kitchen.

I'd been here less than twenty-four hours ago, but now it was a different world altogether. Instead of a group of friends eating together, taking solace in community, it was the Nancy Reed solo show. She had sandwiches lined up and was putting them all together. I smelled cookies and bread baking, and noticed that both oven timers were about five minutes away from releasing delicious goodies. My lack of hunger flew out the door and my stomach growled.

"Ruth, what are you doing here?"

"I volunteered to help Moira get the dishes done. It gave me an excuse to come back and say hello." I opened up the industrial dishwasher and loaded it like I had been taught. "Is she all right? She was a little weird with me."

"Rumors are flying around town about you and Jeff Paisley," she said, efficiently slicing a sandwich in half. "They don't sit well with her."

"Are you kidding me?" I asked. I stopped loading for a moment, but went right back to it. "Obviously, Pat hasn't been in this morning."

"Not yet. He's out at the cottage."

"Getting a clock ready to be moved. I know. I saw him

there, this morning, right before Caroline drove me into town. I stayed with her last night."

"But your car was at your shop," she said, arranging tomatoes on a BLT.

"Where it's going to stay, until I get someone to jump the battery." I rinsed out the gray tub and dried it lightly. "I'm going to take this back out front and see if I can get some more dishes. May as well run a full load. One thing, Nancy. It sure would be nice if people asked me a question directly, instead of being a gossip."

I walked back out front, to the other busing station. Half the tub was full of dishes, so I swapped them out and then wandered over to three empty tables. Honestly, what was the matter with people? They can't bring their own dishes up? Yeesh. As I went back to the kitchen with a full tub of dishes, I walked by Moira, who was spraying a table down with cleaning solution.

"By the way, Moira, I stayed with Caroline last night. Next time you have a question, ask me." I saw her back stiffen for a moment before she returned to her cleaning.

I went back into the kitchen and over to the dishwasher, which I finished loading. I took a little bit of my hostility out on the dishes and felt better once the dishwasher was running. I rinsed out the tub and then washed my hands. Doing this kind of work was satisfying. There was a mess, it got cleaned up. Would that life worked like that.

I turned around and Nancy was standing there, offering me a fresh cookie.

"No, thanks," I said. "I've got to get back to the shop. Caroline will be there shortly."

"Don't be like that, Ruthie. I'm sorry we all jumped to

conclusions. I'm not even going to try and explain. We're all tired and our nerves are raw. We should have known better."

"Or minded your own business? How does that sound?" I asked, still a little wound up. "What's going to happen if I ever did have anyone stay with me at the shop? Will there be a special edition of the *Orchard Gazette* printed? Yeesh."

"Printing's too expensive. It would be a banner ad on the website. Flashing. Probably red type." Nancy smiled and pushed the cookie forward. "Come on, Ruthie. We're all in a state this morning."

"That's an understatement," I said. "You were right. Beckett is selling clocks."

"What? Sit down and tell me."

So I did. The whole story, starting from Kim's phone call and ending with Beckett's store. I left out some parts, like the information about the watch, that weren't mine to share. I ended with the coffee area in the store.

"What kind of coffee area? I thought I put a stop to that," Nancy said.

"It looked like there were urns of coffee, or going to be, once it was set up."

"There are ordinances about that, you know. He can't sell coffee without permits. He must have found a way around the rules. No doubt with Kim's help."

"What does Kim have against all of us?" I asked. "For a town manager, she seems determined to put some of us out of business. I thought that would stop when we derailed the development plans she had."

"From what I hear, she's looking at different chains, trying to get them to come to Orchard."

"But the entire point is that we are all unique."

"A point that is being made, and resonating with folks. The open house yesterday was testimony to that. At this point, she's trying to do things out of spite more than anything else. You know, she refers to you and your grandfather as 'those Clagans' as if your grandfather is orchestrating our actions from beyond the grave. Her face turns kind of purple when she says it."

"Nancy, that shouldn't make you so happy. I hate to think I'm stirring so much up in town. That wasn't my intention."

"It's your birthright. Seriously, Clagans are one of the oldest families still living here. Your people have always been stirring the pot. In a good way. Glad to see that Thom passed it along. It's one of the things that keeps Orchard on track, and honest. Maybe you should run for the Board of Selectmen. I've heard that Dottie is going to retire—can't stand working with Kim. We need to get someone on there with a backbone."

"Why don't you run, Nancy?"

"Me? Folks wouldn't vote for me."

"Of course they would. You've got the vote of everyone downtown. Seriously, Nancy, think about it."

"I'll think about it. Now, before you go, let me pack you a couple of sandwiches for lunch. Don't say no. It will make me feel less guilty about earlier. I made this spread today. Chickpeas, green olives, olive oil, garlic, some hot pepper flakes. Fresh turkey breast, this spread, a good midwinter sandwich."

"Actually, winter is only a week old," I said.

"Don't remind me. Every year I say to Pat, maybe we should go and visit my sister in Florida for a few weeks. You know what he says?"

"What?"

"'Your sister drives me crazy. I'd rather shovel snow.' Truthfully, she drives me crazy too, but at least we'd be warm. Anyway, let me know what you think of the sandwich. And tell me, what else is Beckett selling that is making you so angry?"

"Clocks aren't enough?"

"Clocks are enough, but if they were nice clocks, you'd probably send customers over. What's the matter with them? Are they electric?"

"I don't mind electric clocks. Don't laugh—it's true. They have their place in the market. I wouldn't sell them, but that's because I'm a clock snob. If he was selling electronic clocks, I'd feel better. What he's selling is much worse than electronic clocks, though."

chapter 17

I thanked Nancy for the food, grabbed my groceries, and went back out to the front of the Sleeping Latte so I didn't let cold air in through the back and freeze Nancy. Moira waved as I walked out, but my hands were full. That's why I didn't wave. Or at least that was my excuse. I walked out the front door and looked to my right, noting the crowd gathered around Ben's shop. There were a couple of TV vans as well. Yeah, not today. I walked down the side of the Sleeping Latte and the back way to my shop. I was surprised that no one was back there, but looking out at the end of the alley I noted that the entrance was cordoned off. Maybe it was because of evidence, or maybe it was Jeff Paisley giving us all a little privacy. No matter what the reason, I was grateful.

As I let myself into the shop, I heard my cell phone ring.

I put down my bags and fished around the front pocket of my dress.

"Hello?" I said.

"Ruth, it's Jeff Paisley."

"Hey, Jeff. Long time."

He ignored me, which was probably best. "You remember that I promised to send you the pictures of the watch by noon?"

"I do."

"How about if I bring you the watch instead?"

Jeff came in the back door about fifteen minutes later. I had a pitcher of water and had set out the sandwiches Nancy sent over. Normally there is a rule about no food in the workroom, but this wasn't normal.

"What's up with the news vans next door?" I asked.

"There are a couple of folks who don't think there is any such thing as bad publicity. Kim Gray is one of them."

"Is she there?"

"She's scheduled a press conference at three o'clock."

"Really? What's she going to say?"

"Not sure. I'm out of the loop on this aspect of the investigation."

"Her choice or yours?"

"Hers. Enough about that," he said, reaching into his bag. "Let's talk about the watch."

"Do you have it with you?"

"I do. The lab ran some tests, but there weren't any prints on the outside of the case. They weren't able to get the case open, and rather than have them force it, I thought I'd bring it to you. You have your tools here in the shop."

"The state police let you take it?"

"They don't consider it important evidence. They are more focused on other events. Anyway, I think they were just as happy to have me leave."

"Making friends with the state?" I said. "Okay, let's take a look."

"You'll have to wear gloves."

"Fine, sure."

He handed me the blue gloves, latex free. I used gloves on occasion myself, so I wasn't unfamiliar with the feeling. I readied the area, a clean glass surface with a dark cloth underneath so that I could see any pieces that came loose. I turned on the lights over the workspace and pulled the magnifier over. I put on my own vision visor and focused it down over my eyes. I looked up and saw a wide grin on Jeff's face. Or it may have been a smirk—images were skewed once I put the visor on.

"Is something funny?"

"No. I have never seen you in gear before. You look like the medical examiner."

"Gee, thanks. Give me the patient. Just remember, I'm not a watch expert."

"You know more than the guys in the lab. One of them wanted to use a screwdriver."

I shuddered. A screwdriver. The horror.

"Let me finish setting up the camera, then we can start."

"Why are you recording this?" I asked.

"In case my hunch is right, and this is a critical piece of

evidence, I want to make sure I've followed procedure. Any issues with that?"

"No, none. You know I'll do whatever I can to help." Jeff pulled out a tripod and set it up. The camera was already set up to snap into place, and he was ready to go in a few seconds. "Now I'm going to hit record, and here we go.

"This is Chief Jeff Paisley in the Cog & Sprocket, with the owner of the business, Ruth Clagan. Ms. Clagan is a horologist, and is going to help us open the watch found near the body of Mark Pine, a victim of foul play. For the record, no fingerprints were found on the watch.

"I am now handing the watch to Ms. Clagan for examination."

Jeff took out the evidence bag and opened it, pulling out the watch and handing it to me.

I held it in my hand. "In the future, a better way to transport this would be in a box, keeping it upright. Hear that clinking sound? The watch shouldn't make a clinking sound."

"Do you know what that is?"

"It could be a dozen different things I know about, and another dozen I have no idea about. We're going to take this slowly. As I said, watches aren't my specialty, but I've worked on a few in my training. See on the back here? This watch was made by the Elgin company, but you probably know that already. See the inscription on the back, along the side? That's how you can tell."

"Is it worth much?"

"All depends on the year, the condition, whether it is working, replacement parts, all sorts of factors. Could be worth as little as three hundred dollars and as much as forty-five hundred dollars. I can take some notes, get you some better numbers."

"How do you open it? Pushing down the stem doesn't work."

"It should. Let me see," I said, turning it around in my gloved hand. "Yes, right, there might be something stuck in the hinge. Let me see, maybe this would work."

"What are you two up to?" Caroline was in the back doorway, shopping bags brimming with party supplies in her hands. She dropped both bags and came over toward us. Her cheeks were aglow from the cold air, but the rest of her face was pale.

"Ruth is helping me with part of an investigation," Jeff said.

"What investigation? Does this have anything to do with Mark's death?"

"We found this watch by his body."

"Oh no. When I saw the drawing in your book this morning, I hoped it was a coincidence."

"A coincidence?" I asked.

"Let me look at this watch."

"Why, have you seen this type of watch before?" I said, looking up at her quizzically.

"I should say so. I may have made it."

chapter 18

"What?" I asked.

"What are you recording?" Caroline asked, gesturing toward the camera.

"Chain of evidence for the watch," Jeff said.

"What? Why?"

"We found it last night," he said. "We can't get it open, and I thought that getting some expert help made sense. Of course, I thought of Ruth. Didn't realize there were other experts in the neighborhood."

"Can you turn it off?" Caroline asked.

Jeff didn't look happy about it, but did as she asked. Knowing Jeff, he was being more cautious than necessary. Still, he wasn't one to break his own rules. He wouldn't have for me, that's for sure.

"Here, Caroline, wear these gloves before you touch the watch. Fingerprints wouldn't help anyone."

"Certainly not me," she said, smiling wanly, snapping on the gloves. "Ruth, could I use a visor?"

"Of course," I said. I grabbed the extra one at the workstation, realizing at the last minute it was Mark's. I hoped she wouldn't notice, but when she hesitated before putting it on, I knew she had.

"This is an Elgin, but I suspect you know that." We both nodded. "Very nice case. Not original."

"How do you know that?" I asked. I knew a little about watches, but not enough to assess the details.

"I don't, but I have my suspicions. I need to get it open to be sure. The release pin is stuck. Likely someone snapped it shut over and over, and the gold wore down over time."

"Isn't that normal wear and tear?" Jeff asked.

"The better way to open a pocket watch is to depress the opening mechanism, close it gently, and then release the stem. Let me do this, and then if I gently press the button here, we should be able to get her open."

I pretended not to notice Caroline's hand shake, but she steadied it soon enough and got the watch opened. The winding vine motif was inside the watch as well. Caroline used her finger to trace the vines, and showed us how it turned into a W. I needed to be shown it; then it was obvious.

"It's mine. Or rather, it's Wallace's."

"Who's Wallace?" I said.

"My first husband. Levi's father," Caroline said.

"Wallace?" Jeff asked.

"Wallace Struggs."

"Does he live around here?"

"No. The last I heard, he was still in prison. In Monaco."

"Prison?" I asked. "What did he go to prison for?"

"A lot of things," she sighed. "Including forgery."

"What did he forge?" Jeff asked quietly. He wasn't writing anything down, but I knew he wouldn't forget any of these details. Or did he know them already? When Jeff had first arrived in Orchard, my grandfather and Caroline had gone out of their way to welcome him. Had he gotten curious about Caroline's past? Or had she confided in him? For that matter, what had G.T. known?

"Clocks. Watches. Paintings. He specialized in mid-1800s antiquities. You both might as well know this now, before it gets out of hand. I helped him, mostly with the watches. I didn't realize what he was doing, believe me, but I did help."

Caroline had been working on the watch all the while, laying out the large pieces as they came off. She'd taken off the bezel and the crystal, and then she removed the inner workings of the watch itself. They came out as a unit, which allowed them to be taken apart if necessary. Caroline turned over the mechanism and pointed to the back. She lowered the large table-mounted magnifying glass over the watch and turned on the light. Jeff and I both leaned in.

"See, here? This is my signature. Caroline Struggs. I took to signing the inner workings of the clocks, trying to help the authorities track the work. That was the deal I made, to keep me out of jail."

"To keep you out of jail?" I asked. I still couldn't get past Caroline expertly disassembling this intricate watch.

Caroline sighed and looked up at us both. She picked up the watch case and absently rubbed her gloved fingers over it.

"Wallace and I met when I was quite young. I was an apprentice in a shop where he worked. The shop was owned by Zane Phillips, the man you talked to yesterday. He was a wonderful mentor."

"An apprentice?" I asked. "So you are a clockmaker?"

"A watchmaker, actually," she said, smiling to herself. "Not that I don't like clocks, but my gift was in watch repair. As with clock work, it is very exacting and delicate. The inside of a watch is about the mechanics, and I found that suited me.

"I had a gift, one which delighted Wallace at first. Zane wanted us to stay with him—we were a great team—but Wallace was restless and wanted to move on. I was in love, so I went with him. We moved to Europe and opened our own shop. At first we focused on both clocks and watches, but soon we were getting more of a reputation for watch repair—"

"Because of you," I said, just starting to wrap my head around this revelation.

Caroline reached over and took my hand, giving it a gentle squeeze.

"Modesty aside, yes, because of me," she said. "We were doing a good business and Wallace was doing clock repairs. Then I got pregnant, and Levi was born. Everything changed then."

"What do you mean?" Jeff asked.

"I was a bit older when he was born, almost forty. I didn't expect to fall as in love with my son as I did, but he became my focus. I kept working, of course, but it is one thing to have a baby in the shop. Quite another to have a toddler. So we set up a small shop at home, and I worked more and more from there. That was when it started."

"What started?"

"When I was in the shop, I was involved in the day-to-day workings of the business. I would meet with the customers and learn about the watches, their history. I would talk to them about restoration work, see if they wanted to try to maintain the value if it was very old, or if they wanted to get it working again. You'd be surprised how differently people reacted once you talked to them. More often than not, people wanted the watch to work. So I would replace the older parts and focus on that. A scratched crystal, a bezel that didn't turn as easily anymore, cogs and gears that were worn down. I'd replace the parts with newer models and get the watches running like new. Of course, I'd keep all of the old parts."

"Why?" Jeff asked.

"In case someone wanted a more authentic restoration," I answered for Caroline. "The scratched crystal may not be everyone's cup of tea, but if you have a two-hundred-year-old watch, you may want the two-hundred-year-old crystal to go with it. Even with a little scratch."

"But, of course, I would always let people know that the parts had been changed. Once I was out of the shop, though, Wallace stopped being quite so careful about the record keeping. At least that is what I told myself when I began to wonder why so many antique watches started to come through looking for restoration work rather than replacement parts. Wallace had started to take some watches of dubious distinction, send them to me for restoration, and then he'd pass them off as antiques. He was doing the same with clocks."

"You had no idea?" I asked.

"I don't know. I knew something was going on, but I

couldn't fathom the scope. I'll never forget the day I found out Wallace was under investigation for forgery and smuggling."

"Smuggling?" Jeff asked.

"Wallace would use jewels from nefarious sources in clocks and watches. He'd even taken to using false bottoms in larger clocks to transport stolen pieces of art."

Jeff let out a slow whistle, and Caroline nodded.

"Long story short, I made a deal. I started helping the authorities by signing my name on the wheels of the watches I was working on. I also went into the shop and did the same on some of the cogs in the clocks. It helped track back the work."

"That must have been difficult, going against Wallace," I said.

Caroline looked up at me and shrugged.

"My marriage to Wallace had become a cycle of abuse," she said quietly. "At first it was verbal. Looking back, that was always there—cruel language, put-downs, bursts of anger when he was frustrated. After Levi was born it escalated into physical violence. He never hurt Levi, but my arms were covered with bruises from where he would grab me.

"I was the weak link in Wallace's operation. Interpol understood that before I did. They offered me immunity, and a new life, if I would help them arrest Wallace and shut down his ring."

"His ring?" I asked.

"Wallace may have been a mediocre clockmaker, but he was a smooth talker and an excellent master criminal."

"How long did it take?" Jeff asked, quietly scratching away at his notepad as Caroline spoke.

"Six months," she said. "At first I was a wreck, but after

a while it became second nature. Do the work that Wallace asked me to do, take pictures and write notes for Interpol, and continue to tag the work with my signature, which I had always done subtly on every piece I worked on. Meanwhile, Wallace grew bolder. Ironically, he finally stopped being so abusive at home."

"He never caught on?"

"He had no idea. Hubris and arrogance were his trademarks, so that shouldn't have surprised me as much as it did. He had no idea until the trial, when I was called to testify against him in open court."

"How did he react?"

"He threatened to kill me. That would have frightened me under normal circumstances—I knew what he was capable of more than anyone—but I knew two things: First, that he was going to jail for a very long time, hopefully forever. Second, I was getting a new life and moving back to the United States."

"So Caroline Adler was born," I said softly, a little in awe of the strength of this small, tidy woman I saw before me. What else didn't I know about her?

"Reborn," she said, smiling. "At first, I tried to completely divorce myself from my old life. I had no living family to speak of, so I thought that would be easy enough. But I missed doing my work. By then, Zane Phillips had moved to Vermont, so I went to visit. He was thrilled to see me and was completely comfortable with helping me create a new identity. He gave me work on the side, kept my secrets. I holed myself up in Vermont and lived in fear for a long time. Then I started to relax.

"Six years ago, Zane talked me into going to a Clockmakers of America society conference. He thought it was high time I started to expand my horizons a bit, especially now that Levi was getting older. Besides, Zane wanted to step back from work and travel. He knew I needed to make my own connections. So I went to the conference, and Thom Clagan was there. He and Zane were good friends, and so the three of us spent a lot of time together, eating meals and talking. This was shortly after your grandmother Mae had passed, and Thom was in terrible shape. Zane invited him up to Vermont for a visit, and we spent more time together. He also met my son, Levi. He was so, so good with the boy. Levi was about fifteen then, and in need of a male role model. Fond of the boy as Zane was, and is, he wasn't much help with the role model part of being with a young person. Clocks made of knives and teenage boys don't exactly mix." She laughed.

"Is that why you both got married? So Levi could have a father?" I asked.

"Ruth, I married your grandfather because I fell in love with him. He was, and is, the best man I've ever known. I know that he loved your grandmother desperately and would never love me the same way, but we had a good marriage. I like to think I made him happy. I think I did. At least I tried my best."

Not for the first time since I'd met her, I was sorry that I had reacted so badly to the news of their marriage and had stopped talking to my grandfather. I should have known that marrying Caroline wasn't a sign of not loving my grandmother. He'd been lonely. I wasn't going to underestimate their marriage, though. From what Flo and Nancy had told me over many cups of tea, Caroline and G.T. were happy. She'd been good for G.T.

"Did G.T. know about Wallace?" I asked.

"He knew everything. Do you think I would have married him without letting him know about my past? He and Zane Phillips are the only two people who know the story. Or they were. Now you know the story too."

"Levi doesn't know?" Jeff asked.

"He thinks his father died in a car accident," she said, shifting her gaze down to the table.

"Okay," I said carefully. "I guess I can understand that. Anyway, your secret is safe with me."

I noted that Jeff Paisley did not chime in at this point. Instead, he continued to make notes while Caroline put the watch back together.

"Caroline, would you mind checking these notes?" Jeff asked, setting the open notebook down in front of her.

"Of course not, Jeff," Caroline said. "Let me pack this up for you first."

Jeff nodded to me, and we both took a few steps away. Jeff never took his eyes off Caroline and the watch. We lowered our voices.

"So, Caroline fixed this watch back in the day?" I said. "What does that have to do with Mark's death?"

"That, Ruth, is the question," Jeff said. "The answer could be 'nothing,' but I find that unlikely. I'll try to figure out some other possibilities."

"Maybe check on Wallace Struggs?" I said, watching Caroline skim the notes.

"Top of my list," Jeff said.

"Jeff, it's all packed up," Caroline said, placing the plastic bag containing the watch into Jeff's palm. "Here are your notes."

"Thank you, Caroline. This has been very helpful. Sort of unexpected, but helpful."

"Let us know if you need any other questions answered," I said.

"Will do. In the meantime, you both take care of each other, all right?"

"You've got it," I said, putting my arm around Caroline's shoulder. "That's what family's for."

After Jeff left, and took the watch with him, I asked Caroline if she wanted to come up for some tea.

"Thank you, Ruth, but I told Flo I would go to Marytown with her."

"Weren't you there?" I asked.

"I was, but Flo didn't know that. She is losing her mind, not being able to go into her shop. She wants to look for some new paint colors for Ben's shop."

"New paint colors? Does he know about that?"

"She thinks that given what happened there last night, to poor Mark, Ben needs to make over the shop once he can reopen."

"Wow, she's moving fast. It happened less than twenty-four hours ago."

"Honestly? We had this shopping trip set up before Christmas. Flo hates the colors of the barbershop and was planning on brightening them up anyway."

"She doesn't like chrome, gray, and navy? Why am I not surprised?"

"You need to remember, that was her shop back in the day. He may have gone a bit overboard when he wanted to make it his own. I like some of the changes, but agree that a different color on the walls could help make it a little cheerier. Besides, I've already asked Ben for his blessing, and his opinion."

"You have?"

"Of course. It's his shop. Flo can, and will, run over him if he isn't careful. He's a sweet guy and loves her a lot. But it's his business. I'm happy to be a go-between for them both."

"You can let them both think they won. Genius."

"We'll see. Honestly, I'm happy for the distraction. Of course, I can stay if you need me? Otherwise, Flo and I will do our shopping and then she is coming over for dinner. You're welcome to join us."

"Thanks, Caroline. I have stuff for stew, and I need to get it made. Go with Flo. Call me when you get home, and we can check in. And, Caroline?"

"Yes, Ruth?"

"Thanks for telling me your story. Your secret is safe with me."

"Ruth, as you said earlier, we're family. I shouldn't have been keeping secrets from you. That's how this whole thing got started in the first place."

chapter 19

I stirred the beef stew around in the pot, taking a deep inhale of the mixture I'd concocted. I could still make out the individual ingredients, which meant it wasn't ready. I didn't cook often, but when I did, I cooked in volume. I'd be eating beef stew for days, but the chopping, sautéing, and stirring had been calming. It smelled delicious, if I did say so, but another hour on the stove would do it good. Of course, it would be even better tomorrow.

I poured a glass of red wine and carried it back to the kitchen table. What a day. I sat down and booted up my laptop. The scent of the beef stew filled the air. It was only five o'clock. Bezel jumped up on the other kitchen chair and stared at me.

"Are you judging me, Bezel?" I said, leaning over and petting her head as she rumbled contentedly. "You're right, it is close to dinnertime to start a new project. You're also right, I won't be done by dinner and may need to keep working. I know that web surfing isn't a good dinnertime activity, but I'm so tired that I am planning on going to bed right after dinner, and I want to get started before I run out of steam. Is that all right with you?"

Bezel put her two paws on the table and leaned in toward me, her dark, questioning eyes peering straight into mine. She had her own mind, but wasn't given to getting up on tables. She was trying to make a point, and did it effectively.

"Okay, you're right. You caught me. I'm too nosy for my own good. I want to try and find out more about Wallace Struggs. I can't wait until I'm done eating to start. Tomorrow I'll work on figuring out what happened to Mark, but I don't have the energy tonight. All right?"

Bezel went back to sitting on her chair, and shook her head a few more times. Then she jumped down and went back to daintily eating her dinner.

Before I'd moved into the Cog & Sprocket, I'd never owned a pet. Sure, I'd visited my grandparents during the summers, and they always had a cat or two. But I'd never had my own pet. My mother was allergic, and my ex-husband wasn't a fan. (Yet another sign of his true nature, which I'd ignored.)

Of course, I didn't really own Bezel. She pretty much owned the Cog & Sprocket and had graciously allowed me to move in. Still, I was amazed that after a few short weeks I was talking to her regularly, and as worried about her eating habits as my own. She was a sweetheart, though she pretended not to be.

I poured myself another glass of red wine and sat back down at the computer. My search for Wallace Struggs brought up no pictures, but I did find a few news stories dating back seventeen years. I read them all and took notes on a pad of paper. These notes weren't going into my notebook—they were too private. Puzzles always intrigued me, and this piece was a huge help in understanding Caroline and her reserved nature. Rather than asking her more questions, it was far better for me to find out what I could on my own.

The most recent article that mentioned him was dated six months ago. There had been a discovery of several priceless paintings, rolled up into a tube and left in a storage bin in Brussels. The reporter wrote that the paintings were first tied to the notorious Struggs art theft gang, during the height of their activities in the late '90s. Forgeries were swapped out with the real paintings, creating a shell game of auctions, private collections, and cross-border smuggling. The rest of the article was about the restoration work on the paintings, though the reporter included the fact that Wallace remained in prison in Monaco.

I went back chronologically, but after reading the first few articles, I knew all there was to know, at least from news reports. I did a few more searches and followed up on some of the thefts that had been tied to Wallace Struggs. His vocation was mentioned, but the real press interest was in the paintings and jewelry that he'd been accused of stealing, not the clocks he'd forged. I needed to take a trip to the library to find out more, but that would have to wait. I'd learned what I could, and it all matched what Caroline had told me.

That would have to be enough, for now.

Surprisingly, it was. I closed the lid of my computer and walked over to serve myself some stew. Bezel came over and wound around my legs, purring loudly.

• • •

Thursday morning I woke up and looked out the back window of my apartment. Sigh. Blue skies. I'd made a deal with myself before I went to bed. If there were bright skies, I'd go out for a walk/run in the morning. I doubted Bezel would tell my secret if I didn't keep my promise, but I couldn't be sure of that. She and Pat were pretty close.

I made a small pot of coffee and drank a half a cup of very thick brew. The bananas on my counter were on the verge of overripe, so I ate one. Most days I let them go into overripe, since that led to a banana cake or muffin, but this close to the New Year, I was trying to be healthier. Just a banana, no bread this morning.

I put my layers on and found the headband that came close to taming my curly mop into submission. Let's face it. I was hardly a fashion plate in this getup, and you never knew who you were going to see. With that in mind, I slathered on a bit of lip gloss and went downstairs to the shop.

As was my habit, when I hit the bottom step I looked over to my left, at the model of the Clagan Clock Tower my grandfather had started, and I'd finished. He didn't call it the Clagan Clock Tower, of course. I didn't either, at least not publicly. But the small group who had been working on the plans with me had started using the name, as an homage to my grandfather. He'd hate it, but then he was never one for public displays of affection. I loved that the citizens of Orchard, at least most of them, didn't agree with him on that topic. I hoped he knew how well thought of he was by people in town.

"Good morning, G.T.," I said, touching the corner of the model. "The New Year gets rung in on Saturday night, the shop reopens next Monday, and I have a lot to do before either of those things happen. I know you'll help where you can, and I thank you for that."

Bezel jumped on the table beside the model and bowed her head toward me. I leaned down to accept the headbutt, which I stopped with a kiss. Bezel nuzzled my face a bit, and then sat back and looked up at me, squishing her eyes. I squished mine back.

"Bezel, I know you'll do your part too. I don't know what I'd do without you. I'll let you hang out down here until I get back, but then you have to go upstairs so Caroline doesn't have an allergy attack."

I put my cell phone in my jacket pocket and took a sip from my water bottle. I caught my reflection in the glass door of a grandfather clock. I certainly looked the part of an athlete, though a little on the softer side. Truth was that I had the gear, part of the wardrobe I owned when I was married to my weekend warrior ex-husband. But these days, I didn't run, I walked with short bursts of jogging. Still, breathing the outside air was always good for clearing the cobwebs. Soon enough there would be too much snow on the ground to go outside, so now was the time.

I walked over to the back door of the shop and looked out the window as I was about to go out. Moira Reed was standing to the right of the stairs, looking up. She had a tray of coffee and a bag with her.

"Moira," I said after I'd opened the door. I plastered on a smile and tried to forget the cold shoulder she'd given me the day before.

"Ruth, I came over to talk to you, but then it occurred to me that you might not be up yet. So I was just standing here trying to decide what to do."

"I have become more of a morning person since moving back to Orchard," I said. "Besides, there's a lot going on. I couldn't sleep."

"Are you on your way out?"

"I was going for a long walk. Do you want to join me?"

"I'd love to, but I'm not really dressed for it," she said, looking down at her jeans and boots. "Besides, I need to get back to the Sleeping Latte soon. The place is really hopping. Do you have a minute to talk? I brought food." She held up the bag.

I sighed. The food from the Sleeping Latte was one of the reasons I needed to get more exercise.

"Come in," I said, backing into the shop. Resistance was futile. And I was hungry.

"Wow, the model looks great," Moira said as she followed me into the shop. Bezel had sat back up, and I could hear her purring. Moira put the food bag down on the counter and said a proper hello to the Russian Blue.

"Thanks, I've been working on it when I can," I said, flicking a little spot of dust from the base. "It helps keep me focused, and it calms me down."

"The details are amazing. I've got to admit, I was having trouble picturing how the figurines were going to come out of the clock tower, but this makes perfect sense. It's like they're on a little conveyor belt, aren't they?"

"For now, yes. Four of them. Eventually, I'd love to have them inside as well, and there to be a little more action. But for now, four figures coming out of a door, turning around, and going into another door is all I can pull off. Actually, I'm hoping I can pull that off."

"Dad said that Kim Gray was giving you the runaround."

"That's one word for it. More like she's adding obstacles

to the course. Apparently any modifications to the building need to be approved by the Historical Council, which is being headed up by Beckett Green."

"Since when do we have a Historical Council?"

"Since Christmas Day, around dessert time. You know, I thought trying to figure out how to navigate academia was tough, back when I was a faculty wife, but Orchard has the ivy walls beat by a mile. I wish Grover Winter had made the Town Hall Trust a nonprofit from the outset. It would have made life easier."

"I wonder why he didn't?"

"Paperwork. Having to maintain a board of directors instead of keeping it in the family. Plus, when the family gifted the Town Hall to Orchard for fifty years, they didn't need the money, and he was the chairman of the Board of Selectmen."

"I still don't see what Kim Gray is thinking, not signing a new lease for the building."

"You've heard her at meetings. She's worried about deferred maintenance, that I will use the money the estate is earning from the sale of the Winters' clock collection to pay for the clock tower—"

"She's calling it Ruth's Folly these days."

"Really?" I said. I looked over at the model and smiled. "Maybe it is. But if it is, game on. I'm making this happen, one way or the other. Anyway, enough about that. What brings you by? And as importantly, what's in the bag?"

"In reverse order: a breakfast sandwich and an apology. Mind if we go upstairs to talk?"

"You know the way," I said. I picked up the bag and followed Moira upstairs. My walk would have to wait.

chapter 20

I handed Moira two plates, and she unpacked two sandwiches onto one plate and some pastries and a fruit cup
onto the second. She brought the sandwich plate over to the
microwave.

"These need to be served warm," she said, smiling.

"I know, the cheese needs to be melted," I said. The first
time I'd eaten one of those wonderful concoctions, Ben Clover had ordered it for me and insisted I eat it hot. I smiled
at the memory, and then chewed on the corner of my mouth.
I needed to add calling Ben to my list of things to do today.
Our last conversation had been strained, and that wouldn't
work, at all.

"Don't tell my mother that I used the microwave. She'd
want me to put them back in a fry pan. The yolks are going
to be hard."

"Your secret is safe with me," I said. When we'd both settled in with our sandwiches, I took a bite, savoring the combination of Italian bread, fried eggs, bacon, and Romano cheese. Just enough seasoning to make it more savory, but not to overpower the simple deliciousness of the food.

"Thanks for bringing this by," I said between bites. "I would have made do with my banana, but this is much better."

"Food is always a good excuse for a visit," Moira said. "But what I really wanted to do was to apologize for believing the gossip."

"Gossip? Was there gossip?" I said into my coffee. Orchard was a small town, and one of our major industries was gossip.

"About you and Jeff Paisley. The rumor mill had him spending the night at your shop and leaving after you'd served him breakfast. That and the lipstick on his face Tuesday night?"

"The lipstick wasn't mine," I said. "It was his mother's. Or his sister's. I don't remember which."

"You asked?"

"I knew you'd want to know. And yes, he stayed here Tuesday night. I let him use the shop as a base of operation since the crime scene was right next door and it's cold outside. I made him breakfast. He did sleep here, in one of the chairs downstairs. Honestly, he could have stayed in the apartment if he wanted to—he could have had the whole place to himself because I was in the guest room at Caroline's—but he is careful not to overstep. Jeff and I are friends, Moira. I'm not going to say 'just' friends, because I value him more than that. But there is nothing romantic going on."

"I know. My mother straightened me out," she said,

playing with the lid of her coffee cup. "I'm in a state, ever since Mark died. My imagination is working overtime."

"You're interested in Jeff, aren't you?" I asked.

Moira nodded her head, a slight frown on her face.

"Why so miserable? He's a little older than we are, but not too much older. He's a good man. You don't have a problem because of his race, do you?"

"No, of course not. You know me better than that. There's just one issue: the fact that he isn't interested. At all."

"How do you know that?" I said. "He smiles every time he sees you. Surely you've noticed that."

"Big deal. I've asked him out three times, and he always says no, sorry, he's busy."

"Maybe he is. He has a life, you know."

"But what is that life? How much do we all know about Jeff, after all? I asked him to come to dinner after the event Tuesday night, but he said he was busy. Why wouldn't he tell me he was going to visit his family?"

"Jeff does play it close to the vest," I agreed. "He's got a tough shell, but it is beginning to crack. Did you ever talk to him about how you felt about him arresting your father for G.T.'s murder?"

"I didn't think we needed to talk about it. He knew how I felt," she said, looking down at her now-empty plate.

"He knew at the time. I remember you yelling at him. But afterward, when the charges were dropped, did you talk to him then? Did you try and see it from his perspective? He was just doing his job, after all."

"Just doing his job? Arresting my father?" she said through clenched teeth.

"Trying to solve a murder. He made up for it by saving

my life, don't you think?" I said gently. "It must be hard, especially in a place like Orchard, where you can never really be off duty. He has to be really careful about public perceptions. Dating must be a minefield."

"Dating is always a minefield," Moira said, stabbing a piece of fruit with her fork. "Listen, Jeff isn't my usual type. I've had a string of relationships with men who ended up not being nice guys. The fact that I find Jeff attractive is disconcerting."

"Disconcerting? That's a twenty-five-cent word," I teased.

"Stop. I try to polish off my college education once in a while. Running the Sleeping Latte was not what I imagined I'd do with my English degree."

"Hey, you can hold a conversation," I said. "I love that I studied horology, but my ex-husband used to make me feel pretty bad about my lack of a college degree."

"Didn't you tell me you took a ton of classes while you were married to him?"

"I did. One more semester and I could finish my degree."

"Maybe that's a New Year's goal?"

"Maybe," I said. I'd been thinking the same thing. Getting some of my unfinished goals done was the new future for Ruth Clagan. Provided I got through this week.

"Anyway, Moira, you and I could have a long conversation about bad taste in men. My ex-husband seemed like my Prince Charming, my knight in shining armor, even, when I married him, but the armor was tinfoil, and the prince was a toad. It's hard to trust someone again. That said, Jeff Paisley is a good man. Seems like a safe bet for a crush. Maybe more. Give it, and him, time. Be his friend. Don't yell at him. Figure out how to give him a New Year's kiss."

Moira laughed. "All right, I've got two days to figure out the kiss. Anyway, I came by to apologize for believing the gossip, and for being rude yesterday in the café. This is a tough time for all of us, and we need to be nicer to each other."

"Agreed. Now, back to the gossip mill. What's the latest on Mark's murder?" I asked.

"There are a lot of people coming in and out of the Sleeping Latte, but no one seems to know anything. One thing I'm noticing: no one really knew Mark, you know? He was a nice guy, but he kept to himself."

I nodded, clearing our plates and bringing them over to the sink. "He did here too. He was a very nice guy, but he made Jeff Paisley look like an extrovert. I'm going to give Nadia a call today and see if she knows more about his family and his background. I want to reach out and see what the plans for a service are, and what I can do to help."

"Keep me posted," Moira said. "And thanks for the pep talk. You're a good friend, and I'll never forget that again."

chapter 21

I walked Moira downstairs and checked the wall of clocks in the workshop. I loved this collection of Willard-inspired clocks, each with its own twist on his creation. The biggest difference was the decoration on the rectangle at the bottom. Some were simple, others incredibly ornate. All lovely. Only problem was, none of them agreed on what time it was. They would before they were sold, but for now, it was around nine o'clock. Still time for a good walk, which I needed now more than ever. I had eaten a little fruit salad, but not nearly enough to mitigate the carbs from the breakfast sandwich followed by a pastry.

Layers back on, and another stretch of the legs. Again, I headed out the back door. This time it was the arrival of Tuck that prevented my foray into fresh air. Maybe the powers that be just didn't want me to exercise.

"Is Nadia here?" he asked without preamble, looking past me into the shop. Tuck Powers had the manners of a ferret. Today he looked exhausted, though. His normally waxed mustache was trimmed short, and his black spiked hair was falling over. The bags under his green eyes were significant, and I felt instant remorse. He and Mark Pine had been friends.

"She isn't here, no," I said, closing the door once again.

"She said she was coming in," Tuck said.

"I was upstairs, but I would have heard if she went up to the office."

Tuck turned and ran up the stairs, and came back down within a minute.

"The door is locked." He sounded accusatory.

"Yes, it is," I said, forcing a smile. "Chief Paisley has asked me to lock up the office until he has time to go through Mark's things." All right, he hadn't asked me to do that. I'd just thought of it, but I should give Jeff a call to suggest it.

"My stuff is up there."

"What stuff?"

"My camera and stuff."

"Were you taking pictures the night of Mark's . . . the night of the open house?"

"You hired me to take the pictures, and I take my job seriously."

"Of course you do," I said. I wondered what else Tuck had taken pictures of. I put my hand on my cell phone, fingers twitching to call Jeff. I needed to get him on speed dial.

"So, can I get my stuff?"

"The chief will need to look through the pictures first."

"Come on! They're my pictures."

"And my camera, or the shop's. You're the one who

talked me into investing in that rig. Was there anything else up there that was yours?"

"My tie. And my cuff links."

"You were wearing cuff links?"

"Of course. If you're going to get dressed up, go old-school. The cuff links mean a lot to me."

"I'll make sure they get back to you," I said.

"Nadia's stuff's up there too."

"You don't know where she is?" I asked.

"No. I sort of hoped she'd be here. She's a wreck." He sighed and studied his shoes. "She and Mark were pretty tight."

I remembered the two of them, Tuesday afternoon, close together, hands touching. "Pretty tight" was one way to put it. "You and Mark went to high school together, right? He was your friend too."

"Yeah, yeah, he was." Tuck rubbed the area between his eyes and crouched down into a squat. Luckily his bruised face didn't look too bad.

"I'm sorry, Tuck," I said.

"Do you want to know what really sucks? Mark and I had that huge fight on Tuesday. He tried to talk to me about it, but I wasn't having any of it. I walked away. I'd been doing that a lot with him, not talking about what was going on."

"What was that fight really about?"

Tuck hesitated and then shrugged. "Nadia, what else? C'mon, Ms. Clagan, you've seen them together. They are— they were—crazy for each other."

"I never thought so." I was lying to Tuck. I totally thought that they had the hots for each other, but how would that help? Besides, I didn't want Tuck to shut down.

"Really?"

"Really. I thought that they were friends. Nadia was able to get Mark to talk. You know what I mean. Beyond small talk. I could never get him to open up. Of course, you're not exactly Captain Chatsalot."

Tuck grunted and stood up, a slight smile on his face. He shrugged his shoulders and walked over to the worktable where Mark had always worked. He ran his hands along the desk, then closed his fist and pounded the table.

"Man, I should have called him back," Tuck said, almost whispering.

"Called him back? When did he call you? After the fight?"

"He texted me that afternoon, and wanted to talk. I told him we'd talk after . . . after the open house."

"Then you had the fight?"

"Yeah, and he went all ninja on me. Nadia took off. I tried to clean myself up, then I went over to the Latte to look for Nadia. Nancy saw me and asked me to take some pictures. I was still pretty ticked off, but I should have gone over and talked to him. He was pretty freaked lately. Maybe I could have helped, or gotten there in time."

"Don't do that to yourself, Tuck," I said. "You couldn't have stopped what happened."

"You don't know that."

"You're right. I don't. Listen, I didn't know Mark that well, but I did like him. A lot. He was a good guy. Maybe instead of beating yourself up, you can help the chief figure out what happened to him."

"Me, help the cops? Not going to happen. Not in this lifetime."

"Sounds like you have a history with law enforcement."

"You could say that."

"How about helping me, then?"

"What do you mean?"

"Was something going on with Mark? You said he was freaked. Is that something the chief should know about? Come on, Tuck, what aren't you telling me? Do you know who did this to Mark? Or why? Tell me what you know. I'll tell the chief. I won't tell him it came from you."

Tuck looked down at his phone and then put it back in his pocket. "I'm going to go find Nadia. We need to talk first, but then I'll come back."

"Sounds like a plan," I said. I was amazed at how calm my voice sounded. What I really wanted to do was shout, and shake him till he told me his secrets, but I felt like I was earning his trust and I didn't want to risk losing this progress. I took a deep breath. Tuck turned to go out the back door. I noticed he opened it a crack and looked through the opening carefully before he stepped out.

"Tuck?" I said.

"Yeah?"

"Be careful, all right? Take care of yourself, and Nadia. Call me if you need anything, day or night."

"Will do," Tuck said. "I'll be back."

I hoped he meant it.

chapter 22

I texted Jeff Paisley, letting him know about Tuck's camera. *I already have the camera*, he texted back. *Is he there with you?*

Just left, I texted. *Coming back later. Any interesting pictures?*

Let me know if he comes back. I have questions for Tuck.

You and me both, I thought. I also have questions for you, but they'd have to wait until we were in the same room, and you couldn't ignore me.

I looked up at the wall of clocks and sighed. If I averaged them all, I still had time for a walk. Once more to the back door. Once more an interruption, this time coming from the front.

I could only hope that the shop would be this busy once we were open. Yeesh. I went to the front and looked through the blinds. A tall, pale, angular face stared back, his face half in shadow due to the wide-brimmed fedora he wore low on his forehead. The man from the party store? I put my foot behind the door and cracked it open.

"I'm sorry, we're not open," I said.

"Ms. Clagan? I'm Zane Phillips. I was a friend of your grandfather. We spoke Tuesday."

I moved my foot from the door and stepped back. I smiled, but didn't feel warmth. Something about the man still didn't sit right with me, despite Caroline's endorsement. Maybe it was the large red scar that was etched on one side of his face. A clock with knives, is that what Caroline said? But maybe the inventor of a clock with knives was a man I'd like to meet.

"Mr. Phillips, come in," I said.

"Thank you," he said. "I don't want to keep you from opening your shop."

"We aren't open today."

"Because of the unfortunate incident next door?"

"You heard about what happened?"

"Oh my dear, yes. Everyone has heard about it. It is all over the news. I understand that the young man worked for you? Terrible, terrible. Very honorable to close your shop in his memory."

"We actually aren't going to reopen until next week. But yes, he did work for us. It is a terrible tragedy."

Zane shook his head. He'd kept his hat on and wore glasses that were slightly shaded, so it was hard to see his face. No doubt he wanted it that way. I noted that his gray hair was straight and touched the back of his collar. He had a goatee that was the same shade of gray. All of his clothes were shades of black. His coat was more of a cloak.

"Did we meet at the party store?" I asked.

"I did see you there," he said, his eyes sweeping over the clocks on display. "I didn't realize who you were until I read that newspaper article. Ruth Clagan. I should have recognized you, of course. You look a great deal like your grandfather. Same red hair. Almost as tall. And a clockmaker. All three things run in your genes, don't they?"

"They do indeed," I agreed.

"Your shop is lovely," he said, taking a few more steps in and looking around. "Really lovely. You've been upgrading it."

"Just refreshing it," I said. "Have you been here before?"

"Of course. Of course. Your grandfather visited my shop many times as well. Tell me, is Caroline still working here?"

"She is, or will be. She's out today."

"A pity. I would very much like to see her. We are good friends."

"So she tells me," I said.

"If you will indulge me, I found this old picture of us, from a few years back." He reached inside his coat and slid a photograph from his inside coat pocket. He handed it to me.

I looked down at a picture of a very, very young Caroline. She was standing between two young men. I recognized Zane right away, even without the scar.

"Who is this other man, here?" I asked, pointing.

Zane looked confused and took the picture back, staring at it for a moment before putting it back in his pocket.

"An old friend. We've had a falling-out, I'm afraid. I haven't seen him in a number of years."

That must have been Caroline's ex-husband, Wallace Struggs. I wanted to ask for the picture back, but I didn't. I closed my eyes for a moment, hoping that my visual memory would help me remember his face. One thing I would not have any trouble remembering was how Caroline looked in the photograph. She was beautiful. She was also happy, free of the burdens that weighed her down now.

"I'm sorry to hear that," I said. I tried to smile, but couldn't. Zane Phillips had an odd energy, one I couldn't read. And I was impatient to get him out and get on with my long overdue walk.

"I would love to see Caroline while I am here," he said. "Will she be in later?"

"She may be, but I'm not sure when. How much longer will you be in town?"

"Only until tomorrow, I'm afraid. My business should be completed by then."

"Business?"

"I drove down to deliver some merchandise and to tie up some loose ends. I am almost finished with that, and then I must be on my way."

"Caroline would like to see you, I'm sure. Are you free for dinner tonight?" At this point I would agree to anything to get him to leave so that I could get on with my day.

"I am free. Dinner would be lovely."

"Let me check with Caroline about plans. How about if I call your cell phone later, after we've talked."

"You could give me Caroline's number," he said.

"She doesn't have a cell phone." I'm really not sure why

I lied to him. I was probably being overprotective of Caroline, but that was part of my job.

"Let me give you my cell phone number," he said. He turned on his phone and then grabbed one of the Cog & Sprocket brochures and wrote along the bottom edge. "Feel free to text if you can't reach me. I'd be happy to take you both out for dinner—my treat. How does that sound?"

"Sounds great," I said. I plastered a smile on my face and practically shoved Zane Phillips back out the front door.

chapter 23

If Zane Phillips had been in the area the night of the party, he might have seen something. I texted Jeff Paisley his number, briefly telling him about Zane Phillips. I'd learned the hard way, the more Jeff knew, the more able he was to do his job. Editing the information I gave him had almost got me killed in October. I wasn't going to make that mistake again. I tried to call Caroline at home, and on her cell, but she didn't pick up either phone. I texted her Zane's phone number, and asked her to call me.

My phone was charged, and I decided to finally make a break for it. I locked the front door and set the alarm. I walked through the shop toward the back, but refrained from looking left or right. I didn't want work to distract me. It would be there when I got back. But a walk/run around town was in order.

I put my earphones in and selected the latest episode in the podcast series I was listening to. The series was terrific, but I kept losing track of where I was in the story, so I'd end up listening to it two or three times. No worries though, the narrator was good company as I went in pursuit of some athletic ability. I walked out the back door and locked it behind me before I headed left to go over the bridge. Looking at the back side of Washington Street, and our shops, from across the river was always one of my favorite views. I picked up speed and then broke into a jog. The pace didn't last long, and I went back into a walk. At some point I needed to really try and train for a 5K. For now, I just kept starting the Run a 5K in Six Weeks program, never getting much past week one.

I kept up the pace, trying to jog a bit more each time. I never ran, but I was getting the jog down. Dare I say, I was starting to enjoy myself a bit? A beautiful winter day, cold but not too biting. No ice or snow to give me pause. The bare trees were desolate guardians of the heart of Orchard. Back in the day, this river ran much higher and was used as a mode of transport for logging companies, deliveries, and rum runners during Prohibition. After the last great flood wiped out most of Orchard for the sixth time, a dam was finally installed farther down the river, harnessing it for power, and protecting the inland community. While I was grateful for the safety, I sometimes wished I could go back in time to hear the fearsome rushing of the water, to see the boats floating by. Back then Orchard was on a major artery. Nowadays, the town was more of an afterthought, a throwback to a time gone by. Still, it was home now.

I ran and walked a bit more, focusing on the podcast,

trying to forget everything else that happened over the past few days. My breathing got a bit more labored, and I slowed down to a walk. I was almost at the place in the podcast that I had left off last time I'd taken a walk/run, and I decided to keep going for a bit longer. Instead of going over the next bridge, I'd go down one more. I passed the turnoff when my phone started to vibrate. I took it out of my pocket and checked to see who was interrupting the interrogation scene on the podcast.

"Nadia?" I answered the phone.

"Hey," she said. Her intonation was never lively, but now she sounded completely flat, without the passion that was her usual undercurrent.

"Nadia," I said after she didn't respond. "You called me. I'm out for a run, on my cell. Where are you? At the shop?"

"I'm hanging around my apartment. I'm not going to make it in today. I know that isn't cool, but I just can't."

"Nadia, please, take care of yourself," I said, stretching my legs against a tree. "Mark's death was a real shock. I know you were good friends."

"We were. Friends, I mean. Not that Tuck ever believed that's all we were. I hope he didn't . . . The police are looking for him—did you know that?"

"Looking for Tuck? I'm sure they have some questions."

"Yeah, well, it didn't sound like it was just for questions."

"Tuck came by the office earlier. He was looking for you and he was looking for his camera."

"His camera?"

"But the office is locked up, so he couldn't get in. Chief Paisley said that he had it at his office."

"But he doesn't have the memory card from earlier in the

night. Tuck used two or three cards last night, and he handed them all back to me for safekeeping."

"And did you keep them safe?"

"I kept them here, with me. I guess that's safe. At least I hope so."

I hoped so too. "Nadia, why don't you bring them over to the chief?"

Nadia's laugh didn't sound jovial, nor did it sound like she thought much of my idea.

"Okay. How about if you bring them to me, and I'll bring them to the chief."

"Later, all right? First I'm going out to find Tuck. We have a lot to talk about. Then I'll go by the station, I promise. But first, I have to find Tuck."

"He wants to talk to you too. Keep trying him. If he comes back here, I'll text and let you know. Meanwhile, you e-mail, call, text me with updates. Whatever works, keep me in the loop. I'm worried about you."

"Thanks. I mean it."

"No worries. Talk to you later."

She paused for a second, keeping me on the line. "Ms. Clagan, Ruth, do you have any idea who killed Mark?"

"I wish I did, but I don't," I said.

Was I telling the truth? I couldn't help but think about Tuck and how squirrelly he had been acting, even for him. What wasn't he telling me?

chapter 24

I sent Jeff another text, letting him know about my conversation with Nadia. I didn't want to pressure her, but those cards could be important. I didn't even wait for a text back. Later I'd need to go by the station to talk to him if I wanted a response.

I turned back and went over the bridge closer to town. Who was I kidding? The next bridge was another mile down the river. Aspirations for another day. As I crossed the bridge, I looked around. This bridge spilled into a five-way stop, which could be a complicated traffic pattern in some areas. Not in Orchard, where there wasn't room for a rotary, and no budget for a traffic light. Most folks actually obeyed the rule and took turns going through the intersection. That was not the Massachusetts norm, but neither was Orchard. Of course, I was a bit prejudiced. I loved my town.

The library across the street was, as always, hopping. Like most libraries, Orchard's had added banks of computers where people could work for free. That, in addition to story hours for kids, a variety of book clubs, and a few writing groups who met there regularly, made it a hub of activity. The only downside was the constant call for quiet by Harriet Wimsey. Moira Reed helped solve the problem by giving anyone with a library card a 5 percent discount to the Sleeping Latte. There weren't volume concerns there.

The hardware store, or what used to be the hardware store, loomed like a gray ghost up ahead. It had closed a few years back, and nothing else had opened in its place, until recently when Max decided to open it back up. There weren't a lot of closed businesses in Orchard, but there were enough to remind folks that times had been tough, and they weren't over yet. Becket Green buying the old bank had been a vote of confidence for the town. Too bad he didn't seem focused on the greater good of Orchard or on being a good citizen.

I turned to my right, behind the hardware store. That's where the access road that ran along the riverbank ended. The lowered riverbed made this access road possible. Though the Cog & Sprocket didn't need regular deliveries, I know that it was a great help to the Sleeping Latte, and now the hardware store. It was barely visible from Washington Street, and any additional lighting came from the stores themselves. This time of day, the road looked welcoming, all sun dappled with the river rushing quietly along beside it. At night, it disappeared. I couldn't help but wonder if that is how Mark's killer got to the barbershop that night. I shuddered, but kept walking down the access road. I'd talk to Pat later and get my motion detector moved up on the Pat Project List.

I walked past the Sleeping Latte. The back door was open, and I was tempted to poke my head in, but then I looked at my phone. It was one o'clock. Lunch hour, their busiest time. I'd stop by later.

I called Caroline. "Hi, I'm heading back to the Cog. Where are you? Call me." I hadn't heard from her since yesterday. Not time to worry. Yet.

I was getting cold, and picked up my pace a bit. I was heading toward Parker's Emporium, the old name for the building that now housed Ben's Barbershop on one side and, on the other, his aunt Flo's new drugstore, which she planned on opening soon. She was still working on the official name, but I kept pushing for her to bring back the Emporium. A grand name, sure, but if anyone could pull it off, Flo Parker could.

As I came closer, I noticed that her car was parked on her side of the building, and her back door was open. I walked over and saw piles of boxes inside. I looked up in time to see Flo coming down the back stairs, holding on to the railing. More like leaning on it. She was dressed in full Flo regalia: a leopard-print down vest straining against her ample midsection over a black turtleneck, her artificially red hair swept up into a beehive with a zebra-print scarf holding it in place, large gold earrings that almost touched her shoulders, and black leggings tucked into short white boots that were covered with long white fake fur. Flo was as short as Caroline was, and a bit wider, though they were about the same age. But where Caroline was closed off, Flo's emotions were always close to the surface.

"Ruthie, aren't you a sight for sore eyes," she said, leaning against the hood of the car heavily.

"What are you up to, Flo?" I said.

"Jeff Paisley told me that the state police were done processing my shop. Isn't that a terrible phrase? Processing my shop, like it did something wrong. Anyway, I told him I needed to keep setting up if I hoped to get it open next week, and so he let me come by and drop off some of the supplies. The rest will be delivered on Friday. Can't believe that's tomorrow already. I just hope all this is over by then. That sounds terrible, doesn't it? You know what I mean. Bad enough that poor Mark died next door. From what I understand, no one has been arrested yet. I sure hope Jeff Paisley is on it, and not letting those out-of-towners take over. If they don't solve it in the first forty-eight hours, it's hopeless."

Whoa. Flo was on a roll. "Who told you that?"

"I watch a lot of true crime television, and read a lot of books. I know about these things," she said, inspecting her flawless hot pink manicured talons.

I had learned long ago that arguing with Flo was useless. A much better approach was to persuade her to think differently. Not that I worried about her blaming Jeff for lack of progress. I was more worried about her trying to beat the clock on her own. Over the past few weeks she'd asked me dozens of questions about what happened at the Winter estate in October. I got the distinct impression that she wished she had been in Orchard last summer, when it all got started. She had implied more than once that things would have ended up differently. Maybe she was right. Flo was a force. The idea of different outcomes was something I dreamed of in my darker nights.

"Are those boxes heavy?" I asked.

"No, not terribly. But there sure are a lot of them." She smiled.

"Let me help you," I said. "Where's Ben? I'm surprised he's letting you do this on your own."

"He's back at my house, sleeping. He's got insomnia, poor dear. Hasn't got a moment's sleep the past two nights. Of course, they keep hauling him in for questions."

"He isn't a suspect?"

"No, he was here with me all night. But it is his shop. He's taking it personally. Besides, this time of year is always a little rough for him."

"This time of year? You mean the holidays?" I took out one of the boxes. Flo was right—it wasn't too heavy. But it was awkward. I tried to find a larger flat box, and started to assemble a few more boxes, like a puzzle. I picked them up and started over to the back steps.

"Yes, the holidays. Has he ever told you about his family situation?" Flo followed me up the stairs, huffing and puffing a bit.

"Should I put them down here?" Flo nodded. "No, he hasn't mentioned his family. Why?"

"It's his story to tell," Flo said, showing unnatural restraint. "Suffice it to say, the New Year is always welcome to him. Though he did seem happier this year, up until Tuesday night."

"Tuesday night was a terrible night for all of us," I said. I didn't push Flo about Ben's story. Not that I wasn't interested. Everything about Ben interested me, perhaps more than it should. I'd found that I never needed to pry a story out of someone. They usually told me in their own good time, in their own way. I'd hate to get the reputation of a busybody here in Orchard. There were enough of them around already.

"It was indeed," she said, shifting the conversation.

"Any idea when he will get his shop back?"

"Jeff is trying to move it along, but he says it will be a few more days. Then we'll need to do some work in the shop," Flo said.

"Caroline told me a little about that part. Nothing too drastic, I hope."

"A fresh coat of paint, some new towels. A refresh. A new start for the New Year. Ben deserves it, and he'll need it, after this week."

"Are you going to start cutting hair again?" I asked.

"I'll help out when I can. Maybe we'll trade shifts once in a while." Flo leaned on the counter and fanned her face. "I can't tell you how much I appreciate the help. These tired old bones are having trouble getting up and down those stairs."

"These tired young bones have a few more trips in them. Let me get the rest of the boxes, and you stay here and keep setting up. No buts about it, Flo. You can pay me back with a haircut for the New Year. Deal?"

"Deal. You know I've been wanting to get my hands on those gorgeous curls for weeks. You've given me something to look forward to."

The gleam in her eyes told me that she'd already decided what she would do. Why did I think a flat iron was in my future? I just hoped I didn't wind up looking like a poodle.

chapter 25

I left Flo fussing over the boxes in her shop. I was tempted to offer to stay and help, but the gears in my brain were starting to shift, and I needed some time to process. I walked the few steps to my own back door and called out when I walked in. Silence met me.

I wasn't used to that. Even though I technically lived alone, I had actually spent very few waking hours alone since I moved back to Orchard. There was always something to do at the Cog & Sprocket or out at the workshop at Caroline's house. A clock to repair, a shelf to clean, a box to unpack. My days were full, as was my heart. I had found my place, and now someone had unsettled it by killing Mark.

I walked up the stairs to my apartment, checking the door on the stairs to the attic. Still locked. I was tempted to go in, but thought better of it, for now. I needed a shower and something to eat. I also needed to start a new notebook.

The notebook habit was part of the Clagan DNA. Large hard-covered sketchbooks, mostly black. Upstairs in the office we had built in shelves around the perimeter of the room, two rows of them, that served as a tabletop for clocks and files. But the shelves themselves were becoming the Clagan family archives. Pat had built them, and he'd added sliding doors on them all. There were locks on the doors—after the events of last fall, we'd both agreed that there were likely a few undiscovered treasures, and perhaps some assorted skeletons, that needed to be protected from prying eyes.

I had gathered all the notebooks I could find here in the shop, and I'd scoured the attic and workshop out at the cottage, with Caroline's blessing. There were over one hundred of them, dating back to when my great-great-grandfather had bought the shop over a hundred years ago. Fortunately, most of the notebooks had a start and end date on the inside cover, so they could be sorted chronologically.

Unfortunately, they didn't have a table of contents. I was still working on a process for chronicling what was in them. I needed to hire someone to help, and I was hoping that Nadia would be that person. She'd been doing a great job on the website. Despite her "whatever" attitude, she was also fascinated by the history of the shop, and loved learning about clocks. There was something holding me back, though. Something I didn't trust. But was it Nadia I didn't trust, or Tuck? I needed to sort that through.

When I took over the shop, I started a new notebook and kept up with the plans for the shop, on the work I was doing, and on the ideas for the future. I noted who was doing what when, but I was careful to keep the gossip off those pages. Or, more accurately, I annotated the gossip. As had my grandparents, and my great-grandfather. *Will stopped by. Business closing.* A simple note made in 1931 by my great-grandfather about the closing of the bank across the street, a move that had started a spiral in Orchard that continued for decades. I found a letter he'd written to his brother that detailed the entire transaction, including the shady dealings that had gotten Will arrested, eventually.

Last summer my grandfather had noted the passing of his friend, Grover Winter, and he'd written a note that said *It came on fast, no one knows the real reason.* I learned later that my grandfather's observations were leading him to a startling conclusion, one that rocked Orchard forever.

So I was trying to adopt the family motto of being cryptic, but today it wasn't working. After I took a shower and made myself some lunch, I sat down at the kitchen table and unwrapped a new notebook. This one was smaller, and turquoise, but still unlined paper. Out of habit I dated the inside cover. I left a few of the front pages blank, hoping to create a new habit of a table of contents moving forward. For now, I rolled my pencil in my hand a few times, and then I started to write. Or rather, to draw.

I took a bite of sandwich. Yum. Curried turkey with walnuts, apples, and raisins. I opened a big bag of chips and put a few on my plate, and then wiped my hands on my napkin. I wrote Mark's name down and a few bullet points about him underneath. Then I wrote Tuck's name. And Nadia's. And every other name I could think of from the past few days. I circled each name, and put a number in the circle.

It wasn't any good. I couldn't concentrate. There was nothing new to add, just a bunch of loose ends. I took my plate over to the sink and rinsed it before putting it into the dishwasher. "I'm heading down to the shop," I called to Bezel. She stretched with her whole body, spreading her tiny pink toes, before snuggling her face even deeper into the sofa cushion, wrapping a front paw around her forehead. Sometimes she was so adorable that it hurt.

Down in the shop, there were a few jobs that needed tending. I looked at one of Mark's unfinished projects and took a deep breath before taking it out of the bin. A lovely antique that kept losing time. The clock movement needed an overhaul, and I had been working on it with Mark a few days before Christmas. I checked the notes that were included in the bin. Just as I'd suspected. The case was with Pat for some repair and careful restoration. Mark had started to take the movement apart, but hadn't finished. I would have chastised him for that. I wished he were there so I could. Instead I did a quick inventory, then I finished taking the clock movement apart. Twenty-six pieces.

I turned on the ultrasonic cleaning tank and took out the mesh basket. I put the pieces in the basket, looking each of them over. What a mess. I could already tell that a few badly done repairs needed to be fixed, and a few pieces might require replacing. I couldn't really tell until they were all cleaned up, and that would take time. I submerged the basket into the tank.

The routine had relaxed my mind, just as I hoped it would. I took out the notebook and opened it to a new page. I sketched out a map of Orchard center, specifically the shops. I looked back at the notes I'd started earlier and put the numbers I'd associated with people inside every shop. I stared at it for a few minutes, but my next steps didn't emerge. I knew from my work patterns that forcing it wouldn't work.

I took the mesh basket out of the cleaning solution. I used a pair of long tweezers and lifted out the clock's count wheel. Still gunked up. A very technical term for a clock owned by someone who used WD-40 instead of bringing the clock into a shop for proper cleaning. I'd let the ultrasonic cleaning tank do its work for a while longer. If I tried too hard to clean the pieces with a brush, I might do more damage.

I went back to the notebook and tried something else. I wrote down the time I found Mark's body in the center of the page. As I started to create a timeline, I worked to the start of the open house, but it didn't satisfy me. I needed to start earlier—maybe that morning?

No, I needed to start earlier than that. Another page. I thought back to when I'd first hired Mark, and wrote down the date. I kept flipping back and forth to the first section, where I'd numbered the people, and used that system as I built a narrative from the first time I met Mark.

I took another look at the clock pieces. The cavitation was complete. I took the pieces out of the cleaning tank, then laid them out, rinsing them in a drying solution. The next step was to use a soft brush and a peg to finish cleaning them up. As I brushed each piece, I laid it out for reassembly. When a thought came to me, I'd go back to the notebook and jot it down. I kept up the dance: writing, brushing, cleaning, writing. I filled page after page with notes, circling some, adding triangles to the side, drawing arrows. I ran out of ideas and clock pieces at the same time.

I turned on my phone. Almost three o'clock. I rolled my

shoulders back and flipped backward through the notebook, amazed by my burst of energy, and of ideas. Using numbers instead of names was inspired, if I did say so myself. Interesting in that they helped me recognize patterns without prejudice. I wondered if Jeff used a similar system. Like I'd ever get enough courage to ask him. I imagined his face when I told him what I was doing, and closed the notebook.

I took out another box, this one lined with cloth. I laid out all of the clock pieces in the box and put a cover on top. Tomorrow I'd look them over one more time, straighten some of the levers, double-check that the pallets were clean, and broach the holes. I made a few careful notes on the repair documents and carefully put everything back in the bin.

I went back upstairs and looked over my notes on the murder. One thing was for sure. I needed to talk to Beckett Green. His number, 6, kept coming up. We needed to straighten out a few things, including his encroaching on my clock business.

Then I heard the bells.

chapter 26

Pat Reed and I had discussed ad nauseam what to install on the front door to alert us of customers. I remembered our first discussion.

"It sounds like a buzzer into a prison—hardly the effect I'm looking for for my customers."

"Ruthie, if you're working in the shop, you need to be able to hear someone come in."

"Since we'll be able to see folks come in, that won't be a problem."

Pat Reed had pursed his lips, but didn't say anything. He'd lost that fight. The front of the shop had a countertop with a pass-through. The wall behind the counter was actually beautiful cabinetry, three-foot-tall cabinets with varying-sized rectangular and square shelves on top. During the Great Depression, the Cog & Sprocket had become a

WPA project for Orchard, with my great-grandfather Harry
stepping in to make sure people kept working. There wasn't
enough clock making work to keep people working, so
Harry found things for people to do, and paid them or bar-
tered clock making services. The cabinetry in the shop was
one of those projects, the first. In short order, Harry moved
over to the old Town Hall and its clock tower, setting free
artisans and craftsmen on what eventually became a destination for the region.

From the shop side, the front cabinets were always open
on the bottom half. That is where finished work was put in
a bin and slid in place for pickup by its owner. When we
were doing a walk-through, we removed the back of the
upper cabinets. I loved the light and the illusion of space,
and decided on the spot that we would keep them open. Pat
disagreed, but I wouldn't budge. The battle of the buzzer
was next.

"What happens if you are upstairs? Don't you want to
know when customers come in?"

"Of course I do," I said. "I don't want to jump out of my
skin dozens of times a day."

"Maybe a dozen. We don't get that many folks coming
into the shop."

"We didn't," I corrected him gently. "We will in the New
Year."

"I like your optimism," Pat said, still not looking entirely
convinced.

"Not optimism—strategy. Anyway, how about some
bells?"

We had gone through four different bell combinations
since our first discussion. I reluctantly had to admit I couldn't

hear most of them, but Pat rose to the challenge and had devised a new system. He'd installed most of it over the weekend, but the bells themselves hadn't been put in place. Pat must have been by earlier and done that, since I heard a cacophony of sound coming from the front of the shop, and I went down to investigate.

Cacophony wasn't a fair term. Rather than a tinkle of a bell, it was actually a combination of sounds that cascaded throughout the shop. As I got toward the bottom step, the bells sounded again. I saw Caroline at the front door, hand on the door handle. She opened and shut the door again.

I looked up and noticed for the first time the series of gears that had been placed close to the ceiling. I could be forgiven for not noticing them before, since the airplane wire that ran throughout the system was almost invisible. A dozen or so bells of varying sizes had been hung throughout the web of wires, not on the wires themselves, but dispersed, so that the movement of the wires triggered them somehow.

"Do it again," I said. Caroline complied, opening and closing the door. The system came alive for another brief moment, but how it worked was still a mystery.

"Pat has outdone himself," Caroline said.

"He must have installed this when I was out for my run. This is fabulous. I wonder how it works." I looked around for a chair, hoping to get closer to the ceiling so I could look at the mechanics.

"Don't," Caroline said, putting her hand on my arm. "Let Pat show you. Don't take his moment away from him."

"You're right, of course," I said, still sort of itching to inspect the mechanism. I reached into my pocket and texted him: "Love the bells! Show me how it works!" I put my phone back in my pocket. I looked over and noticed my car keys on the front counter, sitting on a piece of paper. *Fixed* was all the paper said, in Pat's familiar scrawl. What would I do without him?

Caroline and I looked at each other. I bent down and gave her a quick hug, which she returned. We both stood up, a little surprised by my display of affection.

Affection it was. Though Caroline was twice my age, I felt protective of her, even more so since finding out about her terrible first marriage.

I wanted to ask where the devil she had been, but I bit my tongue. "How are you?"

"I know you left me a message. I'm sorry I haven't called you back," Caroline said. "I needed to take some time. Do you mind if we sit?"

"Let's go upstairs and have some tea," I said. Caroline headed up as I confirmed that the front door was locked before following her up the stairs.

Caroline was busy setting down two large bags when I reached the top of the stairs.

"Yeesh, Caroline, I didn't realize you were carrying so much stuff," I said. "I should have helped you."

Caroline picked up one of the bags and put it on a chair. She put her hands on the handles and twisted them closed. She was biting her lower lip, which looked dry and cracked. Her hair was in its normal twisted bun, but the normally smooth top had bumps, and there were chunks of flyaway hair. She looked like a hot mess. Usually that was my role.

I walked over to the sink and filled up the electric

teakettle and switched it on. I pulled out a plate and took out some cookies from the tin. One of the good things about knowing the Reed family is that I get test cookies delivered for my opinion, or extras at the end of the day. It was also the bad thing about knowing the Reed family. After the holidays I had given up wearing pants that buttoned. Leggings were part of my look, sure. But they also had an elastic waistband. Desperately needed these days.

I poured a little milk in my white porcelain creamer and put it in front of Caroline. I spooned some loose tea into the matching teapot, and poured the hot water over it. There was something about her that called for a level of formality. She probably would have been fine with the carton on the table, but it wouldn't kill me to use some of the pieces, like the creamer and teapot, that my grandmother left me.

I was tempted to ask Caroline if she wanted something stronger, but I refrained. I used the strainer and poured her a cup of tea. "Caroline, why don't you sit?"

"I hope that you don't think less of me, after my story yesterday."

"Of course not," I said. "I understand bad marriages and how they can suck you in, better than most."

"Not that. Not only that, I mean. I participated in perpetuating a fraud. I broke the law. Dozens of laws, in fact."

"Did you know you were breaking the law when you were working on the pieces?"

"No," she admitted. She poured a dollop of milk in her tea and stirred it absently. "I had no idea he was selling the pieces as originals. I thought we were creating excellent replicas."

"You never had doubts?"

Caroline took a sip of tea. "One day I came home early and found two people searching our apartment. They ran, but I called the police, gave them the best descriptions I could. Wallace was more concerned about what they'd taken than he was with my safety. That didn't sit well with me. I didn't think more about it, but then we went to Prague.

"Wallace didn't like me to come with him on business trips, but I'd insisted. I'd even left Levi with a babysitter for a few days. It was the first time we'd done that, but I'd always wanted to visit Prague. Anyway, he told me he had business all day, and that I should keep myself occupied. I went to the Astronomical Clock first, of course. Have you ever seen it?"

"Not in person, no."

"You must, someday. Extraordinary. Built in 1410, and still working. Really a marvel—"

"I'll add it to my bucket list. What happened in Prague?"

"I talked to a few people and explained my interest in clocks and watches. One very nice man gave me the name of a private museum, which had limited hours when it was open. I think about that sometimes. If I hadn't met that man, and hadn't heard about the museum, and then the museum hadn't happened to be open when I was there, would I ever have discovered the truth?"

"I'm not following you."

"I went to the private museum, which was really quite lovely. There were a number of pieces, all of which proclaimed to be originals. Then I happened upon a Biedermeier Vienna wall clock. I recognized it as something I'd worked on a couple of years ago—"

"How did you recognize it?"

"I recognized the workmanship on the weights."

"What do you mean?"

Caroline looked miserable and took a long sip of tea. "It was filigree pattern. I was pretty good about matching patterns, and taking weights of the same age and making them match. Again, I have to emphasize, I thought we were making replicas. Anyway, on this particular clock I'd had to do a lot of work and decided to have some fun. I kept it in the pattern, but added my initials: *CAS*. It was part of the leaf. You needed to know it was there, but once you did, it was obvious."

"So maybe the collector knew it was a replica?"

"And displayed it as original? I thought the same thing. I asked a couple of questions, but I was assured that the clock was original. The docent was quite adamant on the point, letting me know that the collector had paid a fair sum for the clock from a private collector."

"Did you ask Wallace about it?"

"No, I didn't. I assumed that the owner was creating his own reality. What did it hurt? It was a private museum, unbound by ethics. The clock wasn't for sale; it was just for display.

"When we got back to the shop, I looked up the sale. I tracked back the receipt, and then I realized that Wallace had a second set of books, a second business, set up. The second business was in the antiques business. He mostly dealt with private collectors, willing to pay exorbitant rates for antique clocks. The gentleman in Prague thought he had an original, because Wallace had sold it as such."

"That wasn't all, was it?"

"No. As it turns out, Wallace had started to do another

side business, using the clocks to smuggle jewels and other works of art. Of course, I didn't know that until much later, during the trial prep.

"A few days after we got back, two men showed up, both wearing suits. They weren't the police. They were with Interpol. It turns out that someone in our shop was actually working for them, and she'd realized I'd been looking at the books and going through the files."

"Why did she tell them about you?"

"The break-in had really shaken me up. She knew me well enough to know that if I thought that Wallace was putting our family in danger, I'd turn on him. She was correct."

"So you began to work with them. That must have been scary."

"Scary, exhilarating, justified, heartbreaking. Stories for another day—is that all right?" she said, and I could see the exhaustion in her eyes. "For now, I want to show you these." She opened one of the bags and handed me a manila envelope. I opened it up and took out the six pictures, laying them out on the table. The clock in the picture was a lovely wall clock. It looked like a Gustav Becker wall clock, either that or a replica. I couldn't tell. The clock also looked vaguely familiar.

"Is that a Becker? Viennese regulator? Lovely wall clock. Dated around 1880 or so?"

"You know your clocks. Yes, it is, but a replica. It was sold as an original."

I whistled slowly. "That's a twenty-five-hundred-dollar difference right there."

"Minimum."

"Your work?"

"Yes. You can tell by the mark here—do you see it?"

She pointed to a place on the clock face. The numbers themselves were ornately painted, with large serifs that had dramatic dips and swirls. Behind the numbers there was fainter scrollwork that covered the edge of the clock. She was pointing to a place that looked a little different. I couldn't see it, but I'd take her word for it. Her mark.

"Why does this clock look so familiar?" I asked, turning the image, trying to get a better look at the clock.

"Because Beckett Green has it hanging in his shop."

chapter 27

"He what?"

  "Let me start from the beginning. Mark had told me about Beckett's job offer a few days ago, and that Beckett needed someone to help get his clocks and watches ready for sale. So I thought I'd go by his shop today and see if I could help somehow."

  "Help? Offer our services, like that?"

  "Yes, like that."

  "Hah! I don't believe you, Caroline."

  "What do—?"

  "I don't believe you because I had decided to go visit Beckett myself. He's number six on my chart." I must have sounded crazy, but that statement had made complete sense in my head.

  "What does that mean?"

"It means we are both trying to figure out what happened to Mark, and we both recognized that Beckett is on a lot of the paths that cross on the way to the truth."

"I have no idea what you said, but it made sense. I know that you and Beckett aren't the best of friends, so I thought it would make sense for me to go over. We chatted for a while. Rina wasn't there."

"I saw her yesterday morning coming out of the Sleeping Latte. She hasn't been around much lately."

"He indicated to me that he was going to buy her out."

"Interesting. The partnership isn't working anymore, I guess."

"Apparently not. I did ask him about Tuesday night, and where he was. He said that he and Rina were in Marytown, having dinner."

"That's what she told me," I said, trying to recall the exact details of our tense encounter.

"I could have sworn I saw Rina's red coat in the crowd during the lantern ceremony, but I must have been mistaken. Why do I always assume that a red coat is Rina?"

"I don't know anyone else with a coat that same color. But if she confirms that they were having dinner, then it might give Beckett an alibi for when Mark was killed."

"Beckett is a loathsome human being, but you don't really think he could have done it, do you?"

"Caroline," I said. "Someone did it."

"But there were so many people here that night," she said as she watched Bezel saunter toward her bowl of food. Caroline must have taken her allergy medication. I was glad, since separating Bezel and food was never easy. "It must have been a stranger."

"The watch that was left makes it personal," I said softly. "Your initials on the watch and now these replicas in Beckett's shop. There must be a connection." The shadow that crossed her face told me she'd thought the same thing.

"So, anyway, what was the tour of Been There, Read That like?"

"It wasn't very extensive. He showed me where the coffee bar was going in. He was trying to breeze by the clocks, but I slowed down and looked at a few of them. That one in particular stopped me. I looked more carefully, and I noticed the mark. The one I'd started to use to tag the forgeries."

"Maybe it's a coincidence?"

"The mark is my initials. I would know them anywhere."

"You're sure?"

"Not a hundred percent. It isn't obvious to the naked eye, of course. But I'd put the mark in some embellishment on the clock face if that was possible. It was more helpful for Interpol agents who were doing the tracking. Anyway, without a magnifier I couldn't be sure. That's why I went back and got these." She pointed to the two bags. "These are my own personal archives from that period of my life."

"Your own archives?"

"I started to have to document what I was doing for Interpol, so I kept a copy for myself. Insurance, if you will. Or maybe it was a record of my work, since I knew that I would lose it all."

She handed me a few more envelopes, and I opened them one at a time, taking a quick look inside. I was shuffling through stunning work, too quickly to really honor it. "You worked with both clocks and watches?" I asked, fascinated by this opportunity to peer through this long-closed window into Caroline's life.

"I did. Watches are my passion. For clocks, I was best at the fine work—painting the faces, etching. It was a remarkable time." She looked absolutely miserable. To do such work, and have it be a misery in your life. It broke my heart.

"Wow, Caroline, you and I have a lot to talk about, don't we?" I flipped through a few more pictures. "What did you say to Beckett?"

"I didn't say anything. I went home, found these things, and came over here to talk to you. Then you mentioned that Beckett is number six, and I have no idea what that means. But it made me feel better, somehow, to know I am not the only conspiracy theorist in this town."

I walked over and got my notebook and handed it to Caroline. She leafed through it quickly and then handed it back to me.

"This new information about Beckett sort of ties him in with Mark's death, because of the watch, don't you think?" I said.

"I do."

"Beckett could have brought the watch over to show Mark and dropped it after killing him. Or it's a warning to someone. In any case, we need to call Jeff Paisley," I said.

If I thought Caroline couldn't be more miserable, I was wrong. Her face crumpled.

"Jeff isn't going to blame you," I said.

"I blame me," she said, her voice raw. "When I saw the watch, I prayed that it had nothing to do with me. Then I went to Beckett's and saw the clock. One has to have something to do with the other."

"Listen, Caroline, we can both make guesses, but where will that get us? Isn't Levi coming home later today?"

Caroline nodded, tears welling in her eyes. "So how about this. We call Jeff and set up a time to talk. Then I'll come out to the house, and we can have dinner with Levi. I am really looking forward to meeting him. Tomorrow, we'll go over and talk to Beckett together. How does that sound?"

I took her nod as an assent, and I called Jeff Paisley. He didn't pick up.

"He could give a girl a complex," I said to Caroline while I listened to his voice mail recording. Caroline was watching me while I left our message. "Jeff, it's Ruth. So, Caroline was visiting Beckett this afternoon, and she noticed that one of the clocks in his shop had some similarities to the watch you brought over yesterday. Call me and I'll tell you more."

"That was fairly cryptic," she said.

"I know. I think we may as well be cryptic on voice mail—don't you agree?"

"In case someone is listening in?"

"Well, I was thinking it would make him more likely to call back. I feel like he's been avoiding me."

Caroline smiled and patted my arm. "I'm sure he's very busy. Listen, why don't I leave all of this with you?"

"Are you sure? It's fine with me, of course."

"I'd rather it be here with you, especially now. You can keep it safe and help me figure out what to do with it after you've looked it over. It is time to work out my past before it takes over my present. I hope all of this is a terrible coincidence."

"I'm sure it is," I said. We both knew I was lying, but it was a necessary lie for now. Believing anything else would break Caroline's heart, and I wasn't sure she could live through yet another heartbreak. On the other hand, the more

I learned about Caroline convinced me that she was probably one of the strongest people I knew. All of those secrets must have been a heavy burden.

"Now, I need you to promise me something," Caroline said, smoothing her hand over her hair, tucking in a few flyaways with practiced fingers.

"Anything."

"Promise me you won't go visit Beckett again until you've talked to Jeff. Don't look at me like that. You know I'm right. If anything ever happened to you—"

"Caroline, nothing is going to happen to me. But if it makes you feel better, fine. I will wait to see Beckett until we talk to Jeff."

Caroline reached across the table and took both of my hands in hers. She may have wanted to see if I was crossing my fingers, but she held them both and squeezed them. I squeezed back.

"I've got your back on all of this," I said. "We'll get through it, no matter what. Trust me."

chapter 28

Caroline scoffed at my offers to bring food for dinner with Levi.

"I've had a brisket cooking all day. That's his favorite. I'll mash some potatoes, and I have roasted vegetables ready to go. I will tell you what, though. Levi loves Nancy Reed's cookies. Maybe you could bring some of them?"

We both looked at the empty plate. We'd polished off most of my stash.

"I'll head down to the Sleeping Latte and see what they've got."

"I'm sure Nancy will have some gossip to go with the cookies. Bring that to dinner as well, won't you?"

"Will do."

• • •

I walked down to the Sleeping Latte. It was almost four o'clock, close to closing, but you wouldn't know it when you walked in. Every table was packed, and there were three people waiting in line for coffee. I was surprised to see Pat Reed busing tables, and I walked over.

"Moonlighting?" I said, smiling.

"Ruthie, you are a sight for sore eyes. Could you grab that tub over there?"

I walked over and picked up the tub. It was full of dishes and coffee cups. I followed him back into the kitchen, and set the tub next to the sink. Three other tubs were on the counter.

"Tuck was supposed to come in this afternoon, but he didn't show up." Pat looked at the dishes and sighed. "I came over for lunch, and they put me to work. They were already understaffed, because of the holiday. But this was supposed to be a quiet week."

"Why don't I take care of the dishes?"

"Know what you're doing?"

"I do. I've been helping out since December when student workers had exams and started calling out on shifts."

"Thanks. I'll go back out front and take over the counter. Nancy isn't the best at customer service."

I found a pair of rubber gloves and grabbed an apron. I heard the sound of a siren wailing down the street, the babble of the crowds in the front of the restaurant, and the ticking of a kitchen timer. I shook my head and tried to block all of the sounds out. I pulled out two racks of clean dishes and walked them out to the front. There were three empty racks waiting, so I gathered them. Moira looked up from frothing some eggnog and mouthed "thank you" to me. I nodded and went back to the kitchen.

It didn't take long to get the dishes into the machine. There was still a tub left. I filled up the sink and started to hand-wash some more cups and saucers to replenish the stock out front. I realized I was going to miss just stopping in to lend a hand once I had the Cog open regular hours and I didn't have as much free time. I left the cups drying in the rack and then added some of the baking bowls that had dried cookie dough stuck inside. I left them to soak for a while and brought the cups and saucers back out front.

"Were you going to close at four?" I asked Pat.

"No, Moira could use the business. We'll close the doors at five."

"I can help for a little while longer. I'll get you ahead of the dishes, at least."

I walked back into the kitchen and saw Nancy sitting on a stool, nursing a large glass of ice water. When she saw me, she started to get up, but I motioned her down.

"Nancy, you look done in."

"I'm too old for this."

"Too old? You? Never. You just need more help around here."

"We really do. I thought hiring Tuck would help us, but then he didn't show up. Ticks me off, it really does. I went to bat for the kid. Even Moira thought he had a talent at the barista bar, which would have been a huge help today."

"He didn't call in?"

"I talked to him last night. I know he was a friend of Mark's, so I told him he didn't need to come in. But he told me he wanted to. He'd quit one of his other jobs and wanted to settle in here. Did he quit working for you?"

"No, not that I know of, but he was sort of working ad hoc in the shop. We have a meeting set up for tomorrow, to go over shots from the open house to use on the site. That is, if we can get the memory cards back from Jeff." I made a mental note to check in with Jeff, and make sure Nadia dropped the memory cards off. Maybe I could use the need for pictures as an excuse to get a glimpse of them all.

"Tuck isn't the most charming guy in town, but he is pretty reliable," Nancy said, interrupting my photo plotting.

"Agreed on both counts." I pulled out my cell phone and texted Tuck: *Call or text ASAP. You OK?* I noticed that I had a call and checked my phone. The ringer volume was practically shut off it was so low, which accounted for the missed call. I stepped out onto the back stairs to check my messages.

The voice mail was short. "Ruth, this is Zane Phillips. Just confirming our dinner plans for tonight. Looking forward to seeing you and Caroline both. Where should we meet?"

Shoot! I had completely forgotten to tell Caroline I'd agreed to dinner on her behalf. Great. Well, I guessed we would have to set an extra place at the table and have him over at Caroline's house tonight.

I hadn't heard back from Jeff about the phone call. I hadn't heard back from Jeff about anything. Where was he, anyway?

I called Caroline first, on her cell. She answered right away. "Caroline, Zane Phillips called. Remember earlier when I called and left you his number? Well, I meant to mention he wants to have dinner tonight. And I said that we were free. Do you think we can have him over to your house just to simplify things?"

"What, oh, I suppose. A little last-minute, but with everything that's happened the past few days it's understandable. And Levi knows him already. It might be nice to have company, take our mind off things."

"Thank you! I feel like anything not directly related to the murder investigation just doesn't fit into my brain these past few days. Is Levi there yet?"

"No, he left a message, and was having some car trouble. Oh, look, that's him now, on the other line. Can you let Zane know the address? Tell him around seven thirty?"

"I'll give him a call," I said.

"Give who a call?" Nancy asked as I hung up the phone and stepped back in. She was back sitting on the stool and was now resting the glass of ice water against her forehead.

"An old friend of hers—Zane Phillips. He's in town and wants to see her."

"That's nice. Levi's there, isn't he?"

"Not yet. He was having some car trouble. But he was calling with an update while I was on the phone with Caroline. Listen, Nancy, I hate to ask, but I actually came by to see if you had any cookies I could take to the dinner tonight. I guess Levi loves them as much as I do."

"Levi is my best taste tester. I'm glad he'll be around for a little while. I have three new cookies I want to try out. Of course I'll send some out with you."

"I'm happy to pay for them," I offered, even though I knew the offer was futile.

"Put your money away. You know how you can help me,

don't you? You can finish up the dishes. And take care of Caroline. She's taking Mark's death hard."

"She is. And I will. Let me get the next load of dishes in."

"I'll put a couple of batches in the oven now." Hot, home-baked cookies. A couple of loads of dirty dishes in exchange for those gems. Yet again, I got the better end of the deal.

The box of cookies was warm in my hands. I knew it would get cool soon enough, but wouldn't it be great if they made it out to the cottage warm? I decided to go out the front of the Sleeping Latte, hoping to have a quick chat with Moira before I left. Her back was to me, at the espresso machine, six drinks in various stages of completion as she carefully steamed some milk. I didn't want to interrupt her rhythm, so I waved at Pat and walked out the front door. I'd catch up with Moira later.

I hadn't walked down the main drag in a couple of days. Though it was more efficient to walk down the back alley, the true spirit of the town didn't exist back there, but rather on this main stretch of road. The Corner Market's parking lot was packed. Of course, there were only six spots, but still, it was good to see. The library was to the left, across the street. I loved that it was still open seven days a week, from eight in the morning till eight at night.

At the last town meeting Kim Gray had tried to propose shorter hours and closing on weekends to save money. She hadn't even gotten to the amount it would save in the budget before Nancy Reed stepped in.

"We have to keep the library open. It's the only place a lot of folks have access to the Internet. It's also warm, which is critical this time of year," Nancy Reed had said. "It's not just a place to borrow books, it's a service to the community." She got a round of applause as she sat down.

"You don't want folks sitting in the Sleeping Latte for hours, using your Internet," Kim had said, smiling as if she were joking. Everyone in the room knew she wasn't. The Nancy Reed–Kim Gray tussles had become a spectator sport at town meetings, and everyone was waiting for Nancy's response.

Nancy stood back up and smiled at the people in the room.

"Kim, the business is Moira's, but I think I can speak for her when I say that we love folks to come in, get a cup of something hot, and sit. We never kick people out. That said, there are some who don't want a cup of coffee or can't pay for it. There are other folks who need a quiet place to work and don't have a computer. Older folks who need access to benefits online, people who need to apply to jobs, kids working on papers and using the resources provided at the library that they can't get at home . . . I can go on and on. If you take away that option, we'll do what we can to take up the slack. But it isn't the same—you know that."

They combed through the budget and they kept the library open by shifting some funds around, including the money that was earmarked for a new office suite for the town manager, Kim Gray herself. She'd tried to slide it through, but not much got past Nancy Reed. That drew new battle lines between the women. Most of the townsfolk were on the Reed side of the fight. A few others sided with Kim Gray, at least publicly. The only person who was completely on Kim's side was Beckett Green. Not joining the POL consortium and participating in the open house had been his attempt at being a conscientious objector. It hadn't won him any fans. I suspected it would also cost him some business once his store was open.

Beckett Green was the other reason I decided to walk back to the shop down Washington Street. I'd made a promise to Caroline, one I intended to keep. But still, maybe Rina was in. I should really stop by and apologize for yesterday. I was rude, taking my frustration out on her, when it was directed at Beckett. If being a good neighbor let me take another look at the clocks, so much the better.

I looked up the street at Been There, Read That. Lights were on. A lot of lights were on. The entire corner glowed. Jeff Paisley's car was parked right in front of the building, blocking other cars from going in or out of Beckett's small parking lot. An ambulance was backing out of the parking lot, lights flashing. As it sped past me, they turned the siren on. Even though I knew it was coming, the sound stopped my heart for a moment.

I looked both ways before crossing the street by rote, but was glad I did when I saw another SUV flying past me. I hurried my pace and caught Ro Troisi as she was getting her gear out of her car.

"Is everything all right?" I asked. "Is someone hurt? Was there a robbery?"

"A robbery? What makes you ask that?" she said, cocking her head.

Ro Troisi was formidable, with dark curly hair that she corralled into a ponytail, and a shirt that always gaped at unfortunate places. Ro and I always grabbed a cup of coffee when we had the chance, and she'd become a friend. I knew that Jeff considered her his right hand, and she was blossoming under his leadership. She had stopped what she was doing and was waiting for my answer.

"Beckett has been bringing in some merchandise that is worth a good deal of money. Since he isn't open yet, I'm not sure if all of his alarms are in place. I figured maybe something was taken."

"So you decided to come over and check it out," she said, cocking her eyebrows.

"Yes," I said. I matched Ro's gaze and smiled. "Given everything that is going on around here, do you really blame me?"

"You do seem to be around for drama," she said with a snort. She looked over her shoulder as Jeff Paisley was coming out the door. She bent over and picked up her gear.

"Troisi, you need help?"

"No, sir. On my way in."

"Good. We need to secure this scene before the state comes in and takes it over. You up to that?"

"I'm on it, Chief." She looked at me and shrugged slightly.

Jeff Paisley came down the stairs, heading right toward me.

"What are you doing here, Ruth?"

"Saw the lights and the ambulance and thought I'd come over and see what was happening. Just curious."

Jeff nodded and looked at me. He and I may be the same height, but his shoulders were twice as broad. His eyes were dark brown with yellow flecks. Though I knew he was at heart a very kind man, Jeff rarely smiled. It was as if he took on the pain of others and held on to it while he sorted things out. Today he looked miles away from even a shadow of joy. I put my hand on his arm and squeezed it gently.

"What's going on?"

He looked around, and then back at me.

"Where were you for the last hour or so? I came by the store a couple of times today to talk to you, but you weren't there."

"Why didn't you call or text?"

"Better in person these days."

"Okay. I was at the Sleeping Latte, helping out in the kitchen. Before that Caroline and I were having some tea. Before that only Bezel saw me."

"This was after the tea with Caroline."

"What was after the tea with Caroline?"

"You'll find out soon enough. Someone tried to kill Tuck Powers."

chapter 29

"Tried to kill him?" I said. I must have swayed a bit, because Jeff put both of his hands on my shoulders. "Here?" He nodded. "When?"

"Within the last hour, best as I can tell," Jeff said, looking over his shoulder. "Caroline came to see me after you'd had tea. While we were talking, I gave Tuck a call and asked him to come by the station."

"Is he going to be all right?"

"No one is making any predictions, but he's still alive. That's a good sign."

"Why Tuck?" I asked.

"I'd already called Beckett to ask him where he got the clocks in his shop. He told me that Tuck had brought them in on consignment."

"Tuck?"

"I take it you know nothing about this?" Jeff said.

"I didn't even know Beckett was selling clocks up until a couple of days ago."

"Clocks and watches, as it turns out."

"Any of the watches like the one that you found with Mark's body?"

Jeff looked at me and shook his head. He took the phone out of his pocket and opened up a text. "I was with Caroline when I got the call. I'd already started to work on getting more information about her ex-husband to find out if he has anything to do with this. I can't get verification that he's still in jail, but official channels say that he is."

"You don't believe them."

"Not sure what I believe. The language is cagey," he said.

"Shouldn't you be able to find this out? It seems sort of basic. He's either in jail or he isn't."

Jeff smiled and shook his head. "You'd think, wouldn't you? But working with a lot of agencies, you'd be surprised how many people get territorial. Some for no good reason, others for very good reasons. I've got a couple of calls in to old friends who can help me cut through red tape. I'm waiting to hear back from them."

"Does Caroline know about Tuck?"

"No. She knows I had to leave. We were planning on continuing the conversation later. She said something about a dinner at her house?"

"Yes, and it's turning into quite a party. Her friend Zane Phillips is in town, and he's coming out to the cottage."

"Didn't you text me his phone number?"

"Yes, in case he saw something."

"Was that the only reason?"

"Well, given everything, I just wanted to make sure he was who he said he was."

"The number belonged to Zane Phillips."

"Alright then." I took out my phone and texted Zane Phillips, giving him the address of the cottage. I'd programmed his number, just in case.

"Sorry," I said, looking up at Jeff. "I forgot to text him the address earlier. Listen, I'm going to head out there. Anything else you need from me?"

"Do you know where Nadia is?"

"Nadia? No, why?"

"We're going to want to talk to her."

"Surely you don't think Nadia—"

"I am keeping an open mind about what I think. What I know is that she knew both men, and one is dead, the other one close to it. They were both attacked in very similar fashions. What I know is that I want to speak with her, ASAP. Got it?"

"Got it," I said. "If I hear from her, I will tell her to call you."

"And you won't tell her about Tuck yourself, right?"

"Chief, what do you think I am, some sort of gossip?"

"Ruth, don't get me started. Just promise me you'll let me do my job tonight. I'll check in tomorrow, all right? We can have breakfast."

"That will start the gossip flying again." I smiled, but he didn't smile back. "Breakfast would be great. Call me whenever you can make it. I do have a favor to ask, though: let me know when you've spoken to Nadia, so I can try and be there for her. She's been through a lot." He nodded once, but that was enough. "Then, I promise I won't call anyone." It was an easy promise to make. I didn't want to be the one to tell Nadia that her boyfriend had been hurt so soon after she lost Mark. Besides, I wanted to be with Caroline before she got the news.

Those old clocks had secrets, and Caroline was the one person who might be able to help figure them out.

I went over to the shop and unlocked the front door. The cascade of bells assaulted me. I'd forgotten about the welcome bells that Pat had installed and almost dropped the cookies on the floor. Yeesh. I was a bundle of nerves. But then, who could blame me?

The news about Tuck finally hit me after I closed and locked the door, safe in my clock haven. Tuck wasn't the most charming of young men, but he certainly deserved better. Besides, he knew the secret of the clocks. I was more convinced of that than ever. I hoped he didn't die and take the secret with him.

I thought back to my conversations with Nancy as I walked through the store. Tuck was supposed to have worked today, but something sidelined him. From what she'd said, he had been planning on working at the Sleeping Latte a lot. Was I making a career move? Was he expanding his business or was he sick of doing odd jobs around town? Had he gotten himself in over his head? Was Mark involved in some harebrained moneymaking scheme with him that had gone bad?

I put the cookies down on the workbench toward the back of the shop, and then I walked up the stairs. Bezel needed dinner before I went out to the cottage. I kept thinking about the last few days. Beckett selling the fake clocks in his shop. The watch by Mark's body, and Caroline's connection to it. Was there a watch in Tuck's hand as well? What had Jeff said? I shook my head, trying not to think about Tuck being attacked, grateful that I hadn't found him. Yet I was still curious about some of the specifics about the attack. What was wrong with me? Since when was I so morbid?

I was at the top step when I heard the noise. It sounded like an injured animal was trapped somewhere upstairs. Just at that moment, Bezel came out and wrapped herself around my ankles, headbutting the back of my knees. She gave one forceful meow. She walked to the left, close to the stairs that led up to the office. I hesitated, but followed her. Bezel was a smart cat, and she wanted me to see something.

I walked past the wall of cabinets. The keening sounds started to get a bit louder, and I looked down, seeing the tip of brown boots peeking out from under a large gray cloak.

"Nadia? Is that you?" I walked over and lifted up the cloak, exposing Nadia's raven black hair. She was resting her head on her knees. I bent down in front of her and put my hands on her shoulders. Again, she made me feel generations older than she was, rather than ten years.

"I didn't know where to go," she said. She sounded miserable and started whimpering again.

"What's wrong? What happened?"

"Tuck's dead," she said. "I saw him."

"Oh, Nadia. He's not. They took him to the hospital." She looked up at me and then a sob broke from somewhere deep inside.

"Come here, come in and sit down at the table," I said. I stood up and hauled her up on her feet. Once she was standing I put my arm around her shoulder and walked toward my apartment area. I sat her down at my kitchen table and then sat beside her.

"Tell me," I said.

"Tuck texted me, told me to come over to the bookstore—he wanted to tell me something. I walked over, and Beckett was there, leaning over him, looking at the necktie in his hand. Tuck wasn't moving. I screamed and ran over here. But you were gone."

"Beckett?" I asked. Nadia nodded and put her head down on her arms, weeping more quietly now.

"Nadia, I am calling the chief. You need to tell him what you saw," I said.

"No, I can't. What happens if he comes after me next?"

"Why would Beckett come after you?"

"I don't know. But first Mark, now Tuck. Why wouldn't I be next?"

Why not indeed? I took out my phone and texted Jeff Paisley, letting him know that Nadia was here.

Beckett Green. Mark said he had offered him a job, and Mark had turned him down. Maybe Tuck was leaving his employ as well? Who was Beckett Green, anyway? We'd all bought his rich-guy-buys-a-bookstore routine, but maybe we'd taken too much at face value. I was about to call Jeff when his text came through. *Don't move. I'll be there in a few minutes.*

"Nadia, Chief Paisley is on his way over here."

"Why did you tell him I was here?" she shouted, standing up so quickly that the table shook.

"Stop. You have to tell him what you saw."

"What happens if he thinks I did it?"

"Why would he think that?" I said. The unmasked grief on her face told me, at least, that she hadn't done it. Poor Nadia.

"Just because. It's easiest. Everyone thought I was cheating on Tuck with Mark. I know what people think about me."

"Stop. He's a fair man. But tell you what. I am going to let Kristen Gauger know that you may need her, all right? Here's her number—put it in your phone. She should be back from her trip by now, so she can help out if you need her. Or she can get one of her partners to help." I read the numbers aloud and then texted Kristen, letting her know that Nadia might be in touch. I didn't give her more information than that. I was already meddling too much.

"Nadia, is there anything you want me to know?" I asked. "Anything about Mark or Tuck that might help us find out who did this?"

"I think it was Beckett Green. I really do. He was so mad when Mark wouldn't help him fix the clocks in his shop, even though that's why Tuck got him his job here."

"What do you mean?"

"Remember when you needed someone, and we posted it? Tuck sent it to Mark—he knew him from back in Vermont. Tuck's uncle bought a clock shop a few years ago, and Mark worked up there. I don't remember the name of the guy who used to own it."

"Was it Zane Phillips?"

"No, that's not the name. This guy was named Wally, I think. Wally, now what was his name, Shruggs?"

"Struggs?" I whispered.

"That's it. Wally Struggs had owned the shop first, but then he moved to Europe. Tuck said his uncle took it over as a favor for Wally. They'd done some business together over the years."

"Wally Struggs?" Holy moley, this was getting stranger and stranger. Did Caroline know Tuck's uncle, this friend of her ex-husband's? She must have come into contact with him. Did she know he was running the shop? I'd think she would've mentioned that.

"Yeah, did you know him? I guess he was some sort of a big deal. Anyway, Tuck's uncle Fred is a jerk, but a few months ago he got a new business partner, and he started to get some great inventory in the shop. They wanted to sell it at the Cog & Sprocket, so they decided to move Tuck down here. At first I thought he came to be with me, but he told me the truth the night of the party. It was all about the clocks. When Tuck came down here, you weren't interested in more clocks." I nodded, vaguely remembering Tuck asking me about adding to my inventory, and telling him that I had more than I could handle at the moment. I had just thought he was making conversation, learning about the business. "So he consigned the clocks to Beckett Green. Fred's business partner was pretty ticked off. Tuck thinks his uncle started working another angle. When Tuck told them all about the job opening over here, Fred decided it made sense to move Mark down here."

"Why did they want us to sell the clocks?" I asked. Was it because they were forgeries? Did Tuck's uncle know who Caroline was, and the story of the clocks? Who was his business partner? This was getting more and more confusing. The knot in my gut tightened. I was missing something, some connection, that would help this story make sense. Right now it was a muddle.

"I don't know. Tuck idolizes his uncle Fred. But the few times I've met him, he's given me the creeps. Tuck always has a million deals going, and he sucked Mark into some of them. Tuck didn't tell me much about his side businesses. Whenever he did, we'd end up fighting. Last night he told me that his idea, Fred's and his idea, was that Mark would work on the other clocks for Beckett, and he'd keep trying to talk you into selling some of them. But then that all went haywire."

"Why?"

"Because you and Caroline were so nice. Mark used to say that you were the real deal, an artist with clocks." I felt a blush rise while tears pricked my eyes. "Mark wanted to learn from you, to become better at his job. He didn't want to help Beckett sell his clocks, and told Tuck he was out of the deal. Even Tuck started to feel bad about the whole thing, so he told Beckett and Fred that he was quitting. They wanted out of all that scheming and lying. They wanted to make honest money and become a part of Orchard."

"When did he talk to his uncle?"

"Today." Nadia started crying again, and I rubbed the top of her back. I heard some pounding on the downstairs door and within a couple of seconds my phone was ringing.

"Nadia, that's the chief. I'm going to let him in. You have to tell him what you told me, all right? Let's go downstairs."

I'd be standing by, making sure she did just that.

A s it turned out, the chief didn't even want me in the room.

"Ruth, I can't force you to leave. It's your shop. But I'm going to need to ask Nadia some questions, and it's much easier if we do it here and not have to go down to the station. Yet."

"So you don't think she did it?" I asked.

"I don't know."

"She said that Tuck used to work for—"

"Don't. Let me hear it from her."

"Do you know where Beckett Green is?" I asked.

"He's down at the station."

"Under arrest?"

"I'm not at liberty to say. Now, didn't you say that you had dinner plans out at the cottage? Go be with Caroline. I'll talk to you both either tonight or tomorrow, I promise."

"If you need more information—"

"If I need more information, I have your cell phone number on autodial. In the meantime, how's about we let Caroline enjoy her time with her friend?"

"Can I tell her about Tuck?"

"Not right away, no."

I thought back to my fragile step-grandmother, and agreed. She wouldn't be happy that I'd kept the news from her, but Jeff was right. Why let it sour her time with an old friend? I walked over to the work desk and took out the extra set of keys, handing them to Jeff.

"Bezel needs dinner and I would love to change my clothes to something dinner appropriate," I said, looking up at him.

"Go on up, feed her, and change," he sighed. "I'm waiting for Ro."

"Waiting for Ro? Won't she stay across the street?"

"I just got word that the state police have taken over the investigation," he said. "Again."

"So Beckett is waiting for them, not for you."

"That's right. Ro and I are visiting our friend Ruth's shop. Supporting the community," he said, a small trace of a smile playing on his lips.

"Who happens to have a key witness visiting?" I said, inclining my head toward Nadia's huddled form.

"Coincidence is a great thing," Jeff said.

"It is indeed. Okay, then. I'll feed the cat and go out to the cottage." I headed back up the stairs as Ro came to the front door. Jeff let her in and locked the door behind her.

"Make yourselves at home," I called behind me.

chapter 30

I fed Bezel and pulled on a simple gray tunic dress over leggings, my Docs, a maroon knit scarf, and some of my most intricate clockwork jewelry. My hair would just have to do as it was. I grabbed the cookies and hustled out the back, to my car. I should have eaten one of Nancy's goodies while they were warm. They were stone cold now. It seemed like hours ago I'd been to the Sleeping Latte.

I hit the button to unlock the doors. They opened. Pat Reed to the rescue again. I turned to lock the back door of the store and looked over to my right, toward the barbershop, adjusting the belt on my thick, black wrap coat. I saw a faint outline of someone standing in the spill of light from my back door. Ben was staring at his shop.

"Ben, is that you?" I asked, even though I knew the answer. No one else had that slightly disheveled appearance that was so darn sexy it took my breath away. I hadn't seen him since he brought the flowers over for Caroline, but it had felt like longer. I realized with a start that I'd missed him, that I wanted to talk to him about everything that had been going on. I finished locking the door and walked down the back stairs to my car.

"I was coming by, but saw Paisley go into the Cog. I didn't want to interrupt."

"Interrupt what?" I asked. I tossed my bag onto the passenger's seat and threw the bag of cookies on top. I turned to look at Ben. I could see his breath, all white in the cold air.

"He's been over at your place a lot lately." Ben dug his hands into his jacket pockets and looked down at the ground. "Just wanted to give you both space."

I stood there with my jaw hanging open. "Space for what?" I looked right at Ben, who studiously didn't look at me. "Ben, Jeff's on duty right now. He's using the shop for a couple of meetings."

"Meetings? Who with?"

I looked down at my watch. "Listen, Ben, I'm late to dinner out at Caroline's. I know, me showing up late, big surprise." He didn't even crack a smile. "Do you want to come with me, and I can tell you the whole story on the way?"

"You don't owe me any explanations." His jaw was set, and he looked frustrated. Which, of course, ticked me off.

"Ben, don't be such a jerk. I've had a really hard day."

"You've had a hard day? My day hasn't exactly been a picnic." His voice rose several decibels, which surprised us both. In response, I lowered my own voice.

"Of course it hasn't. Things have been terrible around here this week for everyone. Awful. Well, never mind." I got into my car, keeping the door ajar. I turned the key and was relieved that the car started right away. It was hard to make a dramatic exit when your car wouldn't start. "I'm not having this conversation with you, not right now. I need to get out to the cottage. Last chance—do you want to come?"

"No," he said, turning back toward his shop.

"Suit yourself," I said. "Jerk," I whispered. I made sure it was loud enough for him to hear.

Tonight the moon was behind a cloud. Even if I wanted to hurry, I couldn't. I tried Caroline's cell and her landline. No one answered, but I left a message on each, telling her I was on my way. Odd. She should be home. Maybe Zane was already there, and they were catching up.

I heard what sounded like a bottle breaking. I looked in my rearview mirror, back on the road, to see if I'd run something over. Then I saw the purple flashing light on my cell phone and realized someone was texting me. Nadia must have been playing with my phone's sound effects again. I'd need to change them back later. Crashing glass was not a great choice, especially while I was driving. Maybe there was a funeral dirge I could use. That would certainly be more fitting. I shook my head, trying to get in a better frame of mind. Tuck was going to be okay, I had to believe that. Everything was going to be okay. That was harder to believe, particularly given the knot in my stomach that kept growing.

I pulled into the driveway, turned off the car, and checked my phone. Was Caroline texting me? Did she need something for dinner? If she did, I could go back to Orchard and get it for her. I scrolled through, but the text was from Jeff.

I opened it and realized he'd texted me a picture. I read the words of the text while I waited for the image to download. Honestly, cell service was a disaster in parts of the Berkshires. I still wasn't used to that.

W. Struggs isn't in jail. Picture left to right—Struggs, Caroline, Zane Phillips. He got out six months ago. Some sort of deal. They've lost track of him.

A chill ran through me. Out of jail? How was I going to break that to Caroline?

The picture finally loaded, and I recognized it from the one that Zane Phillips had shown me earlier. But that wasn't right. Maybe it was backward, because Zane Phillips was definitely the man on the right, just many years older and with scars on his face. I could barely breathe when I called Jeff.

"Jeff, the picture. Left to right. Zane Phillips is the guy with the black shirt, right? Call me," I said to his voice mail. I looked at the picture again. Neither one had scars. That's how I'd known Zane was Zane—the scars. That's how I'd described him to Caroline. I hadn't noticed much more than the scars. I texted Jeff again.

The guy in the black shirt, he introduced himself as Zane Phillips. Is that him or not? I texted again, after a minute.

Jeff, I texted the black shirt guy Caroline's address. He's probably there already.

I sat in the car and waited. After a minute I called again, but it went right to voice mail. I left another message, telling Jeff to get to the cottage as soon as possible.

I sat in my car, waiting for Jeff to call me. My phone rang. It was Caroline.

"I'm waiting for a call back from Jeff—" I said.

"Run, Ruth! Get away from here!" I heard a scream and the phone went dead. The voice was Caroline's and so was the scream.

No more waiting. I called 911 and gave the dispatcher my address.

"We'll get you help as soon as possible," the dispatcher said. "It will be a few minutes. Wait for the officer, all right?"

"Could you call Jeff Paisley and tell him to listen to his messages?" I said. I hung up, but I couldn't wait. Caroline was in trouble. I couldn't let her face her abusive ex-husband all by herself.

I stuffed my phone in my coat pocket and searched the glove box looking for something, anything I could use as a weapon. The pointy metal nail set. I kept it in case I ever went off a bridge and had to break a window. I'd watched too many disaster shows than were good for me, but I'd always figured the four-dollar tool carpenters used to push nails into wood was worth the just-in-case investment. It felt ridiculous as a weapon, but it was the best I could do.

I shoved my keys and the nail set into my other pocket and turned off the interior light. I slipped out of the car and onto the driveway, closing my car as quietly as I could. I locked the car by rote and glanced at the two cars parked beside mine. I recognized Caroline's, but not the one with the Vermont plates.

I tiptoed to the front door and peered up through the front window. No one was in the living room but all the lights were on. I tiptoed around to the other side of the front door and peered through that window. The dining room looked empty, but the only light spilled from the living room. The door to the kitchen was closed. I hesitated for a moment. To look into the kitchen I'd have to step up on the deck. I wasn't sure why I was hesitating, but I trusted my gut. I needed to find another way into the house.

My heart was pounding. I had trouble swallowing. I forced myself to stop, close my eyes, and take a deep breath. Then another. It helped a little. Not a lot, but a little. Where was Jeff? Where were the police? I retraced my steps back to the living room area of the house and walked around the side. There was a large three-season porch on the side of the house, and I walked over toward it. Again, only the light from the living room illuminated the porch. I creeped over, bent in half to stay below the windowsill line. Once I got closer I lifted my head up and peeked in the window. No one was in there, but someone must have been earlier. The bookcases under the bench seating were cleared. Books were strewn around the room. Was that where the books that Caroline brought out to me had been kept? The ones filled with all of the evidence from the investigation into Wallace Struggs's criminal dealings and her part in them? Had they been hiding in plain sight this entire time?

I walked around to the back of the house, again ducking under windows. It was tough since the rear of the house faced the water, so there were a lot of large windows. Big windows. I crouched lower and walked like a duck. My thighs screamed from the effort. I paid attention to my path, trying to avoid sticks or leaves, anything that might give me away. It was slow going, but I didn't want to rush. Where was Caroline? Who was with her and why was she so scared?

I was halfway around the house. In a few more feet I'd

reach the side of the deck, the one that led out to the small shed where Caroline kept the garbage cans in the back of the house, close enough for convenience but impossible for raccoons to reach. Maybe she had something I could use as a weapon in the shed? It was worth a look. Just one more step. Boom. Floodlights turned night into day. I blinked my eyes, trying to refocus quickly, but it was no good. Damn, the motion-sensor lights were on. How could I have forgotten about them? I froze and let my eyes adjust. I turned to retrace my steps and go and wait for Jeff.

A shadow swooped in front of me, blocking the light, stepping toward me.

"Ruth, come join us. Caroline, you were wrong," he said, calling into the house. "She's out here."

"Oh, hello, Zane. I was just checking on . . . something." Brilliant conversationalist, that's me. Quick on my feet as always. I looked up, but he was standing behind the lights, so I saw only a shadow. Why wasn't Caroline answering? Could she even hear him?

"I'm sure you were. Come in."

"I forgot something in the car," I said dumbly, turning to go back around the house.

He covered the three steps to my side in a single movement. Once he stepped in front of the lights, I could see him more clearly. I could also see the gun in his hand.

chapter 31

I thought about making a run for it even though my legs were still cramped. I remembered reading that most people are terrible shots when they were surprised. It was dark out. But as if he could read my mind, he grabbed me by my upper arm and dragged me toward the open kitchen door, tossing me into the room. I didn't fall, but I did hit the kitchen table with my left hip, hard. I made an effort not to wince, and I turned to look at him. I avoided staring at the gun, but it was tough. Caroline was nowhere to be seen. What had he done to her?

"Zane, surely we can—"

"You can cut the 'Zane' crap, Ruth. You wouldn't be sneaking around the house, peeking in windows, if you didn't know the truth."

"Okay, Wallace Struggs. You've got me," I said. I clenched my jaw tight, trying to keep the rising bile at bay.

A terrifying, joyless laugh erupted from the middle of Struggs's chest. "You got it in one. I'm surprised you didn't figure it out sooner."

"I'm sorry I didn't," I said. Wallace Struggs. I needed to start trusting my gut more. Caroline's affection for her caring friend Zane Phillips and the uneasy feeling I had about the man whom I had met never quite fit. My gut was right. Wallace Struggs was a creep. And he had a gun.

"Where's Caroline?" I demanded.

"She's fine, just fine. You'll see her soon enough. Let's us catch up, shall we? We're practically family, after all."

Family. Was he kidding? I looked at Wallace. The scars I'd noticed before seemed so fake now. As if he could read my mind, he brushed the bottom of his face with his free hand. He wasn't wearing a hat now. His dark glasses were sitting on top of his head. I could see his entire face. His looks were compelling, but the blue eyes that stared at me weren't human. His mask was literally slipping as a fake scar peeled off into his hand. He had been wearing Halloween makeup and I had fallen for it.

"Let me see Caroline," I said.

"I told you I wanted to talk!" he shouted suddenly, smacking his free hand down on the countertop. "I make the rules here. Me. Don't you want to ask me about Zane?"

"What happened to Zane?" I whispered.

"Caroline asked the same thing. He's fine. I'm sure someone will find him soon. It must be difficult for him, since I have his phone with me, but still. One would hope that his absence from society will be noticed sooner rather than later."

"What do you mean?"

"I suppose you might as well know. I left him locked in his basement," he said with a little chuckle. "With food and drink. Provided he survived the fall, I'm sure he's fine."

"So you didn't kill him." I looked around the kitchen, hoping to be able to grab a knife or a rolling pin. Something. No such luck. There wasn't even a pan out on a counter.

"Of course I didn't kill him. I merely taught him a lesson. As I will with Caroline. A valuable lesson." His eyes twinkled.

I shivered. "Why are you staring at me?"

"You don't remember me, do you?"

I shook my head. "No, should I?"

"Years ago, you were about eight, visiting Thom and Mae for the summer. I came by to visit. You obviously don't remember me. Your grandmother hustled you out of the room pretty fast."

"Why?"

"Why indeed? Thom was a bit of a stick-in-the-mud. But you knew that." He waited for a response, but I wasn't going to give him one, even though he was right, in a way. Grandpa Thom had a very strict moral code. If Wallace Struggs went against his code, G.T. would have shielded me from him.

"What happened?" I asked, after a pause. Wallace wanted, demanded, a conversation. I had to buy some time so that the police could arrive. I needed him to keep talking.

"I tried to sell him some merchandise, but he questioned the provenance. Can you imagine that?" Wallace cackled at the memory.

"He was always meticulous about record keeping."

"He couldn't prove anything. He never could. I was careful."

"Sounds like he had you figured out, though."

"Thom Clagan had trust issues. Or maybe he didn't like my style."

"So this was what, twenty-two years ago, if I was eight. That's right around the time you moved to Europe and opened your business there. Tell me, is my timing right?"

"Just about, yes."

"Huh." Where was Jeff? I glanced over at the clock and was horrified that it had only been ten minutes since I'd left my voice mail. Even if he left right away, it was a twenty-minute ride to the cottage.

"Did you blame my grandfather for your having to leave? Is that why you are targeting me?"

"He had nothing to do with me having to leave. He was a little man who noticed a slight flaw in my product and called me on it. It made me better. If anything, he helped me create my business model."

"Business model?"

"We all have a business model, Ruth," he said, absently peeling another scar from his face. "My first business model was to hone my craft and provide people with what they wanted. Private collectors are amazingly narcissistic. They can easily be encouraged to think that their taste, their expertise, has helped them make an amazing find. They are willing to pay for their brilliance."

The frightening thing was, I followed his logic completely. It didn't give him the right to con people, of course. But he had tapped into the human fallibility of hubris. Of course, I needed to remember that it wasn't just the clocks that had put Wallace Struggs in jail. He'd broken more laws than that.

"Now, wasn't that nice? We had a chance to get to know one another. It could have happened earlier, but Caroline was very difficult to pin down, and I had other business here that prevented me from waiting around. Honestly, is she ever alone? Now, be a good girl and give me your cell phone, and your car keys."

I slid my phone and keys out of my pocket. Wallace leaned toward me, reaching for them both. I tossed them at him, aiming for his head. He ducked, and they missed. I tried to jog to one side, but he anticipated my move. He grabbed me by my arm and twisted it behind me. I screamed with pain, which only made him twist harder. He propelled me forward, and I stumbled a couple of times. He held me up.

"No you don't," he chided. "You're a handful, aren't you? Time to join Caroline down in the basement. She'll be glad to see you." He opened the cellar door and tossed me down the stairs, hard.

I grabbed the banister and kept from tumbling into the dark abyss.

He slammed the door and threw the locks. My breath came in short pants, so I tried to slow them down. My head felt fuzzy, but passing out would be a disaster. I looked around. Trying to break through the door was just a waste of energy. It was steel. Most people didn't lock basement doors, but my grandmother had insisted dead bolts be installed. No, I wasn't getting out the way I came in. I'd figure out another way.

First I had to find Caroline.

chapter 32

My perch on the cellar stairs was darker than the inside of a pocket, as my grandmother used to say. I stood still for a minute, hoping that my eyes would adjust, but without much luck. Dark was dark.

"Caroline?" I whispered. No reply. No sound, for that matter. I tried to tamp down the panic as I struggled to acclimate myself and feel my way up the stairs to find the light switch.

"Caroline?" I called again, this time louder.

I tried to figure out where the light switch was, and felt along the wall. The plaster was more of a stucco finish, very rough. I had to lighten up my sweeping motions so I wouldn't cut my hands. After a dozen swipes I found it and flipped it on. Ugly fluorescents flooded the space. I blinked in the bright light. Caroline was crumpled motionless on the landing below.

I ran down, stumbling. I grabbed the banister to steady

myself. Years ago my grandfather had installed a bumper wall at the bottom of the stairs, foam padding that helped protect large pieces as they turned the corner. The padded wall wasn't pretty, but hopefully it had done its job one more time.

I climbed over her and knelt down, feeling for a pulse. I found it. Thank heaven. I didn't dare to try and move her, since she was lying at an odd angle. I bent down, putting my hand on top of her head. "Caroline, it's me, Ruth. I'm here. Jeff is on his way. Hang in there." Caroline's eyes fluttered, and she stared up at me.

"Levi . . ."

"Is he down here with you?" I asked, looking around. I had assumed that the car with the Vermont plates was Wallace's.

"No. Wallace . . ." Caroline squeezed her eyes shut, opened them, and looked up at me again. She was looking more awake, but her color was still terrible.

"Wallace what?" I asked.

"Wallace might not know who he is. He's desperate. I don't think he'd hurt Levi, but maybe? Wallace wasn't done looking yet."

"Looking for what?"

"For the notebooks I brought to you. If only I'd kept them here he'd be gone now. Levi would be safe," she said, grimacing in pain.

"Did you tell Wallace where they were?" I said, crouching beside her and carefully smoothing her hair away from her face.

"I told him I wouldn't tell him anything until he promised to leave us alone. We were fighting about it when you drove in."

"So you called me? How?"

"You're on my speed dial. I took out the phone and hit the button. I wish I could have called Levi and warned him to stay away. I never should have invited you out here for dinner. If I hadn't, you wouldn't be here, trying to help me. It's all my fault. Everything's my fault."

I blinked back my tears and did my best to hold my face in a neutral position. Pity wouldn't serve Caroline, and she wasn't looking for sympathy.

Caroline tried to sit up, but I held her back. "Don't move, Caroline. Something could be broken. So after you called me, what happened?"

"Wallace grabbed my phone and hit me." I winced. "It wasn't the first time, of course. He saw you get out of your car, so he threw me down the stairs."

"I wonder why he didn't kill me when he had a chance?" I said.

"He doesn't know you."

"Gee, Caroline, thanks. To know me is to want to kill me?"

"No, of course not." At least I got her to smile a little. "Wallace has a terrible temper, but his wrath is saved for those who have done him wrong. Besides, he needs you alive. He'll figure out that you have the books soon enough."

"Do you think he'll try and kill you? Or Levi?"

"Not Levi. Never Levi. Believe it or not, he loved his son. He may not recognize him though."

I didn't argue with Caroline, not then. But I had to wonder if telling Levi that his father was dead had really been the kindest thing. Surely now Levi would have to learn what the truth was. There would be time to talk to Caroline about that later. First we needed to get out of this basement.

"I wonder where Jeff is?" I asked. "I know the state police are a ways away, but they were supposed to call him. He should be here by now."

"What do you mean?"

"I texted him and left him a voice mail. He may be ignoring my messages until he is less busy."

"Busy?"

"Oh, Caroline. There's no easy way to say this. Tuck Powers was attacked tonight."

"Is he—" She shifted her weight and groaned.

"He's not dead. Just stay still, Caroline. He's at the hospital." Caroline began to cry softly. I put my hand on her arm and rubbed it slowly.

"We've got to get out of here," I said. "Wallace will kill us. First he killed Mark, then he tried to kill Tuck. And right now he's getting angrier and angrier looking in vain for books that are in my shop . . . I really hope Jeff got my message. I'm sure he did. But just in case he doesn't get here for a while, we need to make a move."

"How? That is a solid steel door. There's no other way out."

"No other way out that you know of, you mean. Of course there's another way out. Two, in fact. One is the window over there. But I haven't tried that since I was about twelve. I don't think I'd fit. You could probably fit."

Caroline tried to sit up again. I tried to stop her, but she shook me off. When she attempted to move her arm she cried out in pain.

"All right, stop. You're hurt. I guess we'll need to use the secret passage."

"Secret passage?"

"When my grandparents built the porch off the living room, it meant that they had to get rid of the bulkhead that led to the cellar."

"That one, over there?" Caroline asked. "I always thought it was stairs to nowhere."

"G.T. was obsessed with safety. He hated the idea of only one way out of here, so he actually built a trapdoor in the porch."

"Really? Your family is fond of trapdoors and secret hideaways, aren't they?"

"We are," I said. "I'm still finding more and more hideaways in the shop. Pat and I found a new one last week. I'll show it to you tomorrow."

"Tomorrow," Caroline said. She sounded doubtful.

"Are you going to be all right here for a few minutes?" I asked.

"I'll be fine. Go get help. Before Levi arrives."

chapter 33

The trapdoor hadn't been used for years, and it protested being recommissioned. I pushed it up, fighting the rug that kept me trapped below. I tried to keep quiet, but moving the rug upended a small table. I closed the trapdoor again and counted to three to see if Wallace had heard me. No footsteps. I reopened the door, pushing harder. I had to get out. Hauling myself up was another reminder that my twelve-year-old self was well behind me. Yeesh, I really needed to go back to the gym. New Year's resolution. New Year's. A couple of days from now. For a second, I wondered if I'd see the New Year, but I shook my head and got rid of the thought. Of course I would. First I needed to get out of here. Easier said than done. After a fashion, I finally found enough footholds and hauled myself up and out of the hatch.

I stayed on my hands and knees, below window level,

listening. I didn't hear anything so I crawled off the porch into the living room, silently thanking Caroline for leaving the door open. The lights were still on in the living room. I looked around for any signs of Wallace. What was he doing now? From my vantage point it seemed he wasn't here. I rose up a little on my knees, taking a sweep of the room. No one was here. I'd made a mistake earlier, thinking that nothing was amiss. On closer inspection, it looked like every item in it had been moved. The books were all askew, in different places, some resting sideways. The room was searched, but not destroyed. From a quick glance, all the clocks were in their rightful places.

I crawled toward the hallway leading to the kitchen. There was a half bath on the left. The door was closed, and I opened it to peek in. Empty. I slowed down and peered around the corner toward the front door. Dark, empty. A few more steps and I was in the kitchen. Empty. I stayed crouched down, which was a bit of an effort. My legs were sore, but rest wasn't on the agenda. Not yet. I opened a few drawers and peeked in. I couldn't find a knife or pair of scissors anywhere. Maybe there was something in the upper cabinets, but I didn't want to risk standing up. I didn't have time to look for a weapon right now. I needed to get help.

I looked around for the phone, but it wasn't on its base. Caroline wasn't the type of person to not return the phone where it should be. I slid into the dining room, staying close to the wall. I went up the stairs and made my way to Caroline's room. The phone was gone. Drawers were open, books were askew. A picture of Caroline and G.T. was lying on the floor, the glass on the frame crushed.

I hurried to the guest room, but wasn't surprised to see

that that phone was gone as well. Wallace was being very careful. The room had been prepared for Levi's arrival, but a search had taken place. Books askew, drawers open.

I looked out the window, toward the barn. What should I do? Wallace hadn't killed me when he had the chance. But he'd thrown me down the cellar stairs and must have plans to come back. Seeing Mark lying at Ben's Barbershop flashed through my mind. I felt sick. Caroline was vulnerable. I couldn't leave her, but I needed to if I was going to get help.

The barn door was open. I could see Wallace pacing around the workshop. He had a full view of the kitchen from there—I couldn't risk him seeing me trying to find a knife. Wallace looked like he was shouting. I thought about the guest apartment. I'd given Caroline a hard time about the landline she insisted on running out there, but I wouldn't do that again. There was a separate entrance to the apartment, and a hidden key. Should I go there, or try to get away?

A car pulled up into the driveway. It barely stopped before the driver had opened the door and turned off the lights. I didn't recognize the car. I tried to cry out, but before I did the figure went into the barn. Was that Levi? Probably. Who else could it be? Jeff Paisley would have shown up with lights blazing. Oh, Levi.

I swallowed the bile that was rising in my throat. Levi was in trouble. I had to go out to the guest house and hope the phone was there. If it wasn't, I needed to figure out how to help Levi, before it was too late.

Time was running out.

chapter 34

Just as I was about to slip out the front door, I remembered the motion-sensor lights. After G.T. died, Caroline was nervous about staying at the cottage by herself. Now that made more sense to me. I couldn't imagine what it had been like for her all these years, looking over her shoulder, living a double life. Trying to keep her son in the dark. For the umpteenth time, I wished G.T. and I had had a chance to talk. What did he think about Caroline's past? I'd never be able to ask him, but I could do what he'd want me to and protect Caroline.

I'd had Pat Reed come out and install the motion-sensor lights. The lights in the back had already showed Wallace where I was. I turned the light off. The last thing I needed was a spotlight while I was trying to be stealthy. I should have pushed harder to have an alarm system put in the house. Budgets had been tight, and that was a next-summer project.

After tonight, I'd move it up. But first, we needed to get through tonight.

I went out the front door and crossed over toward the barn. The building was lit up like a Christmas tree. To avoid the light I scurried through the front yard, looping back toward the back of the barn. I walked by my car. The alarm light blinked inside. Hitting the alarm button was a habit from living in the city. As was not putting a Hide-a-Key on the car itself. Pat Reed always teased me about the habit, but given all that had been going on, the habit was a good one. Not very helpful at this particular moment. I didn't want to touch the car and scare Wallace Struggs away just so he could come back again and inflict revenge. We needed him behind bars again for Caroline to be safe.

The back of the barn was windowless, with one door for access. The windows were on the lake side of the building so the occupants of the guest apartment could have a nice view. Tonight the water was flat and dark, no moon reflecting on it. Ice hadn't formed yet, but would soon.

There was a key hidden in a false rock that had been part of the landscaping. Caroline had told me about it when I moved back to Orchard. The crushed-gravel walks that wound around the property had breaks that featured native plants, small bushes, mulch, and rocks that made it look like it had been there forever. I'd tried to avoid the gravel paths because of the noise, but after I tripped for the third time, I decided to risk it. I held my breath. I was near the back of the barn. Where was the stone? I got down on my hands and knees, riffling through the mulch to the right of the door. No fake stones over there. I moved to the left of the door and found a clump of three stones. My hands were numb, so it was hard to tell which stone was the hiding place for the key. The second rock was the right one. My fingers had difficulty grabbing the sliding door, but I finally did it. When did it get so cold?

I stood up shakily, leaning on the side of the barn to hold me up. I pulled the storm door open and blocked it open with my body. I felt my way to the door handle and found the lock. I fumbled with the lock a couple of times, desperately afraid I'd drop the key. I finally got it in and turned the door handle.

I pushed the door open. I took a deep breath, grateful for the smooth operation of the hinges. I hoped that no one felt the frigid air flowing by me. I walked in. I closed both doors behind me, keeping my hand on both to ensure silence. Thankfully there was light from the barn that illuminated the lake side of the barn. I took a step into the room and again let my eyes adjust for a moment.

If the house had been searched, the apartment had been destroyed. Furniture had been overturned. Lamps were on the floor, the kitchen table was askew. All of the chairs were tipped over. The apartment had two large closets. One was cedar lined, and used for off-season clothing. The other was lined with shelves, and used for family storage. Their doors were wide open, and it looked like every box had been taken out and opened. Heaps of clothing and detritus were piled all around the room. I hurried across the room to the landline. Damn, the base was empty. I should have been prepared for that, but I was still crushed. I ran to the kitchen, sliding open the cutlery drawer. The knives were gone. I looked over at the knife block. Empty.

I brushed back tears of frustration. I hadn't found Levi but I had to go for help. I couldn't stay here any longer worrying about what Wallace's next move would be. This area was busy in the summer months, but there were only a few hardy souls who stayed during the winter, despite the beauty of the landscape. Most of the houses weren't winterized. I racked my brain. Was Jimmy Murphy here or did he go down to DC to spend the holidays with his son? Why couldn't I remember? He was the closest neighbor, but if he wasn't home, then I'd have to double back to get out to the main road. Unless I could break into his house. People were notorious for leaving keys around. Better to—

What was that noise?

I looked around the room. No one had come in. I heard it again. A breathy grunt. I looked down at one of the piles of clothes on the floor. It moved, and groaned again. I walked over carefully and realized that the heap was actually a person. Wallace. He was out cold. I put two fingers against his neck. He had a pulse, but his eyes didn't open at my touch. I ran my hand along the back of his head and felt something warm and sticky. Blood.

"Wallace?" I whispered as softly as I could, right into his ear. He didn't flinch. When did this happen? Did Levi do it? I almost called out, but stopped myself. I hadn't really seen who got out of the car. I scanned his body quickly, patting his pockets. His gun was gone.

I stood and headed for the door. My boots weren't perfect for running, but running they'd do, because I needed to go and get help. And I didn't even know whom I needed to be saved from anymore.

As I opened the back door, the door from the main space flew open, flooding the room with light. I looked up and saw Rina Sanske at the same time she saw me.

"Could this day get any worse?" she said, flipping her perfect ponytail. She moved her hand toward me. The shadows played games, but the shape of the gun was clear.

chapter 35

"What the hell are you doing here?" Rina asked me.
"I could ask you the same thing," I said, almost tripping over myself as I backed away from her.

"Beckett doesn't even know how to do his own laundry," she said. "Yet again, I'm cleaning up his mess. I guess you know the story behind this family reunion."

"I do," I said. Unlike Wallace, Rina wasn't out of her mind. She was steady, focused, and reasonable. Which made her even more deadly. Better to keep her talking.

"How long have you known about Caroline's troubled past? Longer than me, I'll bet. Amateurs. I can't believe I got this idiot out of jail so he could live out his own revenge fantasy."

"You got him out of jail? How?"

"You're a curious one, aren't you? Let's just say I was

able to help Wallace make a deal with the authorities that got him an early release. I fed him some information that he could use as leverage."

"So he came back here?"

"We needed him back here to help us run part of the operation. Or, I thought we did. I should have known that Orchard was too good to be true."

"What do you mean?"

Rina paused, and shrugged her shoulders. "May as well tell you. You won't get a chance to tell anyone. My business partners decided to use Orchard as one of the nexus points for our operation," she said, sounding bored. "Close enough to Boston and New York, but far enough away to be out of the limelight. Wallace was the one who suggested it. Idiot. I'm surrounded by idiot men. Was your ex-husband an idiot too? I've heard all about your little sob story. Gossip is seriously the only thing that has kept me sane in this sleepy town."

"What did you do to Wallace?" I asked.

"I didn't do anything," she said. "He did it to himself. If he'd done what he was supposed to, and gotten the documents, we'd both be on our way up north now."

"Documents?"

"Don't play dumb with me, Ruth. You're smarter than most of the people in this godforsaken town. Here, make yourself useful. Tie the idiot up." Rina reached over and grabbed the roll of duct tape that was sitting on a box, tossing it toward me. I caught it and walked over toward Wallace. With the lights on, I could see more of his injuries. His lip was bleeding and his right eye was swollen shut. The man who had tossed me down the stairs was gone.

"You're pretty tough," I said, looking over my shoulder at Rina. "He's almost twice your size."

"I am used to being underestimated. It used to piss me off, but now I use it to my advantage. Play the helpless female and get a bunch of men to do my bidding. And take all the risks. Get to it—tie him up." She motioned to him with the gun.

I tore off a long piece of tape and bound Wallace's feet together. "That's good enough. Now get up and come with me. I'll deal with him later."

I walked over to Rina, who stepped back, keeping the gun trained on me.

"What about Beckett?" I said, walking down the hall toward the workshop. "Where does he fit in?"

"He's the biggest idiot of them all. Talk about spoiling a good thing. We were all set up to be a perfect distribution center in a quiet, unassuming little bookshop, then he decides to get smart and start shaking things up and working with Kim Gray, making grand plans and drawing attention to himself and to me. Yeesh."

"So he's in business with you?"

"No, he's a front. I've been using him for years—whatever business he happens to be running at the time. He seems to think that he just pulls money out of thin air—that his businesses do well because of his skill. Can you imagine? Do you think he came up with the idea to open up this bookstore on his own? Of course he didn't. I suggested it. Even drove him past the old bank a few times. He took credit for the idea, of course. I could play him like a fiddle. He thinks a great deal of himself and has never once questioned why someone like me would be with a toad like him. Now, keep moving."

She almost made me feel bad for Beckett. Almost.
"Where do you want me to go?"

"I need you to find the documents Caroline kept on the
clocks."

"Documents? Clocks?"

"Don't play dumb, Ruth," she said, growing impatient.
"It doesn't suit you, and it aggravates me. One thing I've
always liked about you is your intellect. Now, where are the
documents? Caroline told Wallace about them, thinking it
would buy her time. Which it did. But time is at a premium,
and the payment is due. Where are they?"

"Caroline took them to my apartment earlier today. We
can go get them."

"And run into Jeff Paisley or that puppy dog, Ben
Clover?"

"I wouldn't call Ben a puppy dog," I said.

"Ugh," she said, disgusted. "Please, just stop talking. We
don't really need them, I suppose. It's just such a shame. All
of that record keeping for years going to waste. Repair meth-
ods and points of contact that could be studied and used as
we build our enterprise . . ." She trailed off as we entered the
workshop. All the lights were on. Crates were open, but from
what I could see, no clocks were damaged in the search. I
suspected Wallace had something to do with that. I doubted
Rina held horologist's aspirations. "Plans are shifting, but
what else is new? First that moron Mark refuses to continue
to help me, even though we'd set him up to do exactly that.
I'd like to know what kind of spell you're casting over at that
shop of yours. Perfectly good criminals going straight for
minimum wage. I tried to make him see reason, but in the
end I took care of that employee-liability problem with a

shiny watch that he just couldn't help but obsess over and one of Beckett's favorite ties. I couldn't exactly have him working right across the street from our enterprise."

"Took care of—you killed Mark? But I thought you were having dinner in Marytown?" I felt sick, remembering Mark's empty eyes staring up at me.

"Sit down on that stool over there and shut up." Rina kept the gun trained on me and walked over to one of the crates that was open. She rummaged around a bit and then pulled out a clock. She turned it over and looked at the base, which was marked with a small black x in the center. "Gotcha." She put the clock on the workbench, next to a couple of others.

"So I guess you and Beckett weren't having dinner?"

"What did I tell you?"

"Come on, Rina. I've got questions; you've got answers. I want to know how you pulled this off."

"Surprised you, huh? Well, I guess since I'm going to kill you anyway. Beckett wanted to hang around, go undercover, and check out the open house. We both agreed to use the Marytown dinner in case anyone asked."

"Beckett didn't catch on?"

"No. I even had him convinced he was the prime suspect, and I was doing him a favor. And now he actually is the prime suspect. I made sure of that this afternoon."

"When you attacked Tuck?" To my horror, rather than flinching she smiled a bit.

"Losing him was such a shame," she said, systematically sorting through the rest of the crate. "I'm going to have to figure out what to tell Fred."

"Fred? Tuck's uncle? Is he one of your partners?" I

realized that she thought that she'd succeeded in killing Tuck. At least I had that over her.

"Fred and I have been friends for a long time." Rina came up with another clock with an *x* on the bottom. It went to the workbench, and she dove into the crate one more time, never taking her eyes off me. "Such a shame about Tuck. He was an integral part of the operation, but far too young to understand the nuances. He was too easily influenced. Imagine wanting to give up the family business in order to stay in Orchard and make coffee? What's wrong with people?

"Oh, I forgot to tell you. Jeff won't be coming to your rescue," she said, lifting another clock out of the box and placing it on the workbench. "I texted him back with your phone and told him you'd made a mistake, the picture was inverted. That you and Caroline and Zane were all having a good laugh about it. Handy thing, texting. No voices to recognize." Oh, Jeff, please don't believe her, I thought. Please be on your way. "Calling 911 was riskier, but I did that too. I let them know that Caroline was safe and sound. I apologized for the false alarm. Apparently there's a lot happening in the Berkshires tonight. The dispatcher was glad she could redeploy the trooper to another location. Of course they have to send someone eventually, but I'm planning on being long gone by then."

"What are you doing with the clocks?"

Rina regarded me with a mixture of contempt and pity. "It's not the clocks I want, it's the cases. Mark packed them for us. Part of the merchandise we were going to try and move."

"What's in them? Stolen jewels?"

"Nothing so exotic. Just plain old drugs." She rolled her eyes. "Don't look so shocked, Ruth."

"I hate it when people use clocks for nefarious purposes," I said.

"Did you just say 'nefarious'? You are hopeless, you know that? Time to join the real world, Ruth. Oh, wait. You'll be leaving it soon enough. You may as well hold on to your ideals."

I looked around the workshop. I'd spent a lot of time out here these past few weeks. Maybe if I could distract Rina for a moment . . . maybe I'd have a chance.

"What are you looking for?" she asked, tensing and training the gun on me again.

"Pat was going to leave one of my models out here," I lied. "We need it for the Town Hall meeting tomorrow."

"It is a shame you'll miss it. If that fool Kim Gray can pull it off with her partner in crime behind bars . . ."

"Pull what off?"

"Taking over the Town Hall. Destroying your business. Now that I have wasted months of work on this town I am happy that Beckett's silly little side plan will drag Orchard down too. As much as I would have preferred him to keep a low profile, at least there is a sort of satisfaction in knowing that your precious, quirky downtown will be replaced by a bunch of shiny chain stores."

"So, what's next? You just kill me and drive away?" I asked.

"Well, since I am actually back in Boston having dinner right now, I couldn't kill you, could I? That would have to be someone else," she said, smirking. "A few friends willing to provide an alibi."

"Business partners?" I said, rolling my eyes. I needed to keep her talking. I looked around, trying to see what I could use as a weapon. There wasn't much, not out. There were a couple of grandfather clocks in the middle of the space. Maybe if I could navigate Rina near one and knock it onto her? If nothing else it could block me from bullets.

"Business partners, yes. Handy people to know, though this particular partner hooked me up with Wallace. Not the best connection he's made for me. I suppose, being fair, how would he have known that Wallace wanted to reconnect with his family so desperately?"

"How did Wallace know that Caroline was in Orchard?"

Rina shook her head. "I hate coincidence, don't you? Apparently there was a remembrance service or something for your grandfather at some clock event or another. Right after he died?"

"At the annual meeting of the Massachusetts Horological Society. Caroline and I didn't go."

"There was some sort of slide show, with a picture of Caroline and your grandfather. Wallace was there. He's the one who brought Orchard up as a possible business site. Suggested using clocks. He had his own 'master plan.' The fool." She snorted and began to count the clocks she'd lined up on the bench.

We both heard the noise at the same time. A slamming car door. Her spine stiffened and I sensed my moment was coming. When she turned toward the door, I darted to the right. She regrouped and shot at me, but her shot was wild. I dove at her midsection, and we both tumbled. I heard the gun clatter away. Rina was strong, stronger than I was. But I had fear on my side, and we kept wrestling. Finally I heard someone calling my name, and I stopped fighting and looked up. Ben Clover was standing there, holding Rina's gun, looking like he wasn't quite sure how he got there.

I rolled off her toward Ben.

"You okay?" he asked, not taking his eyes off of Rina, who appeared to have lost consciousness at some point during our struggle. Thankfully. It seemed like she would never stop talking.

"Been better," I said. "Is Jeff here?"

"He's on his way."

I rolled over to my knees and sat back on my heels. "I don't think I've ever been so happy to see anyone," I said to Ben. He offered me his solid, warm hand, and pulled me up to standing. "What are you doing here?"

"You were right, earlier. I've been such a jerk. I came out to see if that dinner invitation still stood. Saw this place all lit up. The instant I shut my door I looked up and I saw Rina standing there holding a gun. And then I saw you—" He paused and I stared right into those gorgeous eyes of his. "Hey, are you all right?"

All of a sudden I felt like I was going to faint. Ben put his arm around me, keeping the gun trained on our dazed adversary with his free hand.

"I will be. It's been a rough night," I said.

chapter 36

I woke up sitting in a chair in Caroline's hospital room. Jeff let me ride with Caroline to the hospital when I promised him we'd talk in the morning and agreed to talk to Ro Troisi when she came by the hospital.

It took me a minute to realize what had woken me up. Caroline was saying my name.

"Ruth?"

"I'm here. Right here."

"Where's Levi?"

"Turns out his car broke down again. Pat drove to get him and will bring him here."

"Where's Wallace?"

"He's in another room, with police guarding the door. Rina clocked him pretty good."

"Rina?"

"It's a long story. She's telling it to the police right now. Or rather, she's probably lawyered up by now. But I'll bet Beckett is singing."

"He's confessing? To what?" she said, rubbing the bridge of her nose.

"To being an idiot, I think. By the way?" I said, stretching my legs out in front of me.

"Yes?"

"You're going to be all right. Nothing is broken, miraculously. But you are really banged up and have a slight concussion. Your shoulder's a mess."

"I was sure everything was going to be all right the minute I saw you in the basement," she said, neatly arranging her blanket around herself, smoothing the wrinkles out.

"Well, I wasn't. I was pretty much terrified."

"I thought Wallace was going to kill me," she said softly. I reached over and took her hand.

"He's going back to jail. This time, here in the States. He'll be gone for a long time. He's not ever going to hurt you, I promise."

"Unless he cuts another deal. He told me that's how—"

"He won't cut a deal," I said, stopping her. "You're safe." I squeezed her hand and did my best to smile.

"How did he find me?" Caroline asked.

"He saw your picture in a slide show at G.T.'s memorial service at the annual meeting of the Massachusetts Horological Society. He found Zane—"

"Is Zane all right?"

"He is, or he will be. Ro came by earlier to get my statement, and let me know they'd found Zane."

"Thank heaven. I owe so much to Zane. When I came

back here, with a different name, a new identity, I tried to make a different life. But I was a watchmaker. I couldn't give that up. I knew it was a mistake to reconnect with Zane, but I couldn't stay away. He was my only link to my old life and Wallace exploited that. He knew I would go back to Zane. I trusted him with my secret, and he kept it."

"He almost died keeping it. Zane didn't tell him where you were. Ro said your phone number wasn't even in his phone. Wallace only knew that you lived in or near Orchard because of that stupid slide show. I'm sorry you've had to go through this," I said. "Now I understand why you didn't want to be on videos for the shop. I can't imagine how hard it has been to look over your shoulder for so many years."

"When your grandfather was alive, I wasn't afraid. Or as afraid," she said, playing with her wedding band.

"I'm so sorry . . ."

"Ruth, let me finish. Do you know what Wallace said to me earlier? That he'd been trying to get me alone for days, but I was always with someone when he saw me around the shop. He knew his disguise wouldn't work on me—you only fell for it because you didn't know any better. He tried to follow me home, but someone was always with me. Wallace was able to control me when I was young because I was alone. I'm not alone now."

"No, you're not. Neither am I." I brushed the tears from my eyes.

"Does Levi know what happened?" she asked, sighing.

"He thinks that there was a robbery gone bad," I said.

"I'd like to keep it that way." She bit her lip.

"Caroline," I said gently. "You have to tell him the truth. You don't have to tell everyone, but you need to stop living a lie. It isn't good for you. You said G.T. knew about what happened in Europe."

"He knew everything."

"That probably meant that you could relax around him and be yourself. I can't imagine how hard it has been to be living a lie for all these years." I leaned over and took her hand in mine. She squeezed it back.

"Not really a lie. Another life."

"Levi needs to know the truth. Together you can make a decision about how to handle it."

"What happens if he wants to see his father?"

"Then he sees his father. Caroline, if I've learned anything these past few weeks it's that you can't control life, or what happens. You also can't control other people."

Caroline was quiet for a minute. "How can I tell him?"

"How about if I tell him what I know and then you can tell us both the rest?" I would try and run interference for Caroline, but I could also be a sounding board for Levi.

"He is going to be angry," she said, her voice breaking a bit.

"I don't think so. If he is, we'll work it through."

"We will?"

"Caroline, we're family. That's what family does. For better or for worse, we stick together."

I was bone-tired and sore all over from sleeping in a chair at the hospital, but I didn't want to leave Caroline alone. Around three in the morning, there was a knock on the door. I turned around and saw a tall, handsome young man fill the doorway. He had his mother's coloring, but looked an awful lot like his father.

"Levi?" I whispered. I stood up.

"Ruth?" he asked. He walked over and gave me a big hug, which I returned. He looked over at his mother.

"Is she all right?"

"She will be, now that she knows you're here safe and sound."

"What happened? I heard something about a robbery?"

"I'll let her tell you. She really is going to be fine," I said. "You may as well go home and get some sleep."

"Nothing doing. I'm sitting with her. You need the rest more than I do. Pat tells me you have a meeting in the morning."

"Yeesh, I'd almost forgotten. All right, you win. Once you've spoken to your mother, give me a call. We have a lot to catch up on."

I went out to the hall and saw Ben sitting on one of the chairs in the hallway.

"What are you doing here?" I asked.

"I came down with Nadia after Jeff was done talking to her. She's with Tuck."

"How is he?"

"He'll be alright, but they're going to keep him here for a few days. How's Caroline?"

"She'll be all right."

"What happened out there?" Ben asked. He hadn't gotten up.

"It's Caroline's story to tell. Complicated family stuff."

"Complicated family stuff. Sounds familiar." Ben looked down at his hands.

"Always happy to swap stories." Ben was silent, so I kept talking. "Well, I'm going to head home and get some sleep before the Town Hall meeting."

"You don't think they'll postpone it?" Ben finally looked up.

I shook my head. "Saturday is New Year's Eve. The lease will be up. They have to come to a decision. Kim Gray has doubled down, and some sort of new agreement has to be in place by midnight, which means we have Friday to hammer out the business details. First we have to have the town meeting in the morning."

"I'm sure it will all work out." Ben sounded distracted and uninterested. Maybe I'd been reading him wrong these past few weeks. I waited for Ben to ask for more details or to offer me a ride home, but he didn't. Granted, it was three o'clock in the morning, but he really hadn't talked to me since the scene out at the barn.

"I didn't thank you for coming to my rescue," I said.

"You didn't need any rescuing," he said. "I felt bad about the way we'd left things."

"I'm glad you showed up when you did."

"I'm sure Jeff wishes it could have been him. He saw me leaving, since he was at your place. Anyway, I told him where I was going. He called me a few minutes later and was on his way out after you'd left him messages. Wanted to give me a heads-up. Is he coming to pick you up?"

"Jeff? No, he's not. Ro came by a little earlier to take my statement, and I told her I'd come by tomorrow to sign it. I'd imagine Jeff's pretty busy."

"Hopefully he'll be able to wrap things up so he can have New Year's Eve off."

"Why, are you doing something with him?" I asked.

"Me? No. I assumed you both would have plans."

"With each other?"

"Yes, of course."

"Why would you think that?"

"You and he have dinner with Caroline every week. Then, the other night, after Mark died, he stayed over. It's cool—I hope you're both happy." He mumbled this last part.

I was too tired to deal with this in a grown-up fashion. Instead, I resorted to Grade School Ruth, frustrated when the obvious remained unnoticed. I whined. "Dude, you've got to catch up on the gossip train in this town. You're way behind. Did you know that Jeff had dinner with Caroline and G.T. once a week? They've included me in the ritual. As for the other night, he did spend the night at the Cog & Sprocket. At my invitation. I spent it out at the cottage, with Caroline."

"But I thought . . ."

"No, you didn't think," I said, stamping my foot a bit. I needed to get back on the rails, fast. "You assumed. Two different things. Yeesh. From now on, Ben, if you have a question, ask me. Don't mope around, all right? We're both too old for that. What is it with people in this town?"

I turned and tromped off down the hall. I walked out to the front of the hospital to see if someone had the phone number of a cab, but I needn't have bothered. Pat Reed was sitting in a chair, arms crossed, sound asleep.

chapter 37

I'd called Kristen Gauger first thing Friday morning and told her about the cryptic conversation Rina and I had in the barn. I'd only had a couple of hours of sleep, but I was wired.

"So, she intimated that Kim Gray and Beckett had hatched a plan, but didn't mention specifics?"

"Right. Maybe you can talk to her? Or to Beckett?"

"Let me call Jeff Paisley and see what the situation is."

I puttered around my apartment while I was waiting for Kristen to call back. That translated to me cleaning the sink twice and thinking about taking out the garbage. Not much was getting done these days.

"Working on it," she said when she finally called. "From what little I could find out, looks like Beckett Green is more of a victim in all of this than a guilty party."

"He isn't going to jail?"

"Not only is he not going to jail, he is shaping up to be the star witness for the prosecution."

"Good to know. What about the Town Hall?"

"I've passed everything on to Nancy Reed. You work on your presentation, do the changes we talked about, get the proposal ready and make copies."

K risten met me at the Cog & Sprocket in the morning. We walked over to the old Town Hall together.

"I thought the meeting was going to be at the school gym?" I asked, smoothing my coat over my thick oatmeal-colored sweater and plum fitted skirt and my run-free tights. That was as professional as I got this early in the morning. The meeting was scheduled for ten o'clock. I was going to get there early, but I was a jumble of nerves.

"They moved it at the last minute. The school has been closed for the holidays, and they decided not to turn the heat on for one meeting."

"I wonder if they were going to tell me."

Kristen laughed. "Probably not."

"I'm glad you're here. I need someone on my side today. Did you get to talk to Beckett?"

"No. By the time I got into town he'd gone home. Or somewhere. I couldn't track him down. But I did have another idea that I hope worked out."

"Care to share it with me?"

"No. I don't want to get your hopes up."

T he town meeting was packed. I'd like to think it would have been anyway, but today there was extra interest. One of the selectmen, Jimmy Murphy, had saved us seats up front.

"You're back?" I said, sliding over and giving him a kiss on the cheek.

"I wouldn't miss this for all the world, darlin'," he said.

The meeting was turned over to Kim Gray, who ran through the three options for the Town Hall. The inflection of her voice betrayed her preference, which was that the operations of the Town Hall be reverted to me completely, unless I turned it over to the town of Orchard to use as they saw fit. The implied "they" being Kim Gray. The other option was that I lease the Town Hall back to Orchard for a dollar a year plus an increased operations budget, but that I be allowed to renovate the clock tower.

"Of course, Ms. Clagan is several key pieces of paper-work short of the required documentation needed in order to get this option fully vetted," Kim said.

"No, she's not." Nancy Reed emerged from the crowd and stepped up to the front of the room. She had on a tweed skirt and black jacket. The black jersey shirt she wore had a slight cowl, and Nancy wore a double strand of pearls that I recognized as my grandmother's.

My grandmother had made few bequests in her will, but one of them was her pearl jewelry. Nancy had apologized for that several times and tried to give them back, but I insisted she keep them. Far be it from me to question my grandmother's last wishes. Seeing the pearls today, I was glad Nancy had them to give her courage.

"What's up, Nancy?" someone called out.

"Mrs. Reed, the conversation has been closed."

"I have new information that I'd like to put before the meeting," Nancy said. "Trust me, you're going to want to hear it. Beckett Green and I had coffee this morning."

"Does the Sleeping Latte deliver to the jail?" someone shouted. Most people laughed.

"Beckett isn't in jail. He is heartsick about what has happened and wants to make amends to all of us," she said, and the room rumbled with whispers. "Now, now, we can debate his sincerity later.

"He let me know about plans he had to take over the Town Hall, tear it down, and move in several chain stores. As many of you know, Beckett's business partner is under arrest for the murder of Mark Pine and the attempted murder of Tuck Powers. Other charges are pending against Mr. Struggs. Anyway, there's a lot of information to go through, but it seems that Beckett had the backing of some of the Board of Selectmen and the town manager, at least according to the one person I was able to contact." Nancy lowered her reading glasses on her nose and looked out into the crowd, taking a slow sweep of the standing-room-only crowd. The room got quiet and Nancy lowered her voice, sounding more conversational. These were her friends and neighbors, after all.

"I can't imagine that's really true, can you?" she continued. "I mean, come on. Choosing the interests of a stranger over Ruth Clagan? Thom Clagan's granddaughter? When the Clagan family is one of the oldest in Orchard? Beckett indicated to me that he is dropping his interest in the Town Hall. He is going to focus on getting his shop open next month. And being a better citizen of Orchard. We talked a lot about that." There was laughter in the crowd.

"We all know that the Town Hall needs work," she continued. "There's a group of us who are willing to serve on the renovation board, making sure the work that Kim Gray has been putting off finally gets done." Kim Gray moved to take back the podium, but Nancy blocked her. "Don't you start with me, Kim. You know the funds have been in place to get a new heating system, finish upgrading the electrics, and to fix the roof. You put them off until the lease dispute was over. Well, I say it's over. Let's get the heating system replaced and get the roof fixed. Finishing the electrics will help with the clock tower, but it will also make the building safer and more viable. There are plenty of taxpaying folks in town who could use the work this winter, so let's get it done.

"Now, friends, since we're here to wrap up some business before the New Year, I think we should take one more vote. There are plans afoot to restore the clock tower. Ruth can talk about them if you'd like, but I think most of you have heard about them. So I think we should vote on that today. Let's get the New Year started with a bang."

"Mrs. Reed, we don't have the funding . . ." Kim Gray said, trying once more to retake the podium. Again, Nancy blocked her.

"No, we don't. But there's a nonprofit that Grover Winter set up a while ago. Some funds have been raised, and we've recently gotten two grants that will match funds—"

"As long as the funds were raised by the end of the year," Kim Gray said. "Last I heard, you were twenty-five thousand dollars short."

"Not anymore." Nancy turned toward the town administrator, giving her a full-wattage smile. "A donation came in today, for fifty thousand dollars."

"I don't believe you," Kim Gray said.

"You don't believe me? Really?" Nancy looked shocked and turned back to the crowd. I bit the inside of my cheek so I wouldn't burst out laughing. "Did you hear that, folks?

She doesn't believe me. Isn't that rich?" A few people laughed, but to her credit, Kim Gray barely flinched. "As a matter of fact, I have a copy of the check. From Beckett Green. The original has been deposited in the Clock Tower Fund account." Nancy handed the copy to Kim, who barely looked at it.

"Well," Kim said, "we still have two options. We all know that this old building is going to be a money pit. I propose that we tear it down, or—" The capacity crowd started to erupt.

I got up and walked to the front of the room. Nancy stepped aside and blocked Kim from my path. I wasn't sure if she was more worried about her or about me. A few people hushed the others, and after a few seconds the room was quiet.

"No one was more surprised than I was when I inherited this old building," I said. "You've all seen the photos of what it was like back in the day, when the clock tower was in operation and the gardens were kept up. Nadia Wint has put the only film we know of showing what it was like when the clock tower worked on our website. It's grainy, it's old, there's no sound. But it's exciting. Really thrilling. The clock tower was a destination for a lot of people."

"I remember it from when I was a little girl," someone said from the crowd. "We'd come every week to see the dancing figures. It was magic."

"I always wish I could have seen it in person. But I felt like I had, from the stories my grandfather Thom would tell me," I said. The crowd grew silent at the mention of his name.

"I think that the clock tower will bring a lot of tourists to town," I continued. "But more than that, look around you. We're all gathered here, at this wonderful old Town Hall, for this meeting. Most everyone has been here at least once this year, whether it was for a meeting, a play, a craft fair, or a speaker from the historical society." Heads nodded.

"We've had the building assessed," I continued, looking around. "It is old, but it is solid. The new heating system and roof are the last two major repairs that need to be made. Plumbing is up to date. The electrics just need to be wired. The wheelchair lift is in place, and the ramps are all up to code. The stage area even has a new light and sound system. Any other work is cosmetic. Paint jobs, some woodwork repair. This building is the heart of Orchard. I don't want to operate it, but I will, if I need to. I'd rather the town keep using it, and operating it, for the greater good of everyone. Orchard is at a turning point. Let's continue along the path you all set out on years ago. We don't want to change Orchard, we want to get her moving again. Now's the time. You all know that the clock tower is a personal dream that my grandfather passed down to me. Now it's become a mission, and a few more folks are as excited as I am. Next December, I want to ring in the New Year from this clock tower. What do you say?"

Mac Clark poured me another glass of wine. He and Ada had come by to check in about the meeting. We'd moved a few chairs into a circle in the shop and were enjoying the basket of goodies the Clarks had brought over. Wine, sharp cheese, tart apple slices, fresh bread. It wasn't the fanciest of lunches, but it was perfect for the day. I was so tired after the meeting I could barely tell which end was up, so I added sparkling cider to my glass of wine. Not very tasty, but not likely to put me to sleep either.

"Tell me that last part again," he said gleefully.

"Mac, she's told us three times already," Ada said, her hand on her lower back.

"I know, but I love the part about the votes being overwhelming to support the Town Hall restoration and the clock tower. I wish we'd been there."

"I wish the baby coming wasn't a false alarm," Ada said, disappointed.

"I do too, for your sake," I said, sipping at my wine concoction. If I added a few mulling spices, it really wouldn't be too bad. "But obviously he, or she, wants to be born in the New Year! Anyway, Nancy is really the one who saved the tower." I raised my glass in her direction. She lifted her glass in return and took a healthy swig.

Pat Reed put his strong, plaid arm around his wife and kissed her forehead. "She was great, wasn't she?"

"She was indeed," I said. "Are you going to run for the Board of Selectmen? I saw Jimmy Murphy talking to you after the meeting."

"I am considering it," Nancy said, playing coy.

We all laughed. Another job for the very busy Nancy Reed, but one for which she was well suited. I looked around this circle of people. My friends. Flo sat on the other side of Nancy Reed, smiling. Moira and Ben leaned against the counter, too busy snacking to join in the chatter. I was actively avoiding looking at Ben, which meant I couldn't keep my eyes off him. He had done his version of dressing up for the meeting, and I had to say, that crisp white shirt and red tie under his standard leather bomber jacket was really doing it for me. He flashed me a smile as he pushed back his unruly reddish blond hair from his forehead.

"That means she's made up her mind," Pat said. He yawned, shook his head, and then looked down at his watch. "I should get going to the hospital to pick up Caroline and Levi."

"I'll come with you," I said. "My car is out at the cottage."

"I'll help you clean up and give you a ride out to the cottage," Ben said quickly. "Five people would be a tight fit in Pat's car," he added, popping another apple slice into his mouth.

"That's fine," I said, feeling my face turn the same color as my hair.

The party broke up shortly afterward. Ben helped carry the leftovers upstairs. Blue and Bezel didn't hear us come in, so we caught them spooning. Blue was excited to see the possibilities of leftovers coming in the door and his tail thumped the floor the moment he heard us put the food on the kitchen table. Bezel tried to pretend she hadn't been sleeping against Blue's side. The two of them stretched languidly and then trotted over in unison.

Ben leaned over and said hello to both of our furry masters.

"Give them some of the cheese—Bezel will be your best friend for a nibble," I said.

Ben went to get it, and I put the glasses in the dishwasher.

"Ruth, I wanted you to know, those flowers were for you," Ben said as he tore up a few little pieces of cheese for Bezel, who hopped onto a kitchen chair, expectantly licking her chops. Blue chomped the piece Ben held out for him, swallowing it in one gulp.

"What flowers?" I asked with my back to him, even though I knew.

"The flowers I brought by the day after Mark died. But then Jeff was with you—"

"He wasn't with me," I said, trying not to break the glasses as my grip tightened.

"I know that, now," he said softly. "I don't normally listen to the rumormongers, but I saw you both that morning . . . I shouldn't have jumped to conclusions and I'm sorry I didn't talk to you. But I'm not the only one who got the wrong impression, you know."

"I know that. I didn't realize I was such a source of gossip for this town."

"Ruth Clagan, you have been the source of gossip in this town since you arrived." I could hear him stepping closer behind me. "You're an enigma."

"Only if you don't ask me what you want to know," I said. I turned and looked at Ben, and didn't try to look away this time. He was one handsome man. Trouble in blue jeans and boots. I reached over and rubbed my knuckles over the buttons of his shirt. "All you have to do is ask," I said, looking up at him.

"Ask you what?" Moira asked, coming up the stairs.

"Ask me if I was seeing Jeff Paisley," I said, clearing my throat and taking a small step back from Ben. "Which I, for the record, am not. At least not romantically. We're friends, good friends. That's all."

Moira had the good grace to look abashed. "It's been a tough few days," she said.

Blue nuzzled against Ben's leg, looking for more treats.

"It has," I agreed. "A really tough few days. At least Jeff is getting some of the credit for breaking the case and exposing this criminal element."

"Thanks to you," she said, allowing Bezel to gingerly sniff her arm for signs of snacks. "Any word on how Tuck is doing?"

"I called Nadia this morning," Ben said. "She said he's still in rough shape, but he's awake."

"I wonder if he'll be in any legal trouble?" Moira asked.

"I have no idea," I said. "I think that it is going to take Jeff some time to untangle all of this. Maybe Tuck can help."

"I don't know about the two of you, but I still can't believe that Rina is a killer," Moira said. "Never mind the rest of it. Can you imagine, Orchard was almost a hub of crime!"

"It's crazy, isn't it? But it also makes sense, now that we know what was going on," I said.

"Maybe to you," Moira said handing me the last glass from the counter.

I shoved some things around and got it in. "Is that all the dishes?"

"I'll hand-wash the serving plates," Moira said. "One more question."

"Just one more?" Ben said, grabbing a towel.

"For now. Why did Beckett help her with her alibi? About being in Marytown and not at the open house? Didn't he know what was going on?"

"According to Jeff, and Nancy, he had no idea what Rina was doing. They both believe him. Beckett didn't want us to know that he was actually slinking around the festivities even after his shop was left in the dark that night. He thought Rina was covering for him, not the other way around."

"It doesn't say much for his intellect, does it? That he had no idea?" Ben said.

"Rina said that Beckett thought everything revolved around him. I think that's true. Why would he doubt for a minute that Rina was on his team?" I wrapped the block of cheese up and put it in the refrigerator.

"Makes me almost feel sorry for him," Moira said. "Almost."

"Fifty thousand dollars goes a long way toward getting us all to forgive him," Ben said, scratching the back of his neck.

"What do you think Beckett's going to do?" I asked.

"I'll bet he's going to open the bookstore," Ben said. "I think he's really into it. Besides, at this point everything he owns is tied up with the shop. Now that he's made his contribution to the Clock Tower Fund."

"He's trying to buy his way back into our good graces," Moira said, looking skeptically down as Bezel attempted to eat the fluff on her boots in the absence of cheese.

"Obviously," Ben said.

"Question is," I said, scooping Bezel up into my arms, "will his plan work?"

chapter 38

I finished putting the candles in the cake and stood back to survey my work. *Happy Belated Birthday, Caroline!* it said in bright blue letters.

"You're sure about the decoration?" I asked Levi for the umpteenth time. The big yellow smiley face in the center of the cake didn't seem very Caroline-like to me.

"I'm sure. It's symbolic. We've decided that next year is the year of the smile. I want to remind her of that."

"This past year was a tough one," I said.

"She's had a tough few years," Levi said. I looked over at this gentle giant. We'd met in person only yesterday, but it had been quite a twenty-four hours. After we'd all had wine and cheese at the shop, Caroline, Levi, and I drove out to the cottage to have a quiet dinner together. We foraged for food and, over the meal, Caroline told Levi the story that she had held back all these years. I was mostly there for support, but I jumped in with details or when it got too hard for her. We got through it. As a family. I stayed overnight at the cottage. I haven't slept that well in years.

"So, how are you doing?" I asked, gathering plates, napkins, and forks, and putting them on the tray with the cake.

"Fine. Really, I'm good," Levi said.

"You're taking this all really well," I said, smiling at him.

"I already knew most of it," he said.

"What do you mean?" I stopped futzing with the cake and turned to look at Levi.

"When I was about seventeen, I started to ask questions about my father. My mother answered some of them, but I caught her in a couple of lies. So I started to investigate on my own."

"Did she know?"

"No, she didn't. It took some work, but eventually I found out that he was in jail, and I wrote him a letter."

"What happened?"

"It didn't have enough postage, so it came back to the shop. Thom got it in the mail, and he asked me about it. So I let him read the letter. He asked me not to send it. Then he told me about what had happened and why my mother had always pretended he was dead."

"G.T. told you everything?"

"He did. And then he asked me to keep it from my mother, to let her live her lie, for the time being. It made her feel safe. He made her feel safe. Thom was great," he said, smiling to himself. "He let me make my own decision about what to do, but he set it up so I'd do the right thing. He trusted me with the truth, but he also wanted to protect my mother no matter what."

"Sounds like him," I said. I nudged him with my shoulder, and he smiled at me.

I looked down at the cake and decided to adopt Levi's theme for the New Year. Only smiles going forward.

We lit the cake, and Levi carried it downstairs to the shop. The party was in full swing. All of the business owners were gathered, ready to welcome in the New Year. Nadia had come by, and busied herself helping replenish food and drink. When I'd thanked her for helping out, she'd shrugged her shoulders. "Just trying to be a better host," she'd said. "My New Year's resolution."

"To be a better host?"

"To be more like you," she said. She gave me a quick hug, and ran up to get more ginger ale for the punch.

Even Beckett was there. He'd shown up with a case of champagne and a lot of humility. I had to hand it to him, the bubbly wasn't the cheap stuff. Nancy wasn't willing to give him a pass yet, but Pat welcomed him at the door.

The model of the clock tower sat on the front counter, welcoming us all to dream about the next steps in restoring the building. The Clock Tower Committee had an open meeting next week at the Town Hall. This was really going to happen. It was thrilling.

When people saw Levi and me walk down the stairs, they started to sing to Caroline. By the end of the song, everyone was looking around. The guest of honor wasn't in the front of the shop. Levi put the cake on the counter and blew out the candles for his mother. I walked around the corner to the workroom. I found Caroline there, bent over a worktable. She was wearing a vision visor and had a light shining down. I walked over to see what she was working on and found three pocket watches lying on a black cloth. I sighed and shook my head. I knew that look.

"These are all part of the Winter collection," she said, not looking up from her treasure.

"They're beautiful. Valuable?"

"Yes, I think so. They could be really valuable, but I'd need to open them up." She looked up at me and removed her visor. She still looked pale, but pain was gone from her eyes. I also noticed that her hair was down, curling slightly under her chin.

"Do you want to open them up?" I asked.

"I do, once I've got both arms working again." She gestured to her sling, and shrugged her good shoulder. "I've missed working on watches. Your grandfather had me help in the shop, but we hadn't taken in watches."

"The Clagans are a clock family," I said. "But we can expand. How about if you hang out your shingle? We can fix clocks and watches. It would be good for business."

Caroline reached over and grabbed my hand. "That sounds wonderful," she said.

"Hey, ladies, we're about to welcome in the New Year. And there's a cake to be cut," Ben said, poking his head into the workroom. He looked handsome, with a black wool jacket over a crisp white shirt. The jeans were black tonight, and they looked fine.

"We're coming," Caroline said. I helped her stand up. She turned and smiled at us both. She maneuvered to the front of the store slowly, to cheers from the crowd. I saw Levi draw her in and give her a kiss on top of her head. She leaned on his chest, and looked up with a smile.

A few seconds later the clocks all began to chime. They

weren't totally in sync, but it was close enough. "Yay!" I said softly.

"Very impressive," Ben said, looking at me. "And the clocks aren't bad either. You're a woman of many talents, Ruth Clagan. Happy New Year."

"Happy New Year to you, barber Ben. Thanks again for coming to my rescue."

"My absolute pleasure," he said. He leaned down and kissed me. I closed my eyes and kissed him back.

Fireworks welcomed the New Year.

about the author

Julianne Holmes is the author of *Just Killing Time*, the debut novel in the Clock Shop Mysteries, and is the pseudonym for J. A. (Julie) Hennrikus, whose short stories have appeared in the award-winning Level Best Books. She serves on the boards of Sisters in Crime and Sisters in Crime New England, and is a member of Mystery Writers of America. She lives in Somerville, Massachusetts, and blogs with the Wicked Cozy Authors at wickedcozyauthors.com. Visit the author at julianneholmes.com.

From bestselling author
Julianne Holmes

Just Killing Time
A Clock Shop Mystery

Ruth's beloved grandfather instilled in her a love of time-pieces. Unfortunately, after her grandmother died and he remarried, Ruth and Grandpa Thom became estranged. She had wanted to reconnect after her recent divorce, but sadly they've run out of time. Her grandfather has been found dead after a break-in at his shop—and the police believe he was murdered.

Now Ruth has been named the heir to Grandpa Thom's clock shop, the Cog & Sprocket, in the small Berkshire town of Orchard, Massachusetts. As soon as she moves into the small apartment above the shop and begins tackling the heaps of unfinished work, Ruth finds herself trying to stay on the good side of Grandpa's bossy gray cat, Bezel, while avoiding the step-grandmother she never wanted. But as old secrets and grudges start to surface, Ruth will have to kick into high gear to solve the killer case before someone else winds up dead…

julianneholmes.com
facebook.com/JAHennrikus.writer
facebook.com/TheCrimeSceneBooks
penguin.com